The LONG ROAD to FREEDOM

Carolyn Harris

PAGE PUBLISHING, INC.
New York, NY

First originally published by Page Publishing, Inc. 2017

ISBN 978-1-68289-739-3 (Paperback)
ISBN 978-1-68289-740-9 (Digital)

Printed in the United States of America

CHAPTER ONE

"C'mon on, Joseph Dale, ifin we's doesn't git a move on it we's both gonna git caught, then all this plan'n wouldn't have meant a thing to us."

"I's can't Bobby Gene, honestly I's can't." He reached for his ankle. "I's knows it be broken. I's can't feel it." Bobby Gene grasped Joseph Dale underneath his arms using his body's weight for support as he tried helping him to his feet. Joseph Dale took one step and fell back to the ground.

"It be no use, Bobby Gene. I's in too much pain. I's can't goes any farther. You's must goes it alone."

"C'mon, man, we's got to give it one more try. I's can't just leave you's like this, we's be friends fer to long it can't end this way does you's knows they's kills you's when they catch you's?"

"I's knows, Bobby Gene, but ain't no need us both dying. We's knows here be where one of our lives will end. But it can be a new begin'n, a new life fer you's." There came a roar of horses' hooves and the howling of dogs in the distance. Joseph Dale put his hand on Bobby Gene's shoulder.

"Listen, Bobby Gene, that noise be a war'n. It means time dun got closer you's must goes while you's yet has a chance." Tears came into his eyes.

"I thought we's both was gonna make it, but fate must have it fer only one of us to git to the other side." He gave Bobby Gene a hefty thrust but he didn't budge.

"I's heard what you's say'n, Joseph Dale. But I's can't leave you's. We's got to give it one more try." Joseph Dale tore himself away from Bobby Gene's grip.

"Does you's understand, man, I's can't go no farther. Even ifin I's could with my leg busted up we's sure to git caught than you's going it alone." The growling of dogs was closing in. Joseph Dale looked directly into Bobby Gene's eyes.

"This be you's last chance, Bobby Gene. This be a good chance fer you's to does some'n fer our people. You's can find ways to make things better fer them. But you's never knows unless you's take this chance. There be two lives here they both doesn't have to end here today." Bobby Gene embraced Joseph Dale.

"I's never thought it would end this way, but I's promise you's this very day that I's does everything in my power to try and free our people." Tears were now streaming down both their faces.

"I's knows you's will, Bobby Gene. Maybe someone else knows too. Maybe that be why its ended here fer me. Now fer the love of God goes. I's try and stall them as long as I's can. But you's knows white folks ain't stupid." Bobby Gene gave Joseph Dale another quick embrace as he started off running in the distance. Joseph Dale sat there until Bobby Gene was out of sight before he started dragging himself out of the pathway mumbling to himself as he went along.

"God please be with you's, Bobby Gene, and protect him fer the rest of his life."

CHAPTER TWO

*E*verything around him seemed to have changed to slow motion. He could even hear the winds whispering in the tall grasses as it passed him by. He could detect the sharpness of the blades of the grass as they surrounded his body. He also detected the sensitivity of the ground, the growling of the dogs, and the sounds of the pounding hooves as they stomped onto the ground, making their way to Joseph Dale. Suddenly everything was back to normal when he heard the familiar voice of one of the overseers. The horses gathered around Joseph Dale as one of the men dismounted his horse.

"Well now what have we here. Not only did one of mama's black crows strayed away from its nest, but has injured himself during the process. What a pity. Boy don't you know we've been on your trail since sunup yesterday. I must admit you've been one hard nigger to track down. But the journey has finally come to an end. Don't you know nigger? This could be your just reward for trying to escape. Apparently good fortune was on our side. The very thing you used to run with caught you up in your own trap. And where did it get you?" The man's keen eyes moved up then down the leg when he caught sight of the large bloodstain just above the left foot. He bent down and ripped the old flour trousers that Joseph Dale was wearing from the seam. The leg was twice its size, and blood was gushing from the broken bones that had caused a puncture to the skin. Joseph Dale lay there in agony as the man deliberately stepped down onto the wound, sending him into more agonizing pain.

"Oh my ankle, it be broken." The man turned his attention to the other overseers.

"What do you think we ought to do with him?"

"I say let's feed him to the master's dogs. The way I've had to restrain them from jumping onto him you'd think they hadn't eaten in days," the man spoke up.

"I don't think that's a good idea. These dogs are only tracking dogs. Not wild ones. The only thing they are liable to do is to gnaw him up pretty good. But he would soon heal. No, I say we shoot him right here and right now. After all, he's no better than a lame horse. He'll be useless to the master if we were to take him back alive. We also know that when a nigger has been severely injured as this, not one slave owner in the whole county will buy him." The man paced back and forth, rubbing his chin as though he was configuring something in his thoughts.

"No I suggest we treat him the way we would a lame horse and shoot him. I'm sure if Dalton were here he'd do the exact same thing," one of the young men who had accompanied him spoke from his horse.

"But, Travor don't you think we should let the master decide what to do before you take this matter into your own hands? After all he's not your nigger." Travor walked over to the young man, almost pulling him from his horse as he grabbed him by his collar.

"Do you dare to question my decision, boy? And what makes you think you can override what I have to say? Were you the one who was put in charge of this outfit?" He looked up at the young man waiting for a reply to the question he had just asked.

"No. But-" Travor interrupted him.

"Good then it's settled." He shoved the young man backward. "Now as long as I'm in charge of this outfit, you'll do as I say or you just might find yourself out of a job. I say we shoot this nigger right here and that's that. Do I make myself clear?" He directed his attention solely to the young man.

"Yes Travor, I read you loud and clear." Travor looked back upon Joseph Dale for a moment, then he walked over to his horse and took his rifle out of the side holster of the saddle and aimed it toward Joseph Dale.

"Before you die, there's just one question I have for you. Where's that nigger friend of yours who took off with you? And ain't no need of your trying to lie about it because we know it were two of you." Joseph Dale looked up into Travor's face.

"I's doesn't knows noth'n about no nigger. It be me all by myself."

"Look, nigger, you know what's about to happen to you, so you may as well come clean with me and tell where that nigger friend of yours has gone." Travor stood there waiting for an answer. Silence fell over the crowd but there was no response.

"Alright, you don't want to tell us anything. That's fine, we'll find that nigger on our own, and when we do he'll wish he'd never agreed to run away with you." Travor cocked the trigger on the rifle and squeezed. The noise of the explosion rang throughout the woods as the sky filled with the sounds of many flapping wings as the birds fled as though to seek solace elsewhere while tiny rodents scurried for shelter as well. Travor broke down the rifle and shook the used ammunition to the ground. Then he looked upon the young man.

"You, sonny, since you've taken a liking toward these black savages, you can carry him back to the master on your horse. I'm sure he'll be pleased with a job well done. But on the other hand, he's going to be disappointed we didn't catch that other nigger."

CHAPTER THREE

"Masser Dalton, Masser Dalton, come quickly." The screen door flung open followed by a large frame of a man.

"What's all this yelling about, Junie? I could hear you all the way in my study."

"It be Masser Travor, he dun come back." Master Dalton stepped down from the porch and stood next to Junie who was jumping out of excitement, looking in the direction of the horses; The glare from the sunlight blocked Master Dalton's vision. He put his hands over his eyes as a shield so that he could see for himself. The sound of snarling horses got closer, even the dogs scurried about, leaping at the bundle that was tied to the back of the young man's horse. The horses approached Master Dalton and stopped. The black faces were more plentiful now as they gathered but keeping their distance. Travor dismounted from his horse and walked up to Master Dalton. He took off his hat as a show of respect, then he got right into conversation.

"I'm sorry to say, sir that the news I bring you isn't good." There was a moment of pause, even a sigh or two as he continued on. "We caught up with one of those niggers that had escaped. But unfortunately I had to shot him." Master Dalton looked pass Travor at the bloodstained bundle on the horse.

"Is that him tied down to the horse?" Travor's demeanor changed as though he knew he was about to be scolded.

"Yes, sir." Master Dalton walked over to the horse and raised the blanket high enough to identify his dead.

"It's Joseph Dale. Are you sure it was necessary?"

"Well, sir. No not at first." Master Dalton stood there trying to understand what Travor was saying then he spoke.

"Ok, I'm without understanding. Either you had to kill him or not." Travor nervously stood there as he continued to speak.

"That's what I was about to tell you. It just so happened that when we came upon him, he was still a great distant ahead of us. I shouted out to him. I even sent out a warning shot into the air. But he refused to stop and kept running. It was at this point when I knew I had no other choice but to shoot. By this time we had entered a clearing, so I shot between the trees. I only meant to wound him. But apparently the bullet went astray." Mr. Dalton questioned the other overseers as to if Joseph Dale's death was imperative. They each agreed that what Travor had spoken was truth.

"But what about Bobby Gene?"

"That's the other bad news. The dogs tracked us to this nigger only. If Bobby Gene was with him, he got away somehow." Master Dalton looked directly at Travor not even a blink as the tone of his voice rose with anger.

"You should have known this would not be acceptable to me! Bobby Gene is one of my prized niggers! Do you think I wouldn't be upset about this? I suggest you do some back tracking or what-ever it takes! But don't come back without that nigger! I'd hate to lose you as an employee! But that will happen if you should come back without him!" He didn't give Travor a chance to reply before he directed his attention toward the black faces that yet lingered before him in the distance.

"Some of you niggers come lend a hand. Take this nigger out back somewhere and bury him. He's sure as hell ain't good to me dead." There was ruffling in the back of the crowd as a voice came from within.

"Let me be. I's knows that be my Joseph Dale, don't try and stop me. I's must goes to him." The crowd of blackness divided as the figure made its way up to the body on the horse.

"Oh God please don't let this be my Joseph Dale. Not my baby. He's be all's I's got." She reached up and grabbed his legs and held on. Master Dalton spoke to her abruptly.

"I have not been one that is known to have patience, and I'm not about to start now."

"Please, Masser Dalton, don't do this awful thing. My boy deserves to be with his people at our own spread. That be where he should be, not just in an old hole out back." The two niggers that had come forward stood there with a look of puzzlement in their faces.

"What you niggers standing there for? Didn't I tell you to get that nigger out back?"

"Yeees, Masser." They went to lift the body off the horse. But was restrained by the woman.

"Please, Masser Dalton, I's begg'n you's. Don't do this thing!" He looked at the woman as though she was transparent then turned and walked away.

"I's never thought I's see'd the day, Masser, that I's curse you's. But this be the day."

Several of the women had come forward to take her away, and to speak wisdom to her.

"Hush, Lucille, does you's knows the Masser will have you's whupped fer sassing back at him." Master Dalton responded to the comment just made.

"You would do well to take to heart what Martha is saying to you." Lucille didn't back down but kept speaking.

"You's gonna pay fer this, Masser, as sure as God be in heaven. You's gonna pay." Master Dalton turned about face quickly.

"I can see that you're as stubborn as you are black, and I have no tolerance for your behavior. I warned you but you didn't take heed. Have you not learned anything about speaking disrespectful to me or any other whites on this plantation? Hasn't watching your forefathers and mothers being beaten not taught you to keep quiet and just obey. How stupid can you truly be? I guess now this is going to cause me to have to take drastic measures." He called several of the overseers by name. Thomas, Benjamin, take this nigger to the barn. You know what to do from there." He turned his attention to all the black faces that had gathered around him, watching as Lucille was being dragged off to the barn.

"Listen, niggers, and listen good. I don't want any of you to try and speak to me in the manner Lucille just did. Nor do I want you to speak of where you bed down as your property. Nothing on this land belongs to you except the clothes on your backs. The only reason you've got those cabins you live in is because I couldn't very well let you stay in the pastures due to certain circumstances. But I consider you nothing better than animals. Now back to work, or I'll have the whip taken to the whole bunch of you." After that remark you could see the niggers scrambling about in their different directions as to which they had come.

CHAPTER FOUR

"Mrs. Lucille, is you's still in here?"

"Who that be?" Lucille replied in a weak but firm voice.

"It be me, Mrs. Lucille, Anna Belle," the voice answered back. She stood there in the doorway of the barn, hesitant for a moment, then she held out the lantern so it would lead her through the darkness to Lucille. When the light met its target, Anna Belle was mortified and ran over to the woman.

"Please, child, take that light away from my face. It be hurt'n my eyes." Anna Belle eased the lantern on the floor to make sure that it would not tilt over and start a fire from the hay that blanketed it.

"Mrs. Lucille, why you's talk back to the Masser like that fer know'n some'n like this would happen?"

"They kills my boy, Anna Belle, they kills my Joseph Dale. He be all's I's has. Then when the Masser says he can't be buried with the rest of his family. He says just throw him in a hole out yonder somewhere. It hurts Anna Belle; nobody knows how it hurts."

"Look at you's face, it be all black and blue, and that eye be look'n pretty bad. You's lips doesn't look none to good neither. You's won't be eat'n much of anything until them cuts heals. I's reckoned the best be fer you's be some broth. I's brung along some cloths to clean those wounds just in case they's be needed." She removed the rags she had stuffed in her pockets as a few drops of water landed on her hands. The pretense was over. She looked at Lucille's swollen face with compassion for her as the tears flowed down her cheeks.

"I's knows you's be upset at the time. But I's loved him too, Mrs. Lucille, or does you's fergit we's to be wed?"

"No young'n, I's doesn't fergit. But now we's knows that ain't gonna happen now, is it?" Anna Belle took the damp cloth and dabbed gently at Lucille's cuts, then she crumpled it tightly in her fist. You could see her hands starting to tremble as her anger rose inside.

"Masser Dalton, I's hate him. I's hate all white folks. They's be cruel and bad. I's could kills the Masser fer what he dun to you's." Lucille interrupted Anna Belle's conversation.

"Listen here, young'n. I's got some'n to says to you's, and I's want you's to listen very carefully. First of all, you's must never says what you's just says to anyone else. Fer as sure as you's speak it. It will git back to the Masser, and he'll have you's out here next. Look at where it got me. Another thing even though the Masser does comes back with Joseph Dale. He doesn't comes back with Bobby Gene. So's that be a good sign he be gone. I's may not be around to see'd it. But I's have a good feel'n that boy's gonna does us niggers some good one day," directing her attention back to Anna Belle.

"Listen, gal, you's be out here fer quite a spell now. You's best be gitt'n back before someone finds you's out here. You's knows what the Masser will have dun to you's." Anna Belle continued to sit there knowing what Mrs. Lucille said was truth.

"But, Mrs. Lucille, I's can't leave you's like this. Ifin you's doesn't git them cuts attended to, you's could git real sick."

"Child, lean closer." Anna Belle did as she was told. "Look around you's. Does you's see'd anyone else come'n to help me? No, 'cause they knows better. You's knows my being loudmouth with the Masser be the reason why I's out here in the first place. You's be wrong ifin you's tend my wounds then the Masser would knows someone be out here. You's knows this place be off limits when one of us be brung out here fer being hard headed and ifin the Masser should find out that one be you's. I's never fergive myself. Now I's want you's to git right now!"

"Yes 'em Mrs. Lucille, I's leav'n. But I's be back early in the morning to see'd you's. You's heard?" Mrs. Lucille moved her head best as she could and replied.

"That be fine, child, now be off." Mrs. Lucille followed the lantern light as far as her eyes could take her for that was all she was able to move. Her head hands and feet were shackled so tightly she was starting to experience a tingling sensation. She realized the less she moved the better chance she had of not cutting off the blood flow, not to mention the numbness she was starting to experience as well. The swelling of her ankles wasn't of much comfort to her either She watched until everything about her became a blanket of darkness once again, floods of tears came to her as she thought about Joseph Dale and Anna Belle. Then she said out loud to herself concerning Anna Belle.

"Don't be no fool, child."

Once Anna Belle was outside the barn, she quickly blew the lantern out for she knew the glare from it would bring several overseers to venture her way. She also knew it would be difficult enough as it was for her to sneak back to their cabin without being seen. She let her sharp vision wander into the darkness before she continued on her way.

Everything couldn't have been better. She didn't know exactly what time it was, and if she had seen the Master's big clock, she still wouldn't have the foggiest idea. There was a gala of laughter in the distance. She knew this was an indicator she had nothing to worry about. Each night when it was late and the overseers thought all the niggers were settled, they'd get together in one another's cabin, drinking, and playing some kind of game with some funning- looking paper with numbers and different-looking pictures on them.

Sometimes they got a bit loud but quickly quieted down, for if the Master heard them, they would be in a heap of trouble. Taking advantage of this opportunity, she fled for their cabin but found herself gasping for air. Everything in front of her seemed to disappear. When her face was covered by a hand followed by a voice.

"I'm going to take my hand away from your face. But if you holler in the least bit, I will kill you right here and right now. You got that nigger?" Anna Belle nodded her head. "Good, then just so we understand each other." He took hold of her left arm and pulled it backwards, forcing her to squirm a bit from the pain she was experiencing.

"That's only a sample of what you're going to feel if you cross me, nigger." He removed his hand slowly from her face but kept a firm grip on her left arm. Anna Belle began to speak.

"Please, I's doesn't knows who you's be or what you's want. But don't hurt me." The voice spoke again.

"If you do as you're told, then won't no harm come to you. But if you try anything, you'll be very sorry. Now move!" He gave her a shove toward the woods. He could tell that she was frightened because of the tightening of her muscles. Anna Belle did as she was told. She could feel herself getting weak in the knees. But she dared not let it show for whomever had abducted her was truly sincere about what he was doing. The walk was short, but to Anna Belle it seemed like miles. The place was very familiar to her because she used to play there with several others when they were children.

"All right we've gone far enough." Anna Belle spoke again.

"I's doesn't understand why we's out here. Ifin you's try'n to scare me. Then it be work'n." The man smiled to himself.

"You niggers are a fright. I knew there was ignorance about you. But I thought you had some common sense within yourselves. I guess I gave you too much credit. Turnabout girl, I don't like to talk to a person's back even if they are niggers." Anna Belle slowly turned, her eyes showed a look of surprise.

"Masser Travor, it be you's. What you's do'n? Why you's grabbed me like that back yonder, and why we's out here in the woods? Doesn't Masser tells you's ifin you's doesn't come back with Bobby Gene you's to stay away?"

"I can say one thing about you niggers. You sure have a knack for gossiping. You're right about something else. I didn't get that nigger boy Bobby Gene yet. But you can bet with him being a nigger. He won't get too far. I came back for only one reason I forgot something." He stepped into the fullness of the moonlight.

You could see the savage look in his eyes watching like an animal stalking its prey.

"You know, I've been watching you for a long time. I can recall the day you were born. To a little girl now a young woman. I watched the way you and that nigger Bobby Gene use to come to this very place. One day I decided to follow you just to see what you were up to. That nigger friend of yours was quite determined to have his way with you. When he tried to even kiss or touch you. You acted like a wild cat tearing into him, clawing at him. Then after convincing him that it was proper to wait till after you were wedded. He decided to go along with you. What the hell do you niggers know about being proper?" Still watching her, he rubbed his chin.

"You must have been about ten then. Weren't you?" Her fear became obvious as she started fidgeting with the bottom of her blouse.

"Yeee sir."

"How old are you now?"

"Thirteeeen, sir." He stood there in silence just staring knowing how uncomfortable he was making her. Using this to his advantage, he let his hands fall to his waist as she watched his every move. She watched him as he unlatched the buckle of his belt and started toward her.

"Please, Masser, don't beat me. I's dun noth'n wrong, and ifin this has anyth'n to do with visit'n Mrs. Lucille, I's knows I's be wrong. Ifin you's let me be, it won't happen again." The expression on his face changed as he threw back his head, the roaring of his deep laughter echoed through the trees and back at her. She just stood there startled, not understanding what was happening.

"Do you think this is about that old nigger Lucille? I could care less about her. My only regret is that I wasn't the one whom Dalton called on to give her what she so deserved. Hell, nobody knows how to teach you niggers a lesson like me. You niggers are incredible." He chuckled again and repeated her words back at her.

"Beat you? I have no intention of beating you." He took another step closer while unfastening his trousers.

"I'm going to do for you what that nigger boy of yours never got the chance to do. I'm going to take you." Before Anna Belle could think she was off and running deeper into the woods. She could hear the crackling of dry twigs behind her as she kept running.

"Come back here, you black heathen. You're just going to make it harder on yourself when I catch you, and I will catch you make no mistake about that." Anna Belle kept running but turned briefly to see if Travor was visible when suddenly she was greeted by a few tree branches. She fell to the ground momentarily blinded.

"Oh my eyes! They's burn'n. I's can't see'd." Using her hands to see with, she felt for some indication of protection or a place to hide.

"There you are, you little black bitch! You didn't think you'd get away from me now, did you? You little fool!" He snatched her up by the hair only for her to be knocked back to the ground by his powerful right fist. His enormous hands clutched her throat as he fell on top of her.

"You certainly have a lot of strength, but apparently not enough." Freeing one of his hands, he started tearing at her clothing. The more she fought against him, the more vulgar he became with lust toward her. When the clothes were fully stripped, he pinned her bucking body to the ground, yelling at her.

"Listen, bitch! I've taken about all I can from you, and I'm absolutely fed up with it! Now you've got two choices here. Either stop fighting me and let me do what I came to do, or end up like that nigger boy of yours. I want you to know it wouldn't take nothing for me to kill you here and now." Anna Belle, still terrified, kept letting what Mrs. Lucille spoke register in her mind.

"Don't be no fool, child." Anna Belle promptly became calm as she tightly closed her eyes, trying to block out what was happening to her. She could feel the pressure as Master Travor entered her, then a moment of pain as she drifted off into unconsciousness.

CHAPTER FIVE

The rays of the sun managed to break through the thickness of the trees and shone down upon Anna Belle's face. She was startled when she had finally awakened to find that the blanket of darkness had been lifted by daylight. Her body felt like someone had taken a whip to it, and small streams of dry blood had formed on the inner part of her thighs. She slowly sat up, eventually getting to her feet. She looked at her tattered clothing, trying to wrap the remains around her body.

The plantation was farther than she had imagined. When she reached the clearing, she wrapped the clothing tighter against her flesh Elsie Jane, who was in charge of the laundry crew, leaned away from her pot for a moment to wipe the sweat that had fallen down into her eyes. She let her head fall to the side while with the bottom of her apron she dabbed at the perspiration on her neck and the crevice of her bosom.

"Land sakes ifin it gits any hotter 'round here. We's all gonna drop dead from this heat." Her eyes wandered a bit before she went back to work. It was hard to sneak a glance especially when there were overseers everywhere. You dare not blink let alone look away from time to time. This time she decided to defy the rules as she stood there scanning the scenery. A loathsome look filled her weary face as she looked on.

"Oh my God." She nudged Bessie who was standing next to her. "Quick, child run to the Masser's house and tell Lorene to git herself here right away."

"Yes 'em Mrs. Elsie Jane. But what be the matter?"

"Hush child, don't be ask'n no questions now. Just does as you's told." As the figure got closer, she stood there watching making sure her vision wasn't deceiving her. Anna Belle staggered closer. She was positive about what she saw. Lorene came up behind her.

"Elsie Jane, what you's want. Bessie says you's said come quickly. This better be good or the Masser gonna have the both of us whupped." Elsie Jane tried to speak, but the words wouldn't come. She pointed in the direction of the image while Lorene eyes followed.

"My Lord, that be Anna Belle. What dun happened to her?" In a flash Lorene was off and running with Elsie Jane not far behind. When they reached Anna Belle, she clutched her tightly.

"My Anna Belle what dun happened to you's?" With shaky hands, she untied her apron she had around her, and wrapped it about her body. Elsie Jane offered hers as well.

"Mama, don't let him hurt me. Please, mama. Don't let him hurt me." She started fighting, trying to escape her mother's grip. "Let me be. Please don't I's beg you's." Anna Belle's mother shook her, hoping to bring her around.

"Anna Belle it be me, it be you's mama." Anna Belle was still hysterical from her terrible ordeal, and trying to combat herself free. "God, please fergive me fer what I's about to does. You's knows I's never dun any harm to her before. But she be half crazed." She slapped Anna Belle as hard as she possibly could, and the batting of her eyes brought her to a soft whimper, Anna Belle's eyes met her mother's.

"Mama, that be you's?" She stared at her, but the distant look was yet in her eyes. Lorene pulled her daughter close again, wishing she could ease the hideous condition she was in. Lorene led her daughter toward their cabin when Master Dalton approached them.

"What's the meaning of this outburst, and why did you leave the house so quickly?"

"It be Anna Belle, she dun been hurt." He squinted his eyes at her.

"I can see that. But there's no need for such alarm. She's probably been fooling around with one of the nigger boys and things got a bit out of hand. I don't expect this incident to interfere with your chores. You get her home and then get back to the house." He then looked at Elsie Jane.

"As for you. I don't see any reason why this nigger is of your concern. I suggest you hightail it back to your chores as well. I want that laundry finished by sundown, or I'll have the whip taken to you." Elsie Jane let Anna Belle's arm fall limp.

"Yes Masser," she responded.

When they had reached the cabin, Lorene took Anna Belle over to her bed and sat her down, then she went and lifted the pot off the burner of the old cook stove, filling the bowl with water. She took the cloth from the nail on the back of the door and ripped a piece from it, placing it neatly back in place. Then walking over to Anna Belle's bedside, she knelt down before her as she started to clean her wounds and bruises. She could see a drop or two of water starting to form in Anna Belle's eyes once again as she spoke to her mother. She looked at the floor and cried out.

"Oh mama it be terrible. It happened so fast, I's thought it be a bad dream until I's wake up in the woods. "I's com'n from seed'n Mrs. Lucille in the barn. I's knows that ifin I's git caught I's be in trouble, so's that be why I's wait till you's bed down, and it be late when no one would see'd me. I's knows ifin I's was to ask you's ifin I's could goes to see'd her. You's would says no. I's knows I's be tak'n a chance. But mama she looked so bad." A sorrowful look replenished her eyes.

"I's just went to wash her wounds and give her some water. When I's be leave'n. I's be grabbed from behind and told to head into the woods." With this she looked into her mother's face.

"Mama, it be Masser Travor."

"Masser Travor, Anna Belle is you's sure of what you's say'n? Masser Dalton dun as good as fired Masser Travor the other day 'cause he doesn't come back with both niggers."

"I's knows, Mama, that be what the Masser tells me. But he says he left someth'n behind. I's doesn't knows what he means till he hurt me." Lorene jumped up in a rage.

"Child, is what you's say'n is that Masser Travor dun this awful thing to you's?" Anna Belle nodded her head.

"Yes, mama the masser he took me. I's tried fight'n, I's even run, Mama. But he catch me. He says ifin I's doesn't do what he says, he's gonna kill me. I's doesn't care, Mama. I's rather die than to let that white man does what he dun to me. Ifin what Mrs. Lucille dun said to me last night. I's would have rather died. I's hate him, Mama. I's hate Masser Dalton too." Lorene tried to comfort her daughter. She took Anna Belle's hands into hers and squeezed them together tightly. Then she told her to look at her.

"Child, don't never says noth'n like that at all. Fer you's knows the masser will have some'n terrible dun to you's. Even worse he could sell you's to someone else. You's knows it not be unheard of. You's even see'd it fer you's self how he be break'n up families. I's doesn't think I's would even want to live ifin some'n happened to you's. Ifin you's hadn't sneak off to see'd Lucille noth'n like this would probably have happened. But I's knows you's lik'n fer folks." Anna Belle also jumped up.

"I's sick of talk 'bout what the masser will do to me. I's heard it from Mrs. Lucille and now you's."

"I's not afraid of Masser Dalton, and ifin I's git the chance, I's gonna run away from this awful place just like Joseph Dale and Bobby Gene." Lorene squeezed Anna Belle's hands even tighter, eyes cold and direct.

"You's best be scared, young'n 'cause the masser he don't play. You's see'd what happened to Joseph Dale, and the Lord only knows what be happened to Bobby Gene." There was a long moment of silence. "Besides there be some'n in my past I's hop'n I's never have to share with you's. But now I's don't see'd any other way but to tell you this." She eased down on the bed, instructing her daughter to sit next to her.

"I's be 'bout in you's same situation you's be in right now." Anna Belle interrupted.

"You's be raped too?" Lorene patted Anna Belle gently on the hands.

"Let's not git ahead of ourselves. But yes, child," she went on. "It be our wedd'n day. You's papa and mine. It be the happiest time on the whole plantation fer us niggers. The masser says since it be our wedd'n day nobody had to work. This be back yonder when the masser be good to us niggers. Everyone git together with us after we be wed. There be food, lemonade, and danc'n. After a spell you's papa says he's see'd and been round enough niggers and excitement fer the time being. He just wanted to be alone with me. Anyhown, the masser says you's papa could build a new cabin fer us as a gift from him. This very cabin to be exact. I's be happier than I's ever be in my whole life. I's love you's papa so very much." Her thoughts purported back to those years of so long ago.

"I guess that be why I doesn't fuss 'bout you's gitt'n spoken fer at a young age. I's could see'd myself all over again. So happy and full of life. Yet know'n ifin you's papa be still alive he'd strongly oppose." She allowed herself to drift back even farther.

"You's papa and I's be enjoy'n one another after which I's suppose we's fall asleep 'cause the next thing I's 'member was a loud noise. You's papa and I's sat straight up look'n at the door from where the noise had come. There stood two of Masser Dalton's overseers. They rushed over and pulled me out of the bed cause'n me to lose my balance. I's falls to the floor, you's papa jumped over the bed and tried to git 'em to let me be. His eyes were huge from anger as he began to holler."

"What yaw do'n? Let her be." He grabbed one of the overseers and his huge fist sent a staggering blow to his head. We watched him as he fell to the ground. Then you's papa attacked the other overseer. There was struggl'n about the cabin. All's I's could do be to look on. I's not even sure ifin I's recall scream'n. Then you's papa turned toward me. I's could see'd the anguish in his eyes as he clutched his stomach and blood appeared through his fingers, he says my name one last time. Then he falls to the floor I's knows when he doesn't move, he be dead. I's crawled over to him unaware of my naked body. I grabbed the quilt hold'n on as tightly as I's could. I's hollered and bucked as they pulled me away from him I's can still remember call'n out his name as they carried me away. Gabriel, Gabriel, my husband. I's later found out that one of the overseers had put a knife to him. I's be scared fer I's doesn't knows where they be tak'n me. I's fought and kicked all the way." There was a break of silence. Lorene stood up again and started to pace back and forth running her hands up then down her arms trying to ease the tension.

"I's finally come to be where they had been ordered to take me. It be the masser's house. They bring me to the masser's study and just dropped my body on the floor. By this time I's be beside myself. I's knows that the masser has aways been nice toward us. I's picked myself up from off the floor, wrapp'n the quilt round my body and look'n at the masser as I's dun so many times when I's see'd the same expression in his eyes that I's see'd in them overseers. I's pulled the quilt tighter. After seed'n so many others before. I's knows what be about to happen to me."

"Let it fall."

"The tone of his voice let me knows that he was not fool'n around. The quilt drop 'bout my feet and I's stood there bare, all of me." Tears started to whelp up in her eyes.

"He started toward me I's wanted to run, but I's knows better not to. Besides, where would I's run to? He walked around me look'n at me like a madman. I's could feel his breath on my neck. I's doesn't knows what to do so's I's started to talk'n hop'n he's take his eyes away from me."

"They kills my Gabriel Masser Dalton. They broke into our cabin and kills my man." With no concern he spoke.

"What pity. Undoubtedly they felt it imperative or they wouldn't have done it."

"I could feel his white hands touch my shoulders. The smell of whiskey be strong on his breath. His hands moved toward the front of my body then to my waist when he pulled me close to him. Fer a long time his hand touched me all about my person while I's stood there hat'n every minute of what was being dun to me. Then he threw me back onto the floor and took me in ways that I's never knows before, laugh'n about it afterward. I's lay there scared to move. The laughter roared in my head, and the picture of you's papa kept play'n over and over in my head, I's be not think'n at all. The masser put himself back together and went to git himself another drink. I's be in a daze, which I's be not aware of at the time. I struck out at him."

"I's picked up one of the glasses and hit him in the face. It immediately turned red with blood, and he started stumbl'n here and there, wip'n his eyes, try'n to keep the flow of blood from gitt'n into them. He tore off his shirt, dipped the sleeve in the glass of whiskey, and put it where he be hurt. All this time I's just stood there not being able to move. He finally managed to git the bleed'n stopped when he looked over at me. His eyes was the picture of fire. He rushed at me."

"You black whore! I'll kill you for this! His hands clenched my throat, and I's could feel myself gitt'n weak. I's no longer could stand on my own. I's falls back to the floor as he started kick'n me. Every time he kicks me, I's felt myself throw'n up my hands try'n to protect other parts of my body. I's be kicked in the face, head, stomach, everywheres. Blood was oozing out of the corner of my mouth, and my body had no feel'n. But I could still vaguely see'd him kick'n at me. Ifin Kalkie Sue hadn't come to help me. I's probably would have died. I's heard a few muffl'n words, and suddenly Kalkie Sue falls next to me."

"They says that day she gave her life fer me. When she tried to stop Masser Dalton from putt'n the blade of his dagger into me, she got it instead. When the doctor came the masser had to git sowed up and was told he would carry that ugly scare with him fer the rest of his life. Unto this day, the masser dun been more cruel toward us niggers." She looked up and managed a smile through the tears as she softly lay her hands on Anna Belle's once again.

"One good thing come out of all this. Although I's must admit I's had my doubts 'bout you's. I's be not sure ifin you's look like you's papa or has light-colored skin like the masser. But thank God you's a Thompson, you's be you's papa. You's see'd how foolish talk like this be."

24

"Oh, mama, I's had no idea you's been hold'n some'n like this inside you's all this time. But, Mama, answer this one thing."

"Ifin I's can. What it be?"

"Why doesn't you's never marry again? Doesn't you's see'd any suitors after papa?"

"No, child, you's papa died fer some'n he felt be right, and I's owe it to him to give my life to him and him only. But doesn't you's go gitt'n no silly ideas in you's head like that." She stood up.

"I's best be gitt'n back to my chores. I's be gone a bit too long. Know'n the masser I's doesn't want to make him upset. There be some hot water yonder, you's need to take a bath and git rid of that filth."

The months traveled quickly like the pages of a fleeting novel blowing through the wind. Everyone was busy canning and making the necessary preparation for the cold months to follow. It was the middle of October, already the trees were losing their beautiful colored leaves. Anna Belle discovered she was with child. Bobby Gene was still missing, and talk around the plantation was that Master Travor had gotten work on Master Wellington's plantation who just happened to be Master Dalton's neighbor.

"It was also brought to Master Wellington's attention from one of the overseers that someone had been raiding his place. Nothing of great value was taken. Mostly food like chickens, eggs, and an assorted amount of vegetables. Plus, the fact some of the slaves' attire was missing.

A young couple who was passing through had gotten robbed and lost all their worthy possessions except for an old trunk with their clothing. Jeffrey and Pauline Turner were their names. Master Wellington gave them jobs that would tide them over till summer and said if he had any need for them after the fact they could stay or continue on their way. He put the young man in charge of catching whomever it was that had been raiding his place for the past few months.

The nights were long and repeatedly lonesome. His wife visited him briefly during the day whenever she could between chores. He insisted she stay in their cabin or visit with some of the younger women of her age around the plantation. She had become quite friendly with some of the nigger women since they had taken up residency amongst them. The only reason they didn't have to submit to the overseers, was due to the fact they were white.

She carried an admiration for the women on the plantation. Their long flared silky dresses with their fancy decors and ivory-white complexions captivated by the aromatic, sweet scent of a hillside of lilac blowing delicately in the wind. Their lips were stained with color, with rosy cheeks to match. Eyes glimmering like emeralds accented with lovely curls so soft one could almost touch them with their eyes.

She sat there gazing into the fire her thoughts still engorged in what she saw. Last but not least was their proper sophistication. The tone of their voices direct but seductive. Their perfect manners, even the look of virginity, wore very well, that's if their fathers hadn't gotten to them first. A piece of twig snapped in the fire disrupting her thoughts. She blinked her eyes several times. Standing up she walked over to the mirror hoping she was one of the beautiful young women. But was soon brought back to reality as she stood in front of the mirror. She lifted out her long straggly brown hair and let it fall bit by bit through her fingers. Then she took a long look at the image in front of her again.

The ivory skin and golden curls had vanished. What she saw was herself. Skin several shades of color from working the fields, and ragged clothing. Not the smell of sweet fragrance but the strong odor of sweat. She let her body flop lazily upon the bed that rested in the corner, speaking loudly to herself.

"Who are you kidding? You'll never make it in a million years." with this she dozed off into a deep sleep.

The moonlight wasn't the only thing that crept its way into the loft but the chilling winds as well. Each night showed signs of winter threatening the plantation. There had been several cold evenings, and freezing weather had destroyed the remaining crops. To cuddle in front of a warm fire would be a wonderful gesture. But for Jeffrey it was only a thought, for he knew he wouldn't be rewarded with the warmth of a fire or his wife until this task was finished.

The last flickering of flames seemed to diminish about the loft of the barn struggling to fight for its last chance of survival as though it knew what its purpose was. Jeffrey, unbeknown to himself, had dozed off. He caught himself as his head nodded. He quickly opened his eyes to notice the faintness of the flame in the lantern. Its supply of oil was almost gone. Jeffrey searched for the oil can. Upon finding it, he blew out what remained of the flame. The whole loft was swallowed up by blackness except for the few strips of natural light peering through worn shingles of the roof. This light would be his means of refilling his lamp with oil again. He replaced the oil and rolled the cotton wick up till some of it came up through the metal teeth, screwing the top back on. His hands were still trembling from the cold, but he managed to retrieve the matches from his pocket. He was about ready to strike the match when he thought he heard a thump. He sat erect and shifted his body toward the right, leaning his ear into the direction as to where he had heard the sound.

He sat there listening as his eyes searched deep into the night with his mind starting to race. For a moment it had swallowed up his thoughts, even the cramping in his hands seemed to disappear. He went back to concentrating on the matter at hand. It had to have been his imagination. The only time there was anyone present was when Master Wellington wanted to speak with him. Or when one or more of his niggers got out of control and were put there awaiting their punishment.

There it came again that thumping sound. It wasn't his imagination; he really did hear something. He didn't move a muscle for he knew the slightest disturbance would cause whomever it was below him to flee. He had to find out what was happening. He sat there impatiently waiting. Whomever it was seemed to be in no hurry to return outside to face that bitter coldness. Finally, everything was quiet again. The only sound he heard was the rapid pounding of his heart. He sat there holding the lantern. His mind confused, but there was still no sound from below.

"What am I going to do?" he thought to himself. "If I don't find the answer to this problem, I'll be spending the better part of my evenings out here in the loft." He got down on his knees and crawled over to the window where he rubbed a spot in the pane, hoping, just by some great miracle, that he would get the chance or break he'd been hoping for months. He had no idea as to what he was looking for or where to begin. But he was sure of one thing. He was not going out into the cold unless it was absolutely necessary.

His sharp eyes searched as far as his vision would permit. Then he saw it bobbing in and out of the dried-up fields. He had to blink several times. Could this be for real? Or could it be that he wanted something to be there so badly that he only imagined he saw something? He leaned in closer to the window pressing his whole face against it. It was someone, he hadn't imagined it after all. Jeffrey took out after him. He knew if he didn't catch whomever it was, he may as well prepare for a long lonely winter. This was his big opportunity, maybe his only chance.

The weather outside was worse than he had imagined it to be. The wind was blowing frantically. Even with the bundle of clothing he wore he could still feel the acuteness of the cold piercing his body like pins. Whomever was ahead of him didn't seem to mind the chilling condition. But Jeffrey himself hoped it wouldn't be much farther. Jeffrey suddenly stopped. He could not make out who was ahead of him because of the distance between them. But the silhouette of the person let him know he was closing in on this person.

Jeffrey folded his body as low to the ground as he could so he wouldn't be seen, as well as trying to dodge as much of the wind as possible while he stared on. The figure was working swiftly, leaving Jeffrey to wonder if he might be moving something with his hands. He didn't seem to be concerned as to if he might have been followed but concentrated on what he was doing; positive he was all alone. Finally, the shadow vanished into the darkness. He arose and crept his way slowly toward the area where he saw the image disappear. As he got closer, his hands searched freely about his body for his weapon to make sure he would be prepared for whatever situation he might be confronted with.

The closer he got he recognized he had stumbled onto an opening of a cave. But where it led he had no idea. He took a step into the entrance but was still surrounded by darkness. He could feel a lump come into his throat, and it became hard for him to swallow as he ventured deeper into the darkness, knowing he would soon be face-to-face with this person. He couldn't allow whomever it was to get away again. But on the other hand he couldn't risk the chance of barging in on this mysterious person for he didn't know what his situation might well be. Whatever it was, he'd cross that bridge when he came to it. His main objection now was to follow as close to his suspect without being noticed. It wouldn't be easy because everything before him was black. He moved about as only the circumstances permitted.

He stretched his hands outward for guidance as he walked on and on like being in a bad dream. But he was awake and everything was real. He tried swallowing again, but the lump was still there. Where was he going? What would he find at the end of this dark passage? He couldn't believe he was actually in this situation. All he had been hoping and praying for months had finally come to the forefront. Now he was questioning his manhood.

"I'm not afraid. I know I must prove it to myself before anyone else will believe it. If I don't start showing confidence in myself, then no one else will believe in me either."

Jeffrey tried again to swallow his fear, but the lump wouldn't leave. If he were to prove himself, he knew he must continue on no matter what might lie ahead for him. He continued his journey through the darkness. The only sounds were the pounding of his heart.

Suddenly he stopped. Could this really be? Or was his mind playing tricks on him again? Either way, he had to make sure he found out who this mysterious person was. If he proceeded, he'll be proving something to himself. The light seemed to sway with his body movement. As he approached closer, the nervousness came back.

"Come on, man," he caught himself saying. "You can't turn back now. You've come too far." His legs became weak, and perspiration popped out all over his body. It was no longer the pain from his body he was experiencing but the overwhelming dread of fear. At first this job seemed so easy. But now suddenly he felt as though he wanted to run and hide. Thinking on how Mr. Wellington had taken him and his wife in and being so generous toward them, offering them shelter as well as food, asking only this one task be done. He couldn't let him down. Not only that, this would prove to Pauline that he was a man. Ever since they had left Philadelphia, she had been on him about if he'd stood up to her father in the first place they wouldn't be going across country just so they could be together.

"I am a man, and I'll prove it to Pauline one way or another. Why should I be afraid of what's on the other side of this cave wall? Whomever it is couldn't be that threatening." He paused a moment. "Or could they?" He shook his head, trying to release the fear.

"Come on, Jeff, if you're trying to talk yourself out of this one you're doing a pretty good job of it. Snap out of it. You're supposed to be a man, so now's your chance to prove it. If I don't do this, then I'll never know the real reason we left. Was Pauline right when she said I was afraid to stay and fight? But instead took his daughter and ran because I wasn't man enough to stand up to him the way I should have.

"Well, that's all ancient history, and this is tonight, now. If I could only be sure of what was on the other side of this wall." He felt his side once again to make sure his knife was in its place. Then he proceeded with caution. sneaking, ducking, dodging as he crept closer in hopes of getting a better look. The fire was much brighter now, and he could see quite clearly inside the cave's room. There was a shadow bobbing about, and his hands were moving quickly as he stirred the fire. Jeffrey studies from what he could see of the room. This was an assurance that it was only one person. He realized the situation at hand was in his favor. The figure sat with his back to Jeffrey still working with his hands. Quietly, Jeffrey entered farther into the room, hoping to see if there might be any signs of weapons.

Unaware that his shadow had now been cast on the wall, he ventured closer and could feel his pulse quicken, and the throbbing of his heart came through again like the pounding of a drum. His shadow swallowed up the shadow that had once lingered there. The stranger jumped up and turned quickly toward Jeffrey. Jeffrey stopped in his tracks and closed his hand on his knife, ready to draw it at any moment. An expression of fear filled the black face as he backed toward the wall. Jeffrey eased his hand away from his knife. The black face stared on into the blue eyes of the white face that stood off in the distance.

Jeffrey could tell from the stranger's reaction that he was scared. They both stood there a long moment studying one another. Jeffrey was just as frightened as this stranger. But he knew he must not let it be known for the fact that he just might be overpowered by this frightened person. The silence was strong, every now and then the crackling of twigs in the fire could be heard.

"I must say," Jeffrey spoke, looking around at the dark smothering walls. "You're pretty clever the way you've camouflaged that opening back there."

"It was you that I was chasing tonight wasn't?" The only response was the movement of his head. Jeffrey could tell by now that the stranger was of no threat so he eased closer toward the fire.

"Do you mind if I have a sit down," he pointed to the fire. "I'm still a bit cold from that weather outside." The young man didn't move but for the second time shook his head. Jeffrey slowly eased his way to the ground not wanting to startle this person in the least bit. Once he was seated he started to pull at the gloves that had now stuck to his fingers, and laid them next to him. He looked up at the young man who hadn't taken his eyes away from him since he entered the room.

"I don't want to sat and enjoy this fire by myself after all it was you whom built it. Won't you please sit down with me. From the way your body's trembling, I'd guess you could use some more of this warmth yourself." The black body moved closer toward the fire and sat on the opposite side of Jeffrey. After being seated he began to unravel the cloth from his feet. The look of pain overwhelmed his face. Jeffrey's eyes widen substantially as he looked on. His feet were spotted in areas. The skin was cracked and broken not to mention the puffiness. Fresh blood was trying to escape from beneath the blood that had dried, leaving a terrible odor.

"My God man, your feet they're frost bitten. Don't you know that if they're not taken care of properly you could lose them? I must go back to the plantation and get something to try and salvage them. that's if it's not too late. If you have any more of that cloth. I suggest you rewrap them and try to keep them as warm as possible." He sat there a few more moments then he pulled his gloves over his fingers to start on his way.

The wind outside has seized, but the bitter coldness still lingered. The darkness was being lifted up like a drawn curtain as the grey of daybreak appeared. Jeffrey pulled his collar up around his neck as far as it would go as well as pulling the coat tightly to his body to try and keep warm. The tiny cabins around the plantation still showed of blackness, but it would only be a matter of time for the walks of like to be stirring. He made his was to their cabin he knew Pauline wouldn't be awake so he would just slip in grab what he needed then quietly leave again, but unfortunately she was awaken.

"Who's there? Jeffrey is that you?"

"Yes honey it's me," he felt his way over to the tiny table where the lantern was and lit it. For a second or two Pauline had to place her hands over her eyes until they could adjust to the light. Jeffrey didn't bother about starting a conversation but went directly to the cub board and started searching stopping long enough to ask Pauline if she knew where the Epsom salt was.

"It's over here honey on the night table. I used it last night to soak my feet they were swollen from being on them all day."

Jeffrey opened one of the drawers and took out several of Pauline's petticoats as she lay there watching. He then took the empty canteen from the nail on the back of the door and dumped it into the water pail till it was full after that he grabbed the extra pair of boots he had rested near the fireplace as he rushed past the bed he briskly kissed Pauline as he headed for the door.

"I'm sorry to have awaken you honey. I had to get these things I'll explain it better when I come back." He then disappeared on the other side of the door. Yellow lights were beginning to fill some of the other cabins. Jeffrey knew he had to go make his move quickly through the plantation before someone saw him. Getting back to the cave was quicker than before since he knew the way and with a new day coming the entrance to the cave would have to be hidden. Being surrounded by the darkness didn't seem to bother him anymore. He entered the room only to find it empty. But he could tell that it hadn't been long since someone had put out the fire due to the steam rising from it. Jeffrey left the room as he called out to the young man. He waited for an answer but instead heard his voice bounce off the walls and back at him.

"It's me, you can answer I'm alone."

"I's here Masser, behind you's. I's heard you's the first time, but I's couldn't take no chance you's be alone." Jeffrey turned around.

"I guess you're right. I possibly would have done the same thing if I were in your shoes." He followed behind the young man as they entered into a different room of the cave. Jeffrey looked around as he spoke.

"I must say you've got a great advantage here. All this space to roam around freely." Jeffrey noticed a look of despair come on the young man's face.

"Why the disappointing look?"

"It be that word free. Many times at the other plantation that be all's I's heard the other niggers talk of being free, but it never happens."

"Why are you sad though, you are free."

"Me free, not really I's has freedom to run about this cave in darkness. But I's want to be with my people I's want to do some'n to help them. Ifin only Joseph Dale were here maybe the two of us together might could of finds a way to help our people. Now it be no good. I's made a promise to Joseph Dale and I's gonna keep it."

Jeffrey sat down in front of the fire and beckoned for the young man to join him.

"Here come and sit with me. I have a few things I brought that I figured you might be in need of." The young man's eyes widen like an excited child as Jeffrey held out the bundle to him. He fumbled with the knots trying to get them loosen so he could see what was on the inside. The first thing he pulled out of the bundle was the canteen. He held it at several different angles trying to figure out what it was, then stretched it out to Jeffrey.

"This thing here what it be used fer. I's see'd it on the Masser's and overseer's horses." Jeffrey found himself wanting to laugh, but seeing the serious expression on the young man's face he felt sorry for him.

"It's called a canteen and its used for carrying water. They're used when taking long trips, or on hot summer days. It's much more convenient for them to be carried with you so you won't have to worry about going back and forth to the well as often."

"Here." He took the canteen from the young man.

"See this part here, that's called a knob, and this is a cap that screws off." Taking the cap off the canteen he continued. "This hole is what you get the water through." With this he lifted the canteen up to his mouth and took a drink of water then he handed it back to the young man. He took it back and turned it up quickly, water filled his face as he grasped from the cold water that had run down into his shirt. This time Jeffrey couldn't hold back the laughter which suddenly filled the room. The young man looked at him pretending to be upset, but found himself laughing also. Jeffrey snatched the canteen away from him.

"Give me that, before you waste it all. I'll show you how it's done again. Then you can practice after I'm gone." He put the canteen up to his mouth slightly lifting it upwards then he brought it down again. "There that really isn't so hard after all now is it?" He said as he replaced the cap. The young man ventured back into the bundle and pulled out the other things as he held up the petticoats.

"I's hope you's doesn't 'pect me to wear these," he said jokingly.

"No you can tear them up and use them for bandages to help your feet. I also brought along these boots. They're a bit worn, but they're better than having none at all. I doubt if you'll be able to get into them until after that swelling goes away but I do believe you just may wear the same size I do. Let's hope and pray they are not permanently damaged. Putting more pressure on them than necessary isn't good for them. You need to stay off them. When I come back I'll bring you some food and get you a different change of clothing. Your appearance indicates that you can use them as well." The young man had a dumbfounded look on his face.

"Do I fascinate you?"

"Faaaascinate," The young man repeated. "What that 'pose to be?"

"It's just that look in your eyes. You seem to be puzzled as to why I came back." The young man gazed into Jeffrey's face.

"Ifin you's doesn't mind my say'n so's. It be not the part of you's com'n back. I's be look'n fer you's to come back with other overseers. I's never knows no white man to want to help a nigger 'cept to giv'n him a good whupp'n. I's doesn't understand why you's be any different. Also you's speak like I's never heard before." Jeffrey stood up put on his gloves and fastened his coat.

"One day I will explain to you why I'm different. But right now I best be going before I'm missed. I don't want anyone to become suspicious and start snooping around here." He made his way over to the rooms' exit and was about to leave when the young man called after him.

"Bobby Gene, that be my name."

"Mine is Jeffrey," he said with a smile hoping this would somehow let the young man know he could be trusted.

The walk back to the plantation now seemed shorter. Even the piercing wind did not penetrate him body this time. By now the whole plantation was in full swing. Jeffrey was hoping to slip quietly into their cabin without being noticed by anyone.

The slaves hurried about to do what little chores needed to be done so they could get back to their warm cabins. Jeffrey eased his way into the cabin only to be greeted by Travor. His face showed of surprise. Travor had made himself comfortable and was leaned back in one of the chairs. He grinned at Jeffrey while he bit at the straw he had between his tobacco stained teeth. Jeffrey walked over and lifted Travor's feet off the table. Travor stood as though he did not approve of what Jeffrey had just done, but instead of a discordant reaction, he calmly walked around him.

"The boss sent me to have you come to the big house. I hope you didn't mind me making myself at home. But when I couldn't find you in the loft. I came here. The little woman was about ready to leave so she said it was okay for me to make myself comfortable till you got here." Jeffrey put on a fake grin.

"I'll go right up. Thank you for the message." He went to the door opened it then turned back to Travor. "You can leave now."

Jeffrey paused before he stepped inside being greeted by one of the house niggers. The fragrance of hot cider filled the whole mansion. Master Wellington was seated in his study as usual. He stood as Jeffrey entered into the room.

"I see Travor finally tracked you down. Come in and close the door behind you. Don't be frightened. I didn't call you here to give you a hard time or anything like that. I was just curious as to why you were not at your post this morning. Or if you might possibly have a lead as to who has been vandalizing my property." Jeffrey could feel chills starting to overtake his body. Had he been found out already. No he couldn't have. Not this soon, or was Mr. Wellington trying to trick him into a confession. Pauline, could she have mentioned what she saw earlier. He was not sure. Would he be able to shrug this off? He knew nothing of the Midwestern ways, but he knew that people were the same no matter where you went."

"Well sir, I'm sorry that I had not gotten back with you on this, but I have been trying to do a thorough job. Nevertheless, to say I have not had much luck." Mr. Wellington walked over to stir the logs on the cherry red fire when he turned back to Jeffrey with a bit of uncertainty in his eyes.

"That's peculiar. When I sent Travor to fetch you from the barn. He said you were not there. Your wife said she had not seen you all evening." Jeffrey knew he had to think of something brisk to say.

"Well you see sir. Last night I thought I heard something in the barn only to find the wind had been blowing the branches of that big old tree against the side of the barn. I guess after that I must have dozed off for a few hours. I was startled by that same pounding sound. I wiped my eyes clear and looked out the window. I saw that day was breaking so I immediately made a few rounds checking the grounds to see if I might find any traces of evidence. But came up negative. This must have been when Travor came looking for me or shortly thereafter." At this time Master Wellington was seated back at his desk.

"That wind was pretty profound, for a while I thought it was going to lift the roof right off this house." The look in his eyes became soft.

"Jeffrey you're a good man and I realize those nights you're spending in the loft would much rather be spent with the little misses, and I empathize with you. No one knows better than myself how lonely it can be when you're away from someone you love. I can't wait till Margaret gets back here myself. She's my wife. But until this mystery is solved. I'm afraid your wife will have to spend a few more nights of being alone. Besides we have a deal. I don't know, but you appear to be a man of his word."

"That I am Mr. Wellington sir, that I am, and believe me Pauline and I both appreciate the help you've given us. I'm sure this mystery will be solved shortly. Whomever it is is bound to slip up some how and when that happens. I'll be right there ready to pounce on them."

Mr. Wellington chuckled. "Never mind the pouncing for you might find it to be more than you can handle. At any rate do the best you can. You may go." Jeffrey thanked him and went for the door when Mr. Wellington called after him.

"Oh one other thing I know it's hard for you, but please try and stay awake as much as possible. The one time you close your eyes could be that one opportunity you just might lose to solve this mystery."

Jeffrey was taken by surprise by the blanket of snow that was covering the ground. As he was blindly making it back to the cabin trying to hide as much of his face from the wet blowing snow. Travor purposely bumped shoulders with him. Jeffrey could see how intimidating his eyes were, his tone of voice was the same.

"If I were you, sonny boy, I would watch my step around here. Trying to take my place with the boss could prove quite dangerous. I see lately he has taken a fancy to you, and I don't like that one bit. I also don't take kindly to whites that are nigger lovers. Tragic accidents have been known to happen. You best be careful, something just might happen to you, or better yet that wife of yours. She surely a pretty little thing. Still young and ripe for the picking. It would be a shame if something terrible should happen to her." Jeffrey struck out at Travor but was pushed back by his powerful arm. He went off laughing as his voice echoed through the passing wind.

The snow had already begun to pile up for the short distance Jeffrey had to go. He stomped his feet at the door before he went inside. Pauline greeted him with a hot cup of coffee and a smile.

"I figured you'd be needing something to warm you from that cold weather out there." He took a sip of coffee and handed it back to her.

"Let me get out of these clothes then we can sit by the fire and enjoy our coffee together. What are you doing back so soon? I wasn't expecting you till mid-day," he said while he took off his clothing making his way over to the table positioning them in front of the fire so they could be good and hot for when he ventured back to the loft.

"I was down at the washhouse helping Elsie Jane when she said she bet you'd be here 'cause of the condition of the weather outside. She said she knew we haven't been spending much time together and told me to come home to be with you. She said if anyone were to come to check on how the work was coming. Which she doubted. She would tell them she dismissed me early." Silence filled the room as Pauline stared into her coffee.

"Honey is something wrong?" Jeffrey asked as he touched her hands.

"I was just wondering, Jeffrey. How one person can be so cruel to another. I mean these black people are treated like animals, neither are they given any respect. It hurts me to see this happening. Just think we left Philadelphia so our folks wouldn't have our marriage annulled and because it was always said living in the West was the best opportunity. Go West, young man. California is the land of milk and honey riches galore. But from what I've seen from the Midwestern ways it doesn't show signs of it getting any better as we make our way to the West. How can one belittle another because of their skin color? Maybe we should have stayed in the north. After all, we are married and our folks would have had to learn how to live with it. Eventually they would have come around. Besides I'm of age.

"I know what you mean honey. We know and believe these people have a great deal to offer than just their services, if only they could get past that frightening phase that all whites are out to do them harm." Pauline's eyes lit up.

"Why, Jeffrey that's surprising of you to say. I didn't know you had become friendly with some of the black men here. As a matter of fact, I've never seen you with any of them let alone talking with them."

"Come on honey, don't be so naive. Of course I have. It may have been in passing. But I can assure you there's been some communication." He then grasped her hands tightly and leaned into her as he spoke.

"Honey listen, what I'm about to tell you. You must not say a word to anyone. Not Elsie Jane or any of these women you've become friends with, is this understood?" Pauline nodded her head.

"Yes Jeffrey, but from the expression on your face whatever it is you're about to tell me seems to be pretty serious."

"It is, Pauline. That's why you must keep quiet about this." He loosened the grip he had on her hands.

"First of all, I found out who's been stealing from Mr. Wellington." Through her excitement, Pauline jumped up.

"Jeffrey that's wonderful! Now we can be together again! Have you told Mr. Wellington yet? Boy, I bet he's really impressed with you. This might even mean a better job for you and a better appearance for myself. I'm so tired of these old dresses!" She whirled about, happily recognizing that Jeffrey wasn't sharing in her excitement. She sat down, realizing she had let her emotions get the best of her as she reached across the table and softly brushed Jeffrey's face.

Oh honey, I'm sorry this thing that you want to tell me would it have anything to do with that trip you made earlier this morning when you took those boots and other things?"

"Yes it does, that's what I was about to tell you when you went into a tailspin. As I was saying I know who's behind this mystery. Last night while I was in the loft I heard this noise. I had dozed off to sleep so at first I thought I might be dreaming."

"Enough small talk. I'll get right to the point. There was someone there. When I looked out the window I noticed this silhouette going in and out of the bare fields, so I immediately took out after him. I followed him to this cave." Pauline could hear the excitement in his voice as he continued.

"I was so frightened due to the fact I didn't know what to expect. Not to mention the darkness that was surrounding me. I walked, and it seemed that I was in the abyss. Then I finally came upon this particular room that shown of light. I realized then I had to proceed regardless of the situation, so I took my time and examined the room as I entered it. I was not aware at the time that my shadow was cast on the wall before him. He jumped and quickly turned toward me. We stood there face-to-face, and he was petrified to say the least. And so was I, not knowing what this frightened person might try and do to me. I tried to act calm, and he never knew the difference. But here's the thing. He's a Negro, and from the way he looked he's been hiding out there for a while I took those boots and Epsom salts to him because his feet were severely frostbitten. He'll be lucky if he doesn't lose them. He's practically gone barefoot. The only protection he's had was some cloth he wrapped around them, and they were pretty ragged.

"So you see, that's why you must not let this get out. Not only could it mean his life, but it could possibly mean the end of our lives too. I can see that whites around here don't take kindly to whites being friendly toward the blacks. That's why it's important we keep this quiet."

"I don't know Jeffrey. You say that our lives could be in danger if anyone ever found out you had a part in this. What if they go to the cave, then what?"

"I don't think they will find it. It's so well hidden. If I hadn't followed him, I wouldn't have ever suspected anything to be there. Besides, he needs help. If I were to turn him over to Mr. Wellington, they will probably kill him. I can't be responsible for having a part in taking another man's life regardless of what color he is. We weren't raised that way, Pauline, and you know it."

"Jeffrey babe, I empathize with you, but this isn't a game we're playing here. Our lives could be on the line. The reality is that cave is well known. How could one not live so close and not know it to be there? My guess would be it could be where many of the children would play or even be a bit curious about it at least." A smile came on her face.

"But if you think you're doing the right thing, then I'm behind you all the way." He stood up and walked around the table where she sat and lifted her off her feet, whirling her around.

"Oh, woman, I love you so much. You know that?" Pauline found herself giggling like a little girl as she was spinning.

"I believe you, Jeffrey. But put me down before we both loose our balance and fall from dizziness." Jeffrey let her down and gave her a big kiss.

"Jeffrey, I have only one question. What will you tell Mr. Wellington when he questions you about it again later?"

"I've already got that all figured out. The only reason why he was stealing in the first place is because he was hungry. I figured if I were to take him some food then that should eliminate the problems then all could be forgotten. After all, the only thing Mr. Wellington is interested in is his property. When the stealing stops, he will have reason to think that whomever it was has decided to move on."

"I admit that's a pretty good solution, but I'm not sure it will work. Mr. Wellington is a very intelligent man."

"I just can't think about that right now, but there's something I do know, and that is there's a frightened man out there that needs help, and as long as I'm able to help, which means food and or whatever it takes, so be it." Jeffrey quickly drank down his luke-warm coffee.

"Now, honey, if you don't mind, I'd like to go to sleep for a few hours. Maybe by then the snow will have stopped so I can take Bobby Gene some food."

He threw his body upon the bed followed by a long yawn, which sent him into a deep sleep. Pauline sat there a long moment, watching him as he slept. Then she got up and went to the cub board to prepare their evening meal. She had been with him long enough to know that when he put his mind to something, it got done or else. The sun had sat when Jeffrey awoke, as he jumped out of bed.

"Goodness, woman, why didn't you wake me before now?" He talked as he put on his boots. "You knew I had plans." He walked over to the window and wiped a spot from the steam that had built up so he could see. The snow had stopped but not before leaving behind a deep white blanket. Jeffrey walked over to the bed and put on the rest of his attire while he spoke to Pauline.

"You can fix up some of that stew. I'll be taking some with me." Pauline didn't answer but did what she was told. She knew that he was upset and didn't want to do anything to make matters worse. After she had filled the little pail with the hot stew, she brought it over to the table.

"Aren't you going to have any? I cooked a plenty."

"No thanks. I've got to be getting to the loft. I should have been there a while ago right at sundown to be exact." He snatched up the pail and pulled his gloves over his fingers. he gave Pauline a kiss as he passed by.

"See you later."

The weather outside was a repeat of the night before; the wind was so strong, it pushed Jeffrey toward the barn. The inside of the barn was very cold he climbed into the loft and cuddled up to the hay for warmth. He took the matches from his coat pocket so he could light the lantern. The wind outside seemed to be playing a tune, leaving a few of its cold, breezy notes to venture through the cracks of the old barn. This made him cuddle more into the hay. The steam from the stew gave him a bit of heat, but he knew it would be only a short time before that would be gone.

Jeffrey's concern was the overseer's cabins. But from this position it was difficult for him to see anything. He sat listening to the wind howling in passing, then his mind drifted to Bobby Gene. It had been several hours since he last saw him, and he was out of food as far as he could tell. He had promised him that he'd come back to check on him. What would he think if he felt he couldn't trust him? Maybe he might have thought he was trying to trick him.

Jeffrey took the stew in one hand and the lantern in the other as he slowly made his way down the ladder. He sat the lantern behind the door and stepped outside where the view would be better. As far as he could tell there was no one in sight. He could guess it was because of the cold weather. He stood there wondering what to do. Thanks to Pauline for letting him sleep so late, was not in his favor. On the other hand, he didn't want anyone to come looking for him only to find him gone again.

"Oh well it's a chance I'll just have to take," he said to himself. He lifted up the lantern from behind the door and snuffed out the light and put it back inside the barn. The moon was hidden by the clouds, so he wouldn't be seen. He hurried through the bare woods, looking back now and then, making sure he wasn't being followed. Bobby Gene had fallen asleep. But he could tell he hadn't eaten. He awakened just as Jeffrey was about to take a seat.

"Hey you, get up and see what I've brought you." The aroma escaped, filling the whole room. Bobby Gene sniffed into the air.

"I's knows what that be. I's can tell by its smell. That be some good old possum stew, ain't it?" Jeffrey was not only amazed at Bobby Gene's sense of smell but also about the excitement he was displaying.

"That's right, but how did you know?"

"Look a here, Masser, when I's be much younger on the plantation, our folks have to fin fer themself. Me and some of the other nigger boys use to catch them ugly critter fer food to feed our families. Sometimes we's even used traps and catch many of them. I's always scared to help clean them because they reminded me of a big rat. But when the womenfolks start cook'n 'em somehow I doesn't worry no more bout the way they be look'n. All's I's knows that we's be in fer some mighty good eat'n." He stared off into the distance, laughing to himself.

"I's member Joseph Dale and I's had one trapped no place to run. Joseph Dale was the kind of nigger who not be 'fraid of no kind of animal. So's he gonna try and catch it by the tail. That old possum turned on him and bit him on the hand. Boy you ought a see'd that nigger jump and took off running. I's doesn't think I's ever gonna catch him. You see'd outside his not being scared he be a fast runner too. Anyhow, we ran all the way home and tells his ma what happened. She looked at the bite and said everything was gonna be alright. It be a scratch, but don't do noth'n like that ever again. Afterward, his ma gave us each a cookie, and we went out back of the masser's house, sat there on the steps, looked at one another, and started laugh'n. That Joseph Dale was one crazy nigger. God rest his soul." As quickly as he had left, he came back to Jeffrey.

"Come now, my stomach is cry'n out fer some of that stew." He handed Jeffrey an old metal plate while he watched him filling it with the stew. "Aren't you hav'n any?"

"No, thank you." Jeffrey made with hand gestures. "I believe I lost my appetite when you mentioned something about a big rat."

"That be fine," Bobby Gene said between bites. Jeffrey sat there silently as he watched Bobby Gene gobble down the stew, licking the plate when he had finished.

"Poor Joseph Dale ifin only you's be here maybe the two of us together might find a way to help our people. Now it be no good. But I's made a promise to you's and I's gonna keep it." Jeffrey stood up.

"I'm going to have to leave now before I'm missed. The next time I come back I'd like to hear about Joseph Dale. It appears you and he were good friends. I'll also bring you that change of clothing I promised."

CHAPTER SIX

*M*any weeks had passed. Bobby Gene and Jeffrey had become the closest of friends. As they sat across from one another, Jeffrey began to speak.

"Bobby Gene, I hadn't brought this up to you anymore because I could see you were mourning. But I do believe since we've become friends, you will feel more comfortable talking to me about this. Do you recall my asking you a while back to tell me about Joseph Dale? Well, if you're ready now, I'm willing to listen."

"Well as you's might have guessed, Joseph Dale and I's be the very best of friends. We be almost like brothers. We's grows up together on the same plantation, and fer awhile we even be sweet on the same gal. Of course, we's has no idea. Anyhow, after many years of watching our folks being beat'n and abused, we decided to try and escape so's we could do someth'n to free our people. So's we's run off. We's would have made it 'cept Joseph Dale broke his ankle. I's be will'n to stay right there with him, but he says to me there be no need us both dy'n that day. That it be up to me to try and help our people. The last thing I's see'd be him ly'n there like a wounded animal and I's had to leave him like that."

"But, Bobby Gene, how do you know he's dead? You're only assuming he is." Bobby Gene jumped up in anger.

"He be dead! I's knows he be fer when I's run'n, I's heard a gunshot! They kills him, Jeffrey, just like that they kills him. But before we's departed I's promise him that I's do whatever it takes to free our people." His eyes started to well up. Jeffrey held out his hand to Bobby Gene.

"We'll do whatever it takes to free these Negroes." Bobby Gene offered his hand in return, but he had a starry look yet in his eyes.

"Bobby Gene, there's something else bothering you. Won't you please tell me what it is?"

"I's doesn't knows. I's guess ever since that first time we's, met you's help me. I's just find it hard to believe in you's, and now you's offered you's hand in friendship in want'n to help me free those Neg-g-groes," he stuttered. "Or however you's says that word, but how come you's willing to help? Does you's knows the danger you's gonna be in ifin the masser or someone were to find out?"

"Believe me, Bobby Gene. I know but there's no way anyone's going to find out. I've been very discreet. Actually, the only one that may cause me any trouble is a guy name Travor. He's already threatened me as well as my wife." A grimace look came upon Bobby Gene's face as he grasped Jeffrey by his shirt collar.

"Does I's just heard you's says the name Travor?" Jeffrey looked down at Bobby Gene's hands.

"I did indeed, and I'd be greatly appreciative if you would remove your hands from my person."

"I's sorry, but when I's heard that name, it makes me want to do someth'n foolish." He had an enhanced look in his eyes. "This Travor, would he be right here on this very plantation?"

"Yes, but why do you ask? You seem to know this person," Jeffrey replied.

"I's does. You's see'd, he be responsible fer Joseph Dale being dead. I's sure of it. He hates Negroes worst than any overseer I's ever see'd." Bobby Gene squinted his eyes at Jeffrey. "You's claim to be a friend. Ifin this be true, then what I's about to ask of you's shouldn't be of any trouble." Kneeling down in front of Jeffrey with intensity and another grimace look on his face, as he kept on with his conversation soft but overpowering at the same time.

"There be this gal who be on Masser Dalton's plantation, which not be too far from here. Her name be Anna Belle

Thompson. Ifin you's be that good friend, you's bring her to me."
Jeffrey was astonished over Bobby Gene's outrageous request.

"You've got to be kidding, right? Do you actually think I am
able to pull off something of this nature? Even if I could, I have no
explanation for wanting to see this woman. I know nothing about
her. Hell, man, I'm not even from these parts. What am I supposed
to say? 'Hello Mr. Dalton sir, my name is Jeffrey Turner, and I just
came to introduce myself. By the way, while I'm here, I was wondering if I might be able to invite one of your slaves named Anna
Belle Thompson over for tea. This act could certainly bring suspicion down upon us if I were to inquire about someone I never even
met." Bobby Gene didn't find this too amusing.

"So you's think it be too impossible."

"Yeah. I would absolutely say so without a doubt."

"Even a fool like myself knows a white man can do anything
he chooses. As far as you's not being from around these parts makes
no difference. Being white gives you's much right. All's you's have
to do is tell Masser Dalton, Masser Wellington be wondering ifin
he might borrow her for a spell. You's can make up any excuse you's
want." Jeffrey stood up.

"I'll be leaving you now. I've got to think about this one,
Bobby Gene. I want you to know if I should decide to do this, I'm
not doing it because I have to or I'm obligated to you in any way. I
owe you nothing."

The sun had set when Jeffrey got to the plantation. he dreaded
going back to that cold, lonely barn knowing there was no need for
him to be there, but on the other hand he had not found a way to
convince Mr. Wellington there was no need to worry about being
invaded again. Right now he wasn't very popular with Pauline.
For the past few months, he spent all his spare time with Bobby
Gene. He sat there in the loft watching the last of another night
disappear as daybreak showed in the east before him. The days were
coming quickly. Even the weather was beginning to get warmer.
There was still some friction between Pauline and himself. He
was still deciding whether he wanted to do what Bobby Gene had
asked of him. He knew he had kept him at bay too long as it was.

He got up and put on his boots. It was a beautiful day. The sun was gleaming down warm and luscious. Jeffrey, still having to be careful, made his way through the familiar path, looking back as usual. Today, he would try something different. Upon his entering the cave's entrance, he stepped in for a short distance, calling out to Bobby Gene.

"Bobby Gene, come up here." Bobby Gene rushed out into the entrance, hiding his eyes from the daylight.

"What is it, Masser? You sound upset."

"I just had a wonderful thought. Come take a walk with me. I'll tell you all about it."

"Are you crazy, Masser? Don't you know what will happen to me if I get caught out there? Is this your way of trying to make me repay you for all the good deeds you've done for me all these months? By going out there, getting myself kilt? No way, Masser, that's out of the question." He turned to walk away.

"Oh I understand. I'm supposed to prove my friendship to you by meeting your almost impossible demand to bring Anna Belle to you but you can't sacrifice something of yourself for me. You act as though your life is the only one at stake here. Has it never occurred to you that every time I come here my life as well as Pauline's is riding on the same line? How can you say you want to help your people when you won't even come out of the dark?"

You're just as bad as they are, wanting to be free but afraid to take a chance. Life is a chance and it doesn't consist of staying cooped up in this cave for the rest of your life. Apparently, those people aren't as important to you as you say. Your only concern is for yourself, and I'm risking everything because I believe in you. Go ahead, crawl back into your hole, and be afraid the rest of your life. You're a loser. I don't particularly care to associate with losers,"

"You don't have to worry about your secret. It's safe with me. I won't tell anyone. Besides, there's no need to turn you over to them. You're going to kill yourself by being a recluse." Bobby Gene turned back to him.

"Loser. Damn it, Masser. Haven't you checked my skin lately? It's not changed. I'm still black. You act like a friend but you speak like a fool. Even if we were to get caught the worse that would happen to you is your getting a whupping. They don't usually hang white men for not being guilty of any crime You can tell them you found me hiding out in this cave, and that you were bringing me to the masser. That be good enough for them since they won't take no nigger's word over yours."

"You selfish bastard! After all I've done for you. You still think I'm out to get you. It's fine for me to possibly lose my life for you. I'm just another one of those white overseers out there to you. You know what I said earlier about you being a loser. Well, I take that back. You're a coward! Maybe that day long ago the Lord took the wrong man."

Bobby Gene stood there trembling with his fist extended nostril flaring, ready to strike Jeffrey.

"Go ahead, hit me. Take your frustrations out on me, but you will still be a coward."

"Coward. I'll show you who's a coward, pal. Just you lead the way."

Jeffrey felt good that his power play had worked. It had almost worked too good.

"I'm sorry you'll find being outside will make you feel better." He touched Bobby Gene on the shoulder before they proceeded. "I'm sorry for what I said about your friend. I really didn't mean any harm." Bobby Gene covered his sensitive eyes from the sun.

"I know."

They walked and walked for what seemed to be miles. Every now and then a chipmunk or rabbit would peek its head up through tiny holes or burrows in the ground, the smell of spring was in the air. Jeffrey stopped and looked on Bobby Gene's eyes grew large.

"What is it Masser? What's wrong?"

"There straight ahead of us about two hundred feet. What does that look like to you?" Bobby Gene squinted his eyes to get a better view.

"Why, it looks like a lake."

My words exactly." Jeffrey turned to Bobby Gene. "Bet I can beat you to it."

"You're on." Bobby Gene replied as they both took off in a run. Bobby Gene was the first to reach the lake. He stopped at its edge as he watched Jeffrey take the plunge. He stood there watching as Jeffrey's head bobbed up then down in the water. Jeffrey waved his hands to Bobby Gene.

"Come on in. It's a bit brisk, but surprising enough it feels quite good."

"No thanks. You seem to be doing just fine for the both of us. Besides it's not hot enough for me to be out there. I'll sit here and watch."

"All right, suit yourself." He swam a bit longer before he came back to land. His wet, stringy hair covered his face. Once he was out of the water, he shook away as much of it as possible from his clothing. Then he grabbed his hair and squeezed the water from it. His body began to quiver.

"Burr, you were right. It wasn't that warm for a swim after all. One thing I know for sure. I can't stand here dripping from head to toe." Taking off his trousers then his shirt, he wrung out as much of the water as he possibly could. "We must go back to the cave so I can get dry."

CHAPTER SEVEN

*W*eeks turned into months, and months turned into spring. Now and again Mr. Wellington quizzed Jeffrey about any findings. His response was always the same.

"Negative."

Pauline was yet none too pleased with his absence but tried to pretend that all was good with them when her demeanor, along with her emotions, told a totally different story.

Jeffrey and Bobby Gene's relationship blossomed into more of a brotherly one than just friends. Even though he knew Bobby Gene hadn't questioned him about the situation concerning Anna Belle was because he didn't want to jeopardize what the two of them had. Not that it would have made a difference to Jeffrey. Things were going great between them, and he had no need of changing anything concerning it. At the same time, he had also convinced Bobby Gene to come out of the cave to take walks with him. Today would be another one of those days.

They came upon the lake they had visited months earlier, when Jeffrey decided he wanted to take the plunge again. To his favor not only did the April flowers start to bring May flowers it bought along with it some unusual hot days. Bobby Gene watched Jeffrey's head bob in and out of the water, and just as the last time they were there, he tried to convince Bobby Gene to come join him.

"Come on, the water feels good."

Bobby Gene shook his head.

"It was no then, and it's still no now." He swam a bit longer before he came to land.

"Burr, you were right again as usual. It wasn't that warm for a swim after all. One thing's for sure. I can't stand here dripping from head to toe. I have to start moving so I can get dry. Lucky for me the wind is fairly strong. Why don't we walk around the lake a bit farther? Better yet, I just had an idea. Let's go fishing," he said with enthusiasm. "You do know how to fish don't you? Besides I can't go back to the plantation till I'm dry, and we definitely can't risk building a fire." Bobby Gene gave him the most baffled look he possibly could.

"Are you joking with me right now? Did I hear you say you wanted to go fishing?"

Jeffrey didn't bite his tongue nor did he stutter.

"Ok, you've made your point. Go yonder where the sun is hot and the wind be blowing hardest while I go in search of some sticks strong enough to hold a catch." Jeffrey stood there as the wind ruffled through his flowing shirt, hearing his name being called.

"Masser Jeffrey, Masser Jeffrey's come quickly." He could hear the terror in Bobby Gene's voice as he took off running in Bobby Gene's direction. He approached him bending over for a few seconds to catch his breath.

"Bobby Gene what is it. What's wrong? You sound as though you've seen a ghost or something."

"Come and see."

Why, what's in there?"

"Just look, why don't you?"

Because he didn't know what to expect he made sure he stayed in position behind Bobby Gene. He pushed back the tall grasses with his foot.

"Oh my God, can this really be? It's a body. How did you find it?"

"I was walking looking for some twigs or falling branches when I tripped over something. I looked up, and there we be face-to-face. How did he get here?" Bobby Gene began to panic, scouting the area.

"Man, what a fool to think nobody knew about this place. How the hell could I have been stupid enough to believe this place was not known by someone else? This is wide open territory. Someone's bound to know this place exists. We found it, surely someone else has too."

Bobby Gene's paranoia became prevalent.

"If they know about this place, they know about the cave. I've got to go. I've got to find someplace else to hide. There could be someone out there watching us right this moment."

"Hold on a second, Bobby Gene. Apparently we are the only ones out here for the time being. Even though you're right about this place being known, we can be thankful that it has served your purpose for all these months. If anyone were watching they would have captured us by now. So why don't you calm down? Chances are the person may have tried to run away from another plantation fell into the water which in turn carried him downstream. This is probably as far as he got. But how he got to these bushes is another thing. Everybody has a story to tell. Let's turn him over and see what his might have been." Bobby Gene threw up his hands as he backed away.

"Not me, Masser, you can do that all by yourself."

"Ok, Bobby Gene, I get you." He knelt down, saying a brief prayer over him as he proceeded to roll the body on its back.

"Just as I suspected, see that stain there? It appears he's been shot through the heart. Unless he was being followed and needed some place to hide. It's possible he dragged himself up here before he died. If I'm right, there should be bloodstains on the ground from here to the water. Let's check it out and see. We truly can't do anything for him now." They could see faint traces of blood directing a path up to the body. It appeared that Jeffrey was right.

"All right, genius. All what you said proved to be true, But there's one problem. We can't leave him here. Someone is sure to find him."

"Correctly said, and aren't we getting educated on me? Even your vocabulary is improving." Bobby Gene beamed with joy.

"That's because of you, Masser. You've taught me a lot these few months. Not only by listening but by watching as well." Jeffrey was pleased.

"I'm glad to hear that. But there is something else I want to teach you. You need not call me Masser Jeffrey anymore. I have been meaning to mention this to you before but something else always came up before I could get around to talk to you about it."

"I'm not your masser and never have been. No man has the right to give himself that title. Be he black or white."

"You see, Bobby Gene, it's only a title a word and nothing more. But that doesn't make me any better or any more superior than yourself. These are all things you will learn in time. Now getting back to what's at hand here." He sat down in the tall grass next to the body.

"You know, buddy, I've figured out what we can do with this body."

"I'm almost afraid to ask what this idea of yours is. But what?"

"Listen, this body can benefit the both of us. I just found a way for Bobby Gene to rest in peace."

"That's it. I'm leaving. You have gone crazy."

Jeffrey grabbed Bobby Gene's arm.

"Come on, man, at least hear me out. After I tell you this, you will agree it's a fantastic one too."

Bobby Gene saw the seriousness in his face. He settled down as Jeffrey began to speak.

"I've never mentioned this to you before because I never felt it imperative. But you have the right to know now. There have been posters of you circulating about with a good, sizable reward for your capture."

"Posters of me, huh? Masser Dalton always said I was worth my weight in gold to him. I didn't understand what it meant till now. So you really have been putting yourself out there for me, haven't you. I didn't know all this was happening. Why didn't you say something about this sooner?"

"I didn't because I knew you needed help. But most of all, I needed for you to trust me. Anyhown, let's get back to what we were discussing."

"All right, go ahead, but I still don't see how a dead man is going to benefit the both of us."

"Here's the plan. He hasn't been dead that long obviously. We will carry his body back to the cave. This is the only time and way we can pull this off. Late in the evening I will come to you for the body. Then our problems will be solved."

"There you go again talking half-crazed. You still haven't told me how that body is going to help us."

"Just this. We know he's only been dead for a short time. I've been looking for a thief for months. I have someone who was caught trying to steal more property, whom by some strange coincidence will happen to be you, and none could be the wiser. The posters of you will come down, and I can spend my evenings back with Pauline the way a husband should." He discussed the rest of their plan briefly, for he needed to get back to the plantation immediately. He knew the hand of God was with him. For he had been able to get away with this secret for all these months. He took nothing for granted anymore. He was speaking of Pauline.

"Quite frankly, Bobby Gene, I'm worried about her. She has been acting even worse than ever these past few months. What we don't need at this stage is a jealous woman to contend with." Bobby Gene tilted his head to the side looking blindly into the sky as though he was searching for it to give up an answer to him.

"This does sound like a great plan. There's a minor problem. Do you possibly think you could manage to carry him back by yourself? The dead have never been one of my favorite people."

"I will do this, but at some point you will have to participate. From the cave, he will be your responsibility to carry him to the plantation. You will be able to manage that when the time comes. Won't you?"

"Ok, I get it, but it doesn't mean I have to like it or agree to it."

"It's time I get back to the plantation. I might have already been missed."

Bobby Gene positioned himself as he extended his arm out to Jeffrey, helping him to his feet.

Pauline was setting the table and had poured some water for Jeffrey to wash. After he had finished, he walked over to the table and embraced her about her waist. She pulled away.

"Come on, Pauline, how long is this going to keep up? I'm telling you I can't take this rejection any longer."

Pauline slammed the coffee cup on the table.

"You're a fine one to talk about being fed up! I'm the one who is fed up! And with good reason. since you have befriended Bobby Gene, I don't see you at all. Between my working during the day and your being gone all evening. I never see you anymore, except mealtimes. This is not good for our marriage. One would think the way you're carrying on about Bobby Gene, you and he were involved."

Before Jeffrey could think, his hand was raised as it connected to the side of her face. She brushed past him and threw herself upon the bed. Jeffrey walked over to her watching her as she wept, her face buried in the pillow.

"Pauline, I'm sorry." He knelt down before her, wanting to take her into his arms.

"I had no right to do that, but you're not the only one who's hurting here. Before this little spat, I wanted to share some news with you."

Pauline sat up wiping her tears away.

"News? What kind of news? She wanted to know.

"Only that after tonight we won't be spending our evenings apart anymore."

Pauline jumped up once again with excitement.

"Really, Jeffrey? Do you mean it? How? Did you decide to turn Bobby Gene over to Mr. Wellington after all?"

"Not exactly, honey. I can't go into details right now all I ask is that you trust me" He gently stroked at her face. "You do trust me, don't you? Now if I hear no objections, I'd like to make love to my beautiful wife."

She responded back with a nod of the head indicating a yes.

Jeffrey was edgy the remainder of the evening. Time as he knew it seemed to be standing still. Or maybe he was impatient to put their plan into action. He had never in all his days wished the evening hadn't taken so long to get there. He also knew this plan, if it were to work, had to have the precise timing. Fortunately, that one thing was evening. Not only did it give them the perfect opportunity, but everyone would be settled in their cabins and ready to bed down for the evening. Yet and still it didn't make the waiting an easier. Everything seemed to be playing out in their favor. Pauline had settled in for the night as well. He leaned over and gave her a kiss before heading to the door. He looked out the window again, hoping everything was ok. It was time for him to make his move. Bobby Gene was anxiously awaiting Jeffrey's arrival.

"Man, am I glad to see you. I've been on edge ever since I let you talk me into this stupid idea, but now that you're here. I can finally put my mind at ease." Jeffrey let out a sigh.

"I know what you mean. I've been anxious myself. I'm just hoping everything goes according to plan. Let's go over it one last time to make sure. We can't afford to make any mistake. Tonight was the first time Pauline and I have been close in months, and I'd like to keep it that way."

"Believe me, man, I've been praying for nothing but good to come out of this."

"All right, you're going to carry him back to the plantation close to the end of the henhouses. This should give you enough time to have gotten to the henhouse, grab a chicken very quickly, take it back to the body. There you will kill it using the blood to cover the upper part of his body, particularly about the wound. This will make the gunshot seem fresh. I will then position myself on the north side of the barn. I will pretend that I caught you trying to sneak into the henhouse. By this time the body should be in an upright position in case someone is watching. When I yell out stop that will be your clue to execute the rest of the plan and my shooting into the air pretending to have struck the image. You then let the body fall and get the hell out of there. I will come to you as soon as I can to let you know if we got away with it or not. Is this all understood?" He assured Jeffrey he understood perfectly.

"Remember, this is where you have to be very, very quiet that you don't disturb the other chickens or get them excited in any way. Are we clear on this as well?"

"Very clear," he assured Jeffrey once again.

"Have I not done a good job in the past? If this had not been the case, I would have been caught by now. Can we just get on with it before I lose my nerve?" He grabbed Jeffrey's hands.

"Good luck, friend."

"To you as well, my very good friend."

All was still on the plantation. Now and then the passing wind would hum a tune through the trees. Jeffrey went back to the barn. Of all evenings, this time would be the most crucial of them all. He could feel his pulse racing and his palms became sweaty. Perspiration was beginning to pop out all over his body. As he lifted the rifle in his hand, he hoped Bobby Gene had completed what he was supposed to have done. His heart was racing even more so now as he made his way to the back of the barn. Taking in a deep breath, he noticed Bobby Gene in position.

"Dear God, please let everything go accordingly." With this, Bobby Gene heard these words.

"Hey you! Stop! Stop, I say, or I'll shoot!" He ran out a bit to make it look convincing, shooting into the air as he went. He saw the body falling as Bobby Gene fled like a frightened animal. Lights began to appear as he stood there with rifle in hand. The chatter of voices was starting to surround him, as one in particular overpowered the others.

"Move out of the way! Let me through! What's going on here?" Mr. Wellington pushed his way through to were Jeffrey was standing with Travor at his side while tying the robe he had threw on in a hurry. He walked up to Jeffrey.

"All right, Jeffrey. What's going on here? I thought I heard a gunshot."

Jeffrey stood there looking on pretending to be in a daze.

"I shot him. I pleaded for him to stop or I'd shoot. I called out a warning to him, but he kept running. That's when I took out after him. I shot as I watched him fall."

Mr. Wellington turned to Travor.

"This kid has gone into shock of sorts. Go out there and see if you can make sense of what he is saying."

Travor took the lantern as he went here and there in search of the body.

"My God," Travor said as Mr. Wellington and the others looked on.

"What is it, Travor? Did you find him?" Everything got quiet. Travor shouted back at Mr. Wellington.

"Yes sir, Mr. Wellington. I found him all right. It's a nigger."

"Is he dead?" Travor sat the lantern down on the ground next to the body so he could get a better look due to the fact when the body had fallen it had landed on its face. Travor turned him over. He was astonished.

"Good Lord."

Mr. Wellington stood there waiting for an answer.

"Well, Travor, I'm waiting. Give me something."

Travor stood up.

"Oh I'm sorry, sir. He's as dead as he's going to get." He walked back up to Mr. Wellington rubbing his chin. "That's odd."

"What's odd? You seem to be a bit baffled."

"Actually it's nothing. But if I'm not mistaken, that dead nigger out there has been on the run for months now."

It was now time for Mr. Wellington to be bewildered.

"What are you saying, Travor? You know that nigger?"

"Yes, sir, and you probably as well. Remember that prized nigger Dalton had at his place? The one with the sizable reward on his head? Bobby Gene Watson. If I'm correct that's who is lying out there. Dalton fired me for not bringing him back with the other nigger that had run away with him. That's why I came here seeking work. I knew I should have told you the truth from the beginning. But I thought if you knew the truth, you wouldn't have hired me."

"You damn right, you damn fool! After all this time I find out I've hired an incompetent overseer for my niggers. Thinking he was the best, when he can't do a simple job as to tracking down some dumbass runaways. I should fire your ass here and now. But you haven't done anything to my dissatisfaction as of yet!" He shook his fist in Travor's face.

"I'm warning you. If you do anything against my principles, I'll fix it to where you will never be able to even dine with the swine. You got that?"

"Yes sir. I got it."

"Now get a couple of niggers, take that body, and put it some-where till morning. If its Dalton's nigger, then I'm sure he will want to know about it." He turned to Jeffrey.

"I can see this has been a tremendous ordeal for you. Why don't you go home and try to get some rest? I will have a talk with you in the morning. Maybe by then you will be ready to tell me exactly what happened here tonight. Some of you niggers take Masser Jeffrey home. As for the rest of you, get back to your cabins. It's only a few hours before sunup. I don't want any of you to over sleep because of your meddling."

Pauline was one of the many who had been awakened by the gun blast. She was pacing the floor when there came a knock at the door. She ran over to the door, leaning her fragile body against it as support.

"Yes? Who's there?"

"It be Willie and Joshua, Mrs. Pauline. The Masser tell us to git Masser Jeffrey home." Pauline quickly swung open the door. There before her stood a sluggish body being supported by the two of them.

"Jeffrey honey are you all right? You look awful." She noticed the rifle at his side. She looked at Willie. "Here, bring him over to the table and sat him down. What is going on here, Willie?"

"I's doesn't knows Mrs. Pauline. The Masser says that Masser here dun gone and kills himself a nigger."

Pauline was stunned.

"What? How can this be? My Jeffrey couldn't have done something like this, are you sure? That will be all, the both of you can leave now, thank you."

"Yes em. We's does hopes the Masser gonna be all right" When they left she ran back over to Jeffrey.

"Is it true? Did you shoot someone?" Jeffrey stared into Pauline's solemn face and started to laugh. He clutched her tightly in his arms.

"It worked. I didn't think we would be able to pull it off. But we did."

Pauline freed herself from Jeffrey.

"Have you gone mad? Just a moment ago when you came through the door you appeared to have been in another world. Now you're all cheerful. Suppose you tell me why the sudden change?" She demanded as she stood there.

"Pauline honey. Come sit down here next to me. I'll try and explain this to you as best as I can. It all began with Bobby Gene and myself taking a walk."

"You see, I finally talked him into getting out of that cave. Anyways we happened upon this lake. I decided to take the plunge, only to realize Bobby Gene had been right all along about it not being warm enough for a swim. There I am out of the water dripping from head to toe."

"When out of the blue I decided it would be the perfect time to try our hands at fishing, plus the fact I needed to dry out. So we went our separate ways. My getting directly in the sun's rays and him looking for something to make fishing poles with. As I was standing there drinking up the sun with my back against him. I heard this most frantic voice ever."

"Jeffrey, Jeffrey, get yourself yonder here!" I made no hesitation but did as was directed. Upon reaching him I bent over to catch my breath for a few seconds, questioning the demeanor of his voice."

"Bobby Gene, what's the matter. You act as though you've seen a ghost or something."

Bobby Gene pointed towards the tall grasses.

"Look over there?"

"Why, what's in there."

"Just look why don't you," Bobby Gene responded. Not knowing what to expect, I followed closely behind Bobby Gene, as I used my foot to push back the grass to see what Bobby Gene was talking about.

"I discovered he had stumbled upon a body. Wheels started turning over in my mind. So I decided to carve out a plan in my thoughts." The shifting of the head let Jeffrey know she wanted him to get right to the point, so he continued.

"We decided to use the body as Mr. Wellington mysterious prowler."

Pauline was still in the dark.

"You still don't understand what I am saying, do you?"

"No, Jeffrey, honestly I don't." She pushed him backward on the bed and placed her body on top of his. If this absolutely means that you're going to be here with me from now on, I don't care what you're trying to tell me. I love you, and I have missed you, Jeffrey Turner."

He gazed upon her.

"I love you too, Mrs. Turner,"

Their eyes met as they passionately kissed.

CHAPTER EIGHT

*P*auline pulled the blanket from the bed and wrapped herself in it as she walked over to the window where Jeffrey was seated.

"Honey, why don't you come back to bed? It's less than an hour before sunup." Jeffrey sat watching from the window.

"Why haven't they all gone back to sleep? I can still see lights glowing from several of the cabins." Pauline knelt down next to Jeffrey, biting at his ear.

"I don't know, honey. Maybe they're too afraid to go back to sleep." She pulled his face toward her, kissing him on the forehead. Then she whispered softly as though she didn't want anyone to hear the conversation.

"Who cares? For what reason those lights are still burning. I'm more interested in other things at the moment." She let her fingers travel through his hairy chest. Jeffrey pulled her hands away.

"Not now Pauline. Can't you see I've got something on my mind? I'm not in the mood right now."

Pauline broke out into a rage.

"Don't tell me." She sighed. "Let me guess! Bobby Gene again, isn't it? You've been setting there all this time staring out that window trying to catch the right opportunity so you can go to him. Well, I've had it up to here with him. Why don't you just up and go to him right now? It's never stopped you before."

She started beating at his body with her fist as the tears poured down her face. "As far as I'm concerned, you and Bobby Gene can both go to hell. Get out of here!" Jeffrey grabbed for his coat as he went to the door.

"I'm sorry, Pauline. Really I am. Although we are feuding, we yet have each other. He has no one. What is happening to you, Pauline? Your behavior has become quite strange lately. This isn't you." As soon as he was outside, he took off running. He had to go and do it quickly as time wasn't on his side at the moment. For some reason the trip to the cave seemed endless.

"Bobby Gene it's me Jeffrey."

"I'm here Jeffrey," a voice came from the dark. "I didn't want to risk the chance of coming up here with a light. I mean after what went on earlier this evening. I reckon we're gonna have to be extra careful till this thing has quieted down."

"I can't stay for very long. It's time for the people to start to work."

"I understand. Come follow me to the light. I think I can guess why you're here." The light shown on their faces as they stood there across from one another eye to eye, smiling, grinning, laughing, then running to embrace one another.

"We pulled it off, Bobby Gene! We got away with it. We're both home free!"

Bobby Gene broke away from Jeffrey. "I can see that look of dismay reappearing on your face. I'd like to know what it's about. I really must be going now. I don't want to take the chance of blowing the lid off this kettle." He looked at Bobby Gene. "That's just an old saying."

Daybreak as usual caught Jeffrey traveling through the woods. The closer he got to the plantation, he could tell the slaves had already begun their day. Running seemed to be a habit with him these days. Pauline had gone when he got back to the cabin. He knew this was her way of ignoring him as well as getting back at him all at the same time, not realizing how tired he was. He threw his body on the bed and fell off to sleep.

"Knock, knock, hello is anybody be heres? Masser Jeffrey, is you's in there?" Jeffrey stumbled blindly to the door and opened it. The person in front of him was still hazy, but he could make him out.

"Oh Willie. What are you doing back here?"

"Sorry to wake you's, Masser. But Masser Wellington says he want you's at the big house right away."

"Thank you, Willie. Take word back to Mr. Wellington that I am on my way." Jeffrey shut the door and walked over to the night table. He splashed some water on his face and grabbed the towel that hung on the side of the table to dry his faced with.

Each hour began to get warmer. The once bare trees were beginning to bloom. Patches of green were pushing their way through the dead brown grasses. The beautiful sounds of birds chirping in the distance could be heard as Jeffrey moved swiftly across the courtyard fastening his shirt in the process. Travor greeted his arrival at the top of the porch.

"You made quite an impression on Wellington last evening. Quite an impression indeed." Travor stood there, biting down on the straw that always occupied his mouth.

"Apparently the warning I gave you didn't seem to sink in. So I'm telling you for the last time. You'll regret it. I can grant you that." He walked past Jeffrey but looked upon him as he threw the pieces of straw to the ground.

"I realize anyone can break a piece of straw. But I've been known to have broken a few heads as well. That's a fact boy." He strolled off.

Mr. Wellington was seated at the breakfast table when Jeffrey arrived. He motioned for him to be seated at the other end of the table, signaling to the black man who stood at his side.

"Jonah, you can tell Maybelline we are ready for breakfast to be brought in now." Jonah folded the cloth towel over his right arm and exited the room.

Jeffrey sat there admiring the beautifully accented Victorian gold velvet chairs that occupied each corner of the huge room. The fireplace was that of white marble with gold flower inlays imprinted within. An elegant wall-to-wall china cabinet displayed authentic trinkets and very old family heirlooms. The best sterling and finest china money could possibly buy. The six-foot matching oak table was handsomely built with a shine so marvelous you could see a reflection of yourself in its oval shape, accented the magnificent white and gold velvet high back thrown chairs that surrounded it.

The centerpiece was a lovely five-tier candle holder with freshly cut flowers that enhanced the pretty-as-a-picture look. Over the table hung the most remarkable chandelier. The pole of individual hanging stems were of pure gold with exquisite marble cups and gold-stained goblets with white candles in each of the eight cups summing it up.

"Mr. Wellington sir, I'm honored to be having breakfast in such luxury."

"That you should be, my boy. It's not often I allow anyone except family or someone who is very special to me to enter in here."

"Breakfast shall be here any minute now. You look as though you could use some coffee. Jonah, pour Masser Jeffrey and myself some coffee. Now back to you. Last night when you left me. You were in a state of shock. How are you feeling this morning?"

"I'm fine, sir. I must admit last night left me a bit shaken, and for good reason I might add," Mr. Wellington interrupted.

"I called you here this morning because I can't express to you enough on how pleased I am. I could see from your reaction you had never done anything like this before. Being from the north. You probably never had any reason to. I realized how traumatic it can be when you shoot someone for the first time. Or any time as a matter of fact. I also know it took a great deal of courage." He stopped himself.

"Listen to me. I could go on boasting. But I didn't call you here for that. I want you to tell me exactly what you experienced last night. that's if you feel up to it."

Jeffrey could feel the nervous twitch creeping upon him again. Taking a sip of his coffee, trying to give himself time to think of what he was going to say, and hoping the feelings he was suddenly encountering would go down with the swallowing of his coffee.

"Well sir, I was in the loft as usual. When I thought I saw this figure moving toward the henhouses. I slipped outside and around to the back of the barn to see if I might get a better look. This time I was sure. He was also looking around to see if anyone was watching. As he reached for the latch to the door, I shouted at him. He took out running, and I followed pursuit and shouted once again, but he kept running. He was too far for me to catch. So I shot. I was aiming for his legs. Then I saw him fall. Mr. Wellington. I had no idea when I fired I'd kill him." He hung his head in shame.

"That's all right, young man. I can see you are still touched by this. The most important thing is that you did what I asked of you. It's a pity for you that it had to turn out this way." Breakfast had arrived, but that didn't stop Mr. Wellington from babbling on.

"Jeffrey, if you hadn't noticed I've taken a great liking to you. You remind me so much of someone I use to know. I recall telling you once there might be a position around here for you if you were to stay on. Well, I'm glad to announce you have just been chosen to be my right-hand man. In case you're wondering what that means. You will be assisting me in my private affairs. Like accompanying me to auctions. Filling in for me whenever I can't. It's whatever the case maybe. It's also contingent on whether you and the little misses decide to stay." Jeffrey was overwhelmed.

"Ah, Mr. Wellington sir, I'm flattered that you think so highly of me. But I know nothing about being a business man. I wouldn't know where to begin. Or how to act."

"Poppycock, young man. How do you think I got where I am today? I was young and inexperienced once myself, you know. I made it work. I was taught in the same fashion I'm willing to teach you. You haven't touched any of your food. Aren't you hungry/"

"I guess it's the news. I'm too excited to eat."

"Good enough. Jonah, you can clear this away. We're finished. as for you, young man. I won't take no for an answer. I'll also be needing the assistance of that pretty little woman of yours, I would like her to help me here at the house. She will be writing letters and taking care of other personals things Margaret did around here. God only knows when she will return. The things I left her in charge of have piled up. I yet have one last thing to say. This is a very large house. It gets a bit lonely here. Especially when there are only servants present. So I've decided that the two of you should move in here with me. I'm sure Margaret will agree with me when she gets back. Margaret is my wife." Jeffrey felt faint.

"Mr. Wellington sir. You're much too kind. Particularly when we are not deserving of it."

Mr. Wellington stood up.

"Let me be the judge of that. Besides, my instinct tells me you're going to do fine, and my instincts are seldom wrong."

"So for your first assignment, should you decide to stay on, I want you to take that body back over to Dalton. If that nigger is truly his. I'm sure he will want to know about what happened to him." He reached into his pocket and pulled out an envelope.

"Take this and give it to Dalton. This should explain everything to him. I've enclosed some compensation for the loss of his nigger. Travor will be accompanying you to show you how to get there. Everything should be ready and waiting for you out front. If I were you, I'd get started right away. You have a busy schedule ahead of you today with your moving and all." Jeffrey walked to the end of the table where Mr. Wellington stood and gave him a firm handshake, as he accepted the envelope."

"By taking this envelope gives me the indication you've decided to stay, at least for the time being. Am I right in saying so?"

"That is correct, and thanks again, sir. I'm sure Pauline will be as excited about this as I." Travor was waiting out front and raring to go.

"Well don't just stand there looking like an idiot. Get up here so we can be on our way." A most peculiar expression came over his persons'.

"Man, I can't wait to see the look on ole man Dalton's face when he sees me. I have got an overdue debt that needs to be collected on. And that is just what I intend on doing while I'm there." Travor laughed out loud as Jeffrey looked on. The trip was rather boring. But with spring just beginning to bloom, at least the scenery made it worthwhile. Several times they had to stop and push the wheels from deep mud puddles created from the melted snow that lingered behind. Jeffrey purposely kept his eyes on the path from time to time, looking for landmarks to use for his long trip back. He could see Travor was none too excited about his traveling companion either. The silence was beginning to wear on Jeffrey.

"How much longer do we have to go Travor? It seems as though we've been on this path forever." He could see Travor looking at him from the corner of his eyes.

"What's the matter, boy? You don't like my company either? Don't worry, you'll be there before you know it. As a matter of fact, when we round that bend yonder, you'll be able to see the house from a distance being the trees are still partly bare." The closer they got, Jeffrey could feel himself tensing up again.

"What will he say? How is he going to handle this situation? Maybe he was able to fool Mr. Wellington and Travor. But would he be able to fool this Mr. Dalton? Being this nigger was supposedly his. If anyone would know his true identity, Mr. Dalton would. The envelope came to mind.

"Maybe this will do it," he said to himself.

"What did you say?" Travor asked.

Barking dogs surrounded the wagon as strange black faces lined up on both sides of the muddy path leading up to the front of the mansion. Travor pulled up even with the man and signaled the horses to halt. The face of the man turned red as he made his way down the steps, totally oblivious to Jeffrey's presence. Jeffrey sat there as the man stepped down from the porch and walked to the side of the wagon where Travor was seated.

'You low down snake in the grass! You dare show your face back here after all this time. I have a good mind to go inside right this minute, get my rifle, and blow your ass all over this plantation. You have a lot of gall coming back here, Travor." His huge hand reached out toward Travor when Jeffrey captured his attention.

"Ahhh Mr. Dalton sir my name is Jeffrey Turner. You don't know me nor I you. But the reason we're here is Mr. Wellington asked that we deliver something to you, along with this envelope." Mr. Dalton shoved Travor back toward the wagon seat and walked around to Jeffrey's side of the wagon. He looked up at him with his sharp, threatening eyes.

"What is this you say about having something for me?"

"Yes, sir. Mr. Wellington specifically expressed that I give you this envelope and to tell you that everything would be explained in it."

"Well, where is it?" He snapped his huge fingers at Jeffrey.

"Let's have it. I'm a very busy man who doesn't have all day." Jeffrey removed the envelope from his pocket. He could feel the sweat in his palms. It wasn't a secret that his hands were trembling when he presented Mr. Dalton with the envelope. Mr. Dalton stood back from the wagon as he opened the envelope and began to read its contents. Upon finishing it, he started back up the steps, waving them off as he did so.

"Go down the path. There you will find some niggers. Tell them I said to bury him." Jeffrey became more intense as he let the words flow out of his mouth. For he knew what he was about to ask could destroy everything.

"But sir, don't you care to check and make sure he's one of yours?"

"If Wellington says he's mine he's mine. I have no reason to doubt him. We've known each other for many years. I know him to be a fair man and that his word is his bond. Just as mine."

Jeffrey silently breathed a sigh of relief as Travor spoke up.

"If this is true, Dalton, then I'm sure you won't object to my collecting on a debt that is due me." Mr. Dalton quickly turned about face.

"Debt? What kind of debt? What makes you so sure I owe you anything except a good old-fashioned ass kicking?"

"I recall your saying to me at the time getting Bobby Gene back was worth any price. It took a while, but he is back. Not in the fashion you expected him I'm sure."

"All right, Travor, I'm intrigued. Since you have the floor, I'll be humored. So say on. What makes up the benefactor of any debt I owe you?"

"Simply this. You have your prized nigger back. I kept my end of the deal, which means you owe me. You have something I want. When I get it then, we can say we're even."

Mr. Dalton was furious.

"You're smarter than I gave you credit for. Seems as though you know a man in my position can't afford to start bad rumors circulating. Not that I would be intimidated by your trivial lies. Plus, we both know no one would believe you anyway. It's just that honestly carries a great deal of weight and honor around here. Which is more than what I can say for some."

"Before I make any deals with you, I want to know what it is I'm agreeing to."

"That's fair enough," Travor said with a wide grin that filled his whole face while chewing on the piece of straw all at the same time.

"You have a black Philly named Anna Belle Thompson. Give her to me, and we can call everything even Steven so to speak.

Mr. Dalton stood there thinking.

"Anna Belle. Why would you want her? She's of no value to you."

"Let's just say for personal reasons. Besides, once a bitch been properly broken in, it's hard for her to get used to a different stud. You of all people should know that. You've tamed quite a few of these black wenches yourself, haven't you?"

Mr. Dalton's demeanor was quite surprising. There was no hesitation or thought over the matter.

"All right, she's at their cabin. She wasn't feeling too good today, so she and her mother are both there." He turned again to walk away.

"I'll also be needing a bill of sale." Travor spoke assuredly. "To make everything legal and all. You know, in case I were to get questioned by the sheriff for some strange reason." Mr. Dalton became enraged again then a moment of silence crept in.

"Don't think you have won, Travor. All dogs have their day. The only reason I'm giving her to you in the first place is because I am a man of his word. So another word of caution to you one last time. If I ever catch you anywhere on or near this property again, you're as good as dead. I hope you grab a hold of it this time. It would also be wise for you to stay out of my sight publicly. My generosity or honorable nature may not always strive with me." He directed his attention to Jeffrey.

"Young man. It was a pleasure making your acquaintance. Hope to see you again. By the way, be careful of the company you keep. You seem to be a good young man. Ain't no need of your getting a tarnished or bad reputation for yourself, by the company you keep, if you know what I mean."

Jeffrey returned the greeting.

CHAPTER NINE

*J*effrey sat there helplessly watching as the door to the tiny cabin was being kicked in, then he saw him disappear. He stood there at the door grinning from ear to ear. Watching Mrs. Thompson back away from him in terror.

"Hello, Lorene. You seem a bit surprised to see me." Anna Belle rushed into the room to see what was going on.

"Mama, is you's be all right? I's heard you's scream." She stopped her words froze in her mouth, as she looked toward the door. The most terrifying look overwhelmed her as her mouth fell open.

"Howdy, Anna Belle. I was just telling your ma here how surprised she looked to see me. But I believe you have her beat." He started toward her as she tried to flee from him, but she had nowhere to go. Grabbing her, he threw her on the pallet that rested on the other side of the room as she let out a bloodcurdling scream her body connected with the floor. Mrs. Thompson ran over striking at Travor.

"Leave her be." She took a flying spin, being knocked out cold as her head hit the handle of the cook stove. All this time Jeffrey sat there on the wagon seat, wondering what to do. Even the others seemed to be ignoring the screaming and scuffling. Travor waited to make sure Lorene was no longer a threat to him. Then he turned back to Anna Belle. He grabbed her by her right wrist and turned her to himself when he noticed something different about her.

"Well I be damned, the wench done gone and got herself with child. How many months gone are you, nigger?"

"This here be my's eight month."

"Eight months, you say." He rubbed his chin. "So that bastard you're carrying is mine?" Anna Belle slowly shook her head.

"Yeees, Masser. I's be with you's child."

"Well whatta you know. Not only did I get myself a bitch. But a bastard child on the way as well." He all but patted himself on the back. "You did good Travor. You did damn good as a matter of fact." He gave her a hard cold stare. "I came here gal to pick you up. You belong to me now, nigger. So I'm giving you five minutes to gather your belongings and get out yonder to the wagon so you can get to your new home." The terrifying look registered with her as she stood there watching Travor walk over to the door.

"Don't forget five minutes." The door slammed behind him. Anna Belle wasted no time gathering her things and threw them into the satchel next to the pallet. She walked over to where her mother was lying. Tears filling her eyes as she bent over to kiss her good-bye. Her mother didn't move. Anna Belle lifted her face to the heavens, closed her eyes and began to pray.

"Dear God. Please doesn't let mama be dead." She wiped away her tears as she squeezed her mother's hands for the last time, then she stood up.

"I's loves you's Mama." She picked up the satchel and went outside. Travor was untying the horse that was hitched to the back of the wagon.

"I've got a few chores to do for Masser. Wellington. This boy will take you to where you need to go." He mounted the horse.

"Don't think about trying something like that nigger friend of yours or you are liable to end up like him." His vicious eyes glared down on her.

"Do I make myself clear? He then looked at Jeffrey. "That goes for you too sonny boy." Anna Belle lowered her head, hoping to shake off the threatening look Travor was giving the both of them.

"Yes, Masser. I's heard you's." he kicked the horse, letting it know he was ready. Anna Belle held tightly to the satchel as she climbed up onto the wagon Jeffrey offered his help, but she rejected it. She sat down next to him as he gave the reins a jerk as the horses started to trot. Anna Belle turned looking back toward the old cabin, watching it get smaller until there was nothing but trees surrounding the plantation. Occasionally she would use the sleeve of her blouse to wipe away the falling tears. Jeffrey watched her clutching tightly to the satchel. He cleared his throat.

"My name is Jeffrey. Yours is Anna Belle, is it not?" Anna Belle kept watching the road ahead.

"Yes, Masser sir."

"There's no need for you to be formal with me. We yet have a way to go before we get to the other plantation. Won't you talk with me?" Anna Belle turned quickly to Jeffrey.

"Masser Dalton says we's never to speak to white folks 'bout noth'n." As quickly as she had turned to him, she turned away.

"That may be true in most white men's cases. I'm different. You can talk with me if you'd like." Jeffrey waited for a response but got nothing.

"If you're afraid I will tell Travor that you talked with me. Then you need not worry. He will never have to know. I have a secret." He leaned into her. "I don't care for him any more than you do." Anna Belle still didn't respond but focused straight way.

"Aren't you even concerned as to where I'm taking you?" This briefly got her attention again.

"Makes me no never mind. I's doesn't has no say 'bout the situation anyhow. So's why should I's be concerned? You's gonna let me go?" It was Jeffrey's turn to be silent. "I's thought not. Then there be no need fer talk'n anymore."

The singing of birds filled the silence. When they reached the plantation, Jeffrey took Anna Belle to their cabin. Pauline was putting the finishing touch of cleaning to it. She stood there, stunned by Anna Belle's presence.

"Pauline," Jeffrey began. "This is Anna Belle Thompson. Anna Belle, this is my wife, Pauline. Anna Belle is going to be staying here in our cabin." Anna Belle curtsied.

"Howdy, Mrs. Pauline." Pauline ignored her and looked at Jeffrey.

"What do you mean she's moving in here? We barely have room for ourselves." Jeffrey could see a guilty expression come on Anna Belle's face.

"Calm down, why don't you, and give a fellow a chance to explain himself before you go half-cocked." He looked at Anna Belle with a smile, in hopes it would bring some comfort to her.

"I haven't exactly talked with Mr. Wellington yet about your staying here. But I'm sure it will be all right." He turned back to Pauline. "As soon as we can get packed, we will have all the room we could ever need. Mr. Wellington has invited us to move into the big house with him."

"Come on, Jeffrey, this is no time for jokes, especially not now with the mood I'm in." But seeing the expression on his face her voice became gentle. "You're serious, aren't you?"

"Of course. Do you think I would joke about something like this?" Pauline ran over to Jeffrey and threw herself into his arms. All the while Anna Belle was yet standing in the doorway, gripping tightly to her satchel.

"Oh Jeffrey. It's finally really happening! All those endless nights of dreaming have finally come true! We're moving to the big house!" She pulled at him.

"Come, let's not tarry! This is an exciting day for us! I want to pack as quickly as we can and get up there!" Jeffrey eased Pauline down to a sitting position.

"Slow down. There's much more. I haven't had the chance to tell you. Not only are we going to be living in the big house, Mr. Wellington has offered us jobs. Good jobs, in fact. I'm to be his executive assistant, and he wants you to be his personal secretary. At least till his wife returns." Pauline grabbed her head this was so overwhelming to her.

"Please forgive my wife's rude behavior. You can take your bag over there and lay it beside the bed. After we are gone you can settle yourself in. When we get moved up to the big house, maybe Pauline will introduce you to some of the women here on the plantation. She has gotten to know a few of them fairly well since our arrival here."

Pauline intervened.

"Oh, honey. I don't believe I will have much time for that. I'm sure they will find out there is a new person here. They will come over and acquaint themselves. Now come on, Mr. Wellington is probably wondering what is taking us so long."

When they got to the big house, Jeffrey and Pauline found out that Mr. Wellington had one of the master bedrooms prepared for them. Pauline stood there speechless drinking in all its beauty.

"Oh Jeffrey. Its magnificent! Neither of our folks back home had anything so elegant and of this magnitude." He watched Pauline marvel over the beauty as he spoke to her.

"Look, honey, I've got an errand to run." He moved toward the door. "After everything has been put away, Mr. Wellington would like to speak with you as soon as possible. If you need me, I'll stick around and help." Pauline practically shoved him out the door.

"That's Ok, honey. I just want to admire all this beauty alone." Jeffrey went back to the cabin. He didn't bother knocking, knowing Anna Belle may not answer due to the fact she was in a strange place. For all he knew, she might have made him stand there. This would be a natural assumption due to the recent ordeal she encountered with Travor. She was seated at the table. Jeffrey could see that fear was yet with her, and that she had been crying a lot.

"Excuse me for just coming in. I didn't know for sure if you would invite me in or not. I promise it won't happen again. I spoke with Mr. Wellington about you. He said it would be fine, no harm has been done, since we have moved to the big house." Anna Belle sat there looking at him.

"Thank you's, Masser Jeffrey. Ifin you's or Mrs. Pauline need some'n, let me knows. I's help in any way I's can. That be ifin Masser Travor don't mind. That Masser, he be a mean one." Jeffrey went over to the table where Anna Belle sat.

"Funny you should mention that. There is something you can do for me. But we have to do it right now before Travor comes back. I can't tell you what its's about because that part of it is a surprise. This is what I want you to do. At the end of the cabins there are some henhouses. I want you to go and wait there till I come. After that we will begin on your surprise." Anna Belle sat there puzzled but agreed to do what Jeffrey had asked. He got up and walked to the door.

"One other thing. Make sure you are not followed. This is most important."

"Yes, Masser Jeffrey. I's does my best." She went over to the window and looked out. To her surprise no one had noticed or paid any attention about her arrival. Or could it have been they had felt the wrath of Travor and was more frightened than anyone could ever imagine. Everyone was hurrying about with sackcloths of seeds.

The days had gotten warmer, so it was time for them to start the crops. Everyone except the house slaves or laundry workers devoted most of their time working the fields, getting them ready for the year. Anna Belle didn't know how long she stood at the window. She didn't care. Her main concern was to do exactly as Master Jeffrey had asked of her. Not to mention the curiosity as to what kind of surprise this stranger would have for her. Especially after just meeting her. Anna Belle made sure everyone had passed then she eased her way to the barn. she ran around the barn and caught her breath. She saw the henhouses in the distance. But she suddenly froze. What was she doing? Why was she here? She knew nothing of this strange man. So what kind of surprise could he have for her? Was this another white man who wanted to rape her? If so, she wasn't going to have it.

She stood there for a long moment just staring at the henhouses, wondering what she should do. Should she trust this stranger, this person? After all, he is a white man, and they aren't usually as pleasant as this one has been. But on the other hand, something inside her was strongly telling her to trust him. He was very nice to her on their way back to the plantation. She finally decided to follow her gut. Looking to see if anybody had followed her, she ran up to the henhouses and went inside. Jeffrey was already there waiting.

"I was beginning to wonder what happened. I expected you to be here a while ago." Anna Belle dropped her head.

"I's sorry, Masser I's only dun what you's says. Niggers kept go'n bye the cabin. I's doesn't want to take no chance of being followed." Jeffrey became empathetic with her.

"Ann Belle, I'm sorry there's no need for you to be upset. I'm the one who needs to apologize to you. You haven't done anything wrong. I'm just a bit nervous. Well, a lot nervous about us not being discovered. Plus, we can't risk you not being at the cabin when Travor returns. The fact is, I'm overly excited about the surprise doesn't help matters either. Before we go, I want to make absolutely sure you weren't followed." He stuck his head out to see if the coast was clear.

"All is well. Now follow me quickly." They ventured deep into the woods. Anna Belle stopped.

"You's lies. There be no surprise. Why you's bring me out here. You's just tell me that so's you's can git me out here." She took off running back toward the plantation, it all seemed like déjà vu to her all over again. Jeffrey caught up to her and hung onto her. She struck out at him vigorously. Jeffrey was astonished by her sudden change of behavior. He shook her, hoping this might snap her back to reality.

"Anna Belle, what's the matter? Why did you run away like that?" Anna Belle kept struggling with Jeffrey but he still had a grip on her.

"I don't understand why the sudden outburst. Until you explain it to me, I won't be able to help. Besides, I'm not letting you go till you give me some explanation. You may as well stop this fighting and tell me what this is all about." Anna Belle hung her head as she had done so often.

"You's want to hurt me like Masser Travor dun. He takes me to a place like this, then he hurts me."

"Anna Belle, look at me." He waited till their eyes met. "I still don't have the slightest notion as to what you're talking about. But I can assure you I didn't get you out here to harm you. I'm going to let you go. You can trust me and continue on with me. Or you can turn and go back to the plantation. Either way, the choice is yours." He slowly removed his hands from her shoulders, and proceeded on toward the cave. He didn't turn around, but he could tell she was still behind him.

"Masser Jeffrey. I's doesn't knows why. I's believe you's. Masser Jeffrey, you's heard me?"

Jeffrey kept on walking. Upon entering the cave, Jeffrey and Bobby Gene were standing face-to-face when Anna Belle came to the entrance.

"Masser Jeffrey, I's be talk'n to you's back yonder. Doesn't you's heard me?"

"Yes Anna Belle, I heard you." Bobby Gene moved his head slightly to the left so he could get a better view. Tears of happiness filled his eyes as his whole body became visible.

"I can't believe my eyes." He extended his arms outward and ran toward Anna Belle.

"Anna Belle Thompson, is that really you?" Anna Belle blinked several times, stunned, she ran toward him as well

"Oh Bobby Gene. You's be alive. Thank God you's be alive. But how? Where you's be all these months? How does you's knows Masser Jeffrey? Everyone says you's be dead."

Bobby Gene put his hand over her mouth to stop the flow of questions.

"Woooo, slow down now. Only one question at a time. But before any questions are answered. Let's go and sit down. I'm sure you and Anna Belle have a lot to talk over. But I must warn you. You have to do it fast for we must be getting back very soon. I'll go up front, so you can visit a bit." He looked at Anna Belle and smiled.

"Thank you's, Masser Jeffrey. This truly does be a surprise. I's won't be long. I's promise."

Bobby Gene offered his hand.

"Thanks, man. I don't know how I will ever repay you for this. I owe you one." Bobby Gene led Anna Belle into his living quarters. She looked around the room.

"Come sit, over here by the fire. I'm sure you'll be much more comfortable. You know I can't understand why it's always so cool in these places. Even when the weather outside is blistering hot." Anna Belle sat there watching Bobby Gene with a questionable look in her eyes but also distraught by what she had just experienced with Travor and her mother. She started to weep bitterly.

"She be dead, Bobby Gene. Mama be dead. Travor just not long ago kills mama. I hate him, Bobby Gene. Ifin I's git the chance. I's gonna kills him. I's will."

"Hush now, I won't have you talking that nonsense. Travor will have his day. I hope I'll be there to partaker of it." Anna Belle pulled away from him.

"What dun happened to you's Bobby Gene? You's look different. You's act different, and you's speak none like the way I's does anymore. Does it have some'n to do with Masser Jeffrey?" She leaned over closer to Bobby Gene to whisper as though she didn't want anyone to hear what she was about to say.

"Ifin I's be you's. I's be careful as to how much trust I's put in Masser Jeffrey. Doesn't you's knows, ain't no white man can be trusted at all as far as us niggers concern."

A flare of anger came over Bobby Gene.

"You're a fine example to question someone," he spoke while looking down at her belly. "You really had Joseph Dale and myself fooled. Pretending to be untouched. When all along you were probably sneaking off with some of the guys that were always sweet on you. Looks like maybe you weren't so untouched after all."

Anna Belle stood up quickly.

"I's has a good mind to slap you's face. Ifin you's were still the Bobby Gene I's knows, then you's knows I's not like them other girls who been broken in at the plantation. I's doesn't knows what that white man have dun to you's head. But you's speak'n crazy. Fer you's information. This here baby be Masser Travor's."

"That be right. After I get the news about Joseph Dale being dead and you's miss'n. I's come from seed'n Mrs. Lucille at the barn, who had been taken there earlier fer a whupp'n, fer talk'n back to Masser Dalton. After hear'n some words of wisdom from her. I decided it was time for me to git myself home."

"Suddenly my face be covered up, and I couldn't see'd anything, someone grabbed me from behind putt'n pressure on my left arm causing me to surrender to his demand. Shov'n me towards the woods. It be Masser Travor he forced me into the woods and raped me. But you's doesn't see'd any fault in that, being he be white and all. Doesn't you's knows they doesn't care noth'n 'bout no nigger? No matter how much a friend you's think they's be."

"That's not true. Jeffrey's not like that! He really wants to help! Listen here, I'll show you." He reached down and picked up the little black book and opened it as he read the words off the paper.

"In the be-ginnn-ing God created the heavvven and the eeearth."

When he was finished he looked up at Anna Belle.

"See what I told you. Anna Belle. He's even teaching me how to read and other things. He said will help me as well as the other Negroes in the long run."

Anna Belle stood there mortified.

"Bobby Gene Watson. You's dun been bewitched. Doesn't you's knows that it not be human fer niggers to say words off a piece of paper like that. Preacher Finley says that every Sunday in the church sermon. He doesn't knows how to read. But he preaches the word just the way his pappy, and his pappy before him. None of them could read. Ifin Masser Jeffrey be such a good friend to you's, why he not tell you's he and Mrs. Pauline dun gone and got themselves an invite to live in the big house?" She could see the surprised look on his face.

"Yes, that be right. I's live in their cabin. What good it be to them anyhown." Anna Belle was about to leave when Jeffrey came for her.

"I think we better be going. We've stayed longer than we should have." Bobby Gene stood there looking at Jeffrey.

"Is it true what Anna Belle says about your moving to the big house?"

"Yes, it's true. I meant to tell you earlier. But after seeing how excited the two of you were to see each other, it didn't seem important at the time."

Bobby Gene's eyes hardened.

"I can see from that look you don't believe me. I'll explain it all when I come back. Which is going to have to be limited since we have moved to the big house." He looked at Anna Belle.

"You had not right to tell Bobby Gene about my move. I was planning on breaking the news to him myself. While you were at it, did you think to mention to him that the move only took place a few hours ago at the same time we offered you our cabin?" He waited for a reply but received none. "Just as I thought. I know what you're trying to do. I hope you haven't succeeded in destroying what he and I have built together all these months." He walked away. Anna Belle looked into Bobby Gene's eyes and grinned.

"You's trusty friend huh?" She called to Jeffrey. "I's be ready to go anyhown. This man be not the Bobby Gene I's knows or care to knows."

CHAPTER TEN

*T*hree months had passed. A lot of changes had come about on Wellington's plantation. Anna Belle had a son whom she named Gabriel after her father. Still insisting she didn't want to have anything to do with Bobby Gene, a telegraph had come for Mr. Wellington. Apparently on her way back from her mother's, the stage Mrs. Wellington was riding on had a severe accident. Everyone was pronounced dead except the driver. His body got pretty torn up. Mr. Wellington unable to accept his wife's death, entered into a world of depression and started drinking again. Any time of the day or evening he could be found in his study. The doctor made urgent trips out to the plantation to check on him and asked Pauline if she might play nurse maid to him. If there were any changes, she was to let him know immediately.

Pauline's attitude had changed altogether. She no longer had time for the women she used to chat with when they lived in the cabin. When she wasn't doing her work or nursing Mr. Wellington, she was ordering clothing from the catalog. Bobby Gene had seen less and less of Jeffrey. His reading and other basic skills improved each day. Travor, now that was a different story all itself. Ever since he had found out about Jeffrey's position, he tried to find ways to manipulate his relationship with Mr. Wellington Jeffrey was standing outside the study door when Doc. McFallon came out.

"How is he, Doc? Is he getting any better?"

"I'm afraid not, my boy. It's not that he's terminally ill. He could come out of this anytime he desires. But he has to be the one to make that decision. Until he does, there is nothing anyone can do. Try and get him to cut back on the alcohol That's my main concern now. If he keeps drinking like this, he's going to drink himself into a state of oblivion or even kill himself. I've left some medicine with Pauline to give him twice a day. This should illuminate some of the depression he is experiencing. But he must take it. Or it won't do any good. That old coot, and I have been friends for quite some time now, and I'd like to keep it that way."

In July and August, it rained severely. Stopping only long enough for the sun to shine a little reassuring everyone it still existed. Mr. Wellington was now confined to a wheelchair due to an illness he had contracted. Was even more intolerable than ever before. It appears one night in July while he was on his way back from a slave auction, had caught what he thought was a cold ended up being crippling pneumonia. Maybelline, one of his house servants, died of old age as did a few of the other old timers. Mr. Wellington sat on the front porch of his twenty-two room mansion and watched the falling endless rain.

"This damn rain. It's ruined everything."

"Did you say something, Mr. Wellington, sir?" Pauline slightly bent over to hear his response. He turned his head to meet Pauline's face; those once cold, vicious green eyes were sunk in his eye sockets, replaced by small red veins where healthy white pupils us to live. The once white hair was gone. His face was shy of being a skeleton, and the blue veins looked like a tattered road map. Showed the wear and tear all over his frame of a body.

"I was just thinking, Pauline. It took a century and better for this place to be where it is today." There was a sound of fury in his voice. "This damn rain has ruined it all. Look at my crops. Cotton, everything's damn near washed away." He snapped his bony fingers. "Just like that." He motioned to Pauline.

"Wheel me into the house now girl. There is some work that needs to be tended to in my study." Pauline doing as she was told but not liking it, tried to speak out on his behalf as far as his health and wheeled him toward his bedroom.

"Mr. Wellington sir. You remember what Dr. McFallon said about you getting the proper amount of rest due to your illness? Mr. Wellington looked up into Pauline's timid grey eyes.

"My illness is all I seem to hear around here these days. The hell with McFallon that old geezer. I'll probably out live him anyway. Now do as I tell you, girl, and wheel me into my study this instant. Besides, I pay your wages. Not that old fool." Once he was in his study, he sat there watching the rain bounce off the windows. There came a knock at the door.

"Come in, it's open."

"Excuse me, Mr. Wellington sir."

"Oh, Jeffrey, my boy. Come in, come in, what can I do for you?"

"Well, sir, I was wondering. If you don't mind, I'd like to go visit with Anna Belle for a bit." Mr. Wellington squinted his eyes.

"Of course, I mind. I'm worried about you Jeffrey. You're not trying to bring out some of that upbringing by being kind to any of my niggers, are you? I do hope not. There's nothing I hate worse than a nigger lover. While at home you can do as you please. But you are in Missouri now, son, and as long as you are a resident here, you will play the game and abide by the rules."

Jeffrey tried to sound convincing.

"Ever since she came here, she has not been allowed to associate with the other women around here. It's not that they wouldn't like to visit her. According to Travor, she's not allowed company from anyone. So I thought I might assure her that the other women on the plantation aren't unfriendly. They were warned about not going around her."

"I see, but why can't Pauline do that? After all, she did befriend a few niggers before your moving up here, did she not?"

"I know, sir. But whenever I have asked her to do so, she's always too busy or has some other excuse." Mr. Wellington chuckled.

"Enjoying the good like, is she huh?"

"Yes, sir, I'm afraid that's all its about with her these days. Seem she has settled into her new lifestyle quite well indeed. She's acting as though she's forgotten where she came from, and that frightens me."

"OK, son. You've made your point. I want you to know this is the only time. I can't have this out of my employees. I need someone who's going to be civil about this situation. If you don't have the stomach for it, you should consider going back to Philadelphia."

"Thank you, sir. I promise I won't ask anything like this of you again."

"I believe you, son I also want you to know that deep inside. I'm not the tyrant everyone projects me to be. I can't show even the slightest emotions for these niggers, or it could be very detrimental. I know there are some niggers as well as the white man who would like to find a weak link in me." Silence fell upon the room for a moment as Jeffrey saw a bit of decency in Mr. Wellington's demeanor.

"I'm not saying I feel for these Negroes in the way that you do. I am concerned for them. In a different way perhaps. Don't think that I haven't been frightened or intimidated by them for years. Knowing if they found one strong nigger amongst the lot of them to convince them to band together in numbers. My life as well as my overseers could have been snubbed out long ago." He shook his head as though he were waking himself up from a trance.

"I'm sorry, young man. I've never expressed that even to Margaret. Or my closest friend. I also told you in the strictest of confidence. It's just something about you. Maybe it's because I'm trying to relive Matthew's life in a way I thought it should have been through you. Why did he have to betray me?" Mr. Wellington seemed to go into a babbling frenzy as he yet spoke.

"Don't you know what you've done, boy? We'll be the talk of the town. The whole damn county. Have you no pride about yourself. Couldn't you have just bred the wench instead?" Jeffrey could see that Mr. Wellington was being engulfed with his reminiscence. Or was he becoming weak-minded? Jeffrey never heard the mention of one Matthew before.

"What did you say, sir? I mean the part about someone named Matthew." Mr. Wellington looked back at Jeffrey.

"Never you mind, sonny. You know how one's mind gets to wondering after a certain age. You best be going before I change my mind. Oh yeah, don't be too critical of your little misses. We're only on this earth for a season. Let her enjoy this time while she has the opportunity." With this he waved Jeffrey off.

The ground outside was like sinking in quicksand. The mud was so deep, Jeffrey wondered why he even bothered to come out at all. He knew by saying that he wanted to check in on Anna Belle would be the only way for him to sneak and see Bobby Gene as well. It had been some time since the two had seen one another. Who knows, Bobby Gene may even think he had betrayed him. Jeffrey made his way to the porch, tripping in the process. The loud thump aroused Anna Belle to come to the door. Looking down at him, she spoke.

"Masser Jeffrey, why you's ly'n on the porch?"

"I lost my balance walking through the mud. The reason why I'm here, I was wondering if I could talk with you."

"Gee, Masser Jeffrey, I's doesn't knows. Masser Travor says ifin he catches anybody here, he's gonna give me a good whupp'n."

"If that's what bothering you, I will speak with Mr. Wellington first thing in the morning about his threat to you. Now it's very important that we talk. Please, I promise Not to stay very long."

"I's guess it be OK. Ifin you's stay only a little spell. As fer them boots, ifin you's please leave them at the door." Jeffrey waited till they were both seated then he began.

"The reason why I'm here, Anna Belle, is because I want very desperately for you to believe in me as well as Bobby Gene. I know you don't trust me or really think I want to help Bobby Gene and your people. I understand why. But I do want to help. Don't you realize Bobby Gene was hiding out in that cave nearly a year, and I've known almost that long he was there? But I didn't turn him in. I had no intentions of doing it then, and I have no intentions of doing it in the future. I know that you are confused by my actions and having a white man to offer his friendship would make me skeptical as well. My wanting to help is genuine. To me a person's color means nothing."

89

"When I look at Bobby Gene or yourself or the other Negroes around here. I see human beings like myself. Not savages or slaves. I know what you were trying to do back at the cave when you told Bobby Gene about our move to the big house, I truly hope you didn't succeed in destroying what Bobby Gene and I have accomplished all these months."

"You see, Anna Belle, Bobby Gene has gotten a taste of freedom and he knows what it's like. He's not totally free. If he were, he wouldn't have to hide out in that cave. He's exploring a whole new world. That doesn't make him bewitched or anything of that nature."

"Mr. Wellington has no more right to buy and sell any of you than you do taking orders from Travor. Or any whites for that matter. There are many things in life one can achieve. But he has to want them badly enough to go after them. Even if it means making sacrifices. Yourself and others can have freedom if you want. I must warn you, it won't come easy. Nothing good worth having never is."

"But, Masser Jeffrey, Bobby Gene he not be the same. He says words from a piece of paper. He does strange things in the dirt says they be letters. He even does some'n he called numbers. Preacher Finley and some the older folks on the other plantation says. Ifin someone besides the white man does that, they's bewitched. Bobby Gene even talks crazy." Jeffrey gently surrounded Anna Belle's hands in his.

"Listen, Anna Belle. There is no doubt you have heard many different things from the old timers because they never had anyone to care enough about them to make them realize they can do the very same things for themselves. Bobby Gene is doing it. It's too late for them anyhow. They have gotten set in their ways, and nothing or no one is going to make them see past the noses on their faces." He looked directly into Anna Belle's eyes.

"With us, Anna Belle, it's different. We're the new generation. The strong generation who shouldn't be afraid to fight for what we feel is due us. The story about being bewitched because a black man can read or write aren't true. It's only a myth. This is the white man's way of keeping you as their slaves and in control."

"How do you know you can't do any of those things? When the white man has never given you the chance."

"Bobby Gene hasn't changed. At least not in the way you think. He's gotten wisdom and some knowledge. Which was never offered to him before. Believe me. At first he felt the same way you do right now. Until he realized after a while he couldn't help anyone the way he had been brought up. This is why he is getting the learning he can, so he will know how to survive when he gets back into the world."

"To survive in this world, you have to play the white man's game, that is what I am here to teach him. He is a bright, intelligent person if given the chance to prove it. So are the rest of you. All your lives you've been taught nothing. Bobby Gene realizes this and is willing to go all the way to get it. He can't do it alone. He needs you especially to be there for him. I can only do so much."

"I know it's hard for you to accept right now, but he truly does care about what happens to you and the rest of your people. All those months he has been hid out in that cave. He has never forgotten you. As a matter fact, he at one time ask me if I might go to Dalton's plantation and bring you here to him. Then fate had it you should show up. That has to be a sign of some sort. Don't blame the old folks because of their ignorance. Now it's time for a change. Time for a new generation to rein."

"I know you probably don't understand what I'm saying to you. But it's the truth. Your people have given up before they have even started. I understand you all are scared. But it's all a power thing. When someone knows they have control over you, they will continue to use and abuse you until you're all used up."

"It may be too late for some of your people. It also can be a wonderful new beginning for the rest. I must warn you again it won't be easy. Life in general isn't easy." Anna Belle sat there more confused than ever.

"Masser Jeffrey, it does be true. "Bout my not understand'n some of the things you's say'n to me. I's may be ignorant when it comes to certain things. Fer as long as I's remember, and from hear'n stories at night by the older niggers, there be noth'n better fer us. The ones who decide to try and find out ifin there be some truth behind the stories about freedom be whupped badly. Maybe even sold to another masser from they's family. Who be worse than the last one he be with."

"When I look in you's eyes I's see'd gentleness. Not the color of fire I's does believe you's are truly here to help us. Ifin Bobby Gene believe in you's as a friend, I's shall also." Jeffrey leaned over and kissed her softly on the cheek as she touched it in amazement.

"Now, Masser Jeffrey. What you's dun gone and does a fool thing like that fer? One might git the wrong thoughts."

"Don't fret none Anna Belle. That was just my way of showing appreciation for your believing and trusting in me. I know it was a difficult choice to make. Now I must leave for I have stayed longer than anticipated." He got up and walked over to the door only to turn and say a few last words before leaving.

"One last thing. You must remember I'm not your master, and I would consider it to be an honor if you would just call me Jeffrey. After all, that's all I am. Just plain old Jeffrey." He disappeared into the night.

Bobby Gene was reading when Jeffrey finally tramped his way into the cave's room. He sat down opposite Bobby Gene as he proceeded to clean the mud from his boots. Bobby Gene laid the Bible down next to him.

"How white of you, Master, to finally come check on this poor old nigger. Life must be really good for you now that you live in the big house. If I'm not mistaken, it even looks like you're wearing some fancy duds these days.

"Anna Belle was right. Ain't no white man can be trusted. No matter how much of a friend he pretends to be.

Jeffrey stood up as he positioned himself as a gesture that he wanted to brawl.

"All right come on. Get up, I'm challenging you. There's no rules in the book that says that friends can't fight. So let's have at it." Bobby Gene sat there appalled, watching Jeffrey.

"Did I not make myself clear? Or must I demonstrate what I'm talking about? You think you can sit there on your black ass and belittle me, especially after all we have been through in the past?" He kicked his boots to the side as he stepped closer to Bobby Gene. Fist erected, Bobby Gene sat quietly on the ground.

"I don't want to fight you, man. Granted I'm not afraid to. I'm just hurt. It's been weeks since I've seen or heard one single word from you. How the hell do you expect me to feel? For a while you were my constant companion. Then all of a sudden you're not there anymore."

"I'm sorry about what I said earlier. None of those things were true. If I had thought about all the things you've done for me in the past few months instead of letting myself get caught up in what happened only a few weeks ago, then I would have realized there are times in our lives when we have no control over certain circum-stances. This thing with Anna Belle has gotten to me more than I'm willing to admit." Jeffrey sat next to Bobby Gene as he put his hand on his shoulder.

"Listen, friend, and I do mean friend in every sense of the word. I understand what it's like to be frustrated, then the minds starts to play tricks on you. If you recall, I told you my trips here would have to be limited. It wasn't because I had moved into the mansion, but to continue to keep you safe. Just because that scheme we pulled off worked doesn't mean we should never be caught off guard. Until you are literally safe, and I mean in all aspects. We must continue to do things at a cautious pace. This does not mean I'm not going to be here for you. It can't be as often. I think you are intelligent enough to understand where I'm coming from."

Bobby Gene turned to Jeffrey. "I do understand, man. I also realize now by learning things from you. Sometimes understanding is most important. Like for instance this thing with Anna Belle. For a moment she had me caught up in the old beliefs again. You weren't to be trusted. Then after you didn't come to prove her wrong, I thought it to be the truth."

"You see, Jeffrey, I know you are truly my friend. But after living your life a certain way for so many years, sometimes it's not so hard to be persuaded to cross back to that other side. If you don't have the mind and will to continue on. Most of all, determination to follow your dreams, all these things I have learned from you. They feel good to me, and I'm going to continue to pursue them to where ever they take me."

"I would like very much for Anna Belle to experience this new and wonderful world with me as well, but if she chooses to continue to believe her way. Then so be it." Water began to form in the web of his eyes.

"I never thought I would ever say this to anyone except Joseph Dale. Let alone a white man." He looked Jeffrey squarely in the eyes.

"I love you, man. Like a brother. I know I'll never be able to repay you for everything you've done for me." Jeffrey found himself trying to force back the tears he felt coming on.

"I love you too, man, I don't want you to ever forget that. Now come, let's dry our eyes. We're acting like a couple of wishy-washy dames. Speaking of which, before you started to insult me, I had some fantastic news for you about Anna Belle."

Bobby Gene's once dreary eyes lit up like candles.

"News? What kind of news? She's all right, isn't she? Has something happened? Did she lose the baby?"

"Relax, Bobby Gene. Everything's fine. The baby is fine. It's a boy, by the way, whom she named Gabriel after her father. She also wanted me to mention she was behind you all the way." Bobby Gene was overwhelmed.

"Really? That's great! Speaking of great, listen to this." He picked up the Bible Jeffrey had given him and began to read. "The children of Israel went away and did as the Lord had commanded. Moses and Aaron so did they." He looked at Jeffrey. "I've really gotten better. I don't stutter anymore when I come across those big words."

"That you have, Bobby Gene, and I'm very proud of you." He looked back at Bobby Gene with approval. "I have a feeling things between yourself and Anna Belle are going to be something you will be proud about also."

CHAPTER ELEVEN

"Masser Jeffrey, Masser Jeffrey, come quickly." Jeffrey ran out of the house, putting on his boots as he went. Emma stood there, waving her sweat cloth.

"What is it, Emma? You seem frightened."

"It be that new nigger, Masser. She be call'n out fer you's."

"What's wrong with her?" Jeffrey asked.

"I's doesn't rightly knows, Masser, but from the way she be look'n, she be beat up pretty bad."

"What?" With this, Jeffrey took off even faster. Anna Belle was lying stretched out on the bed when Jeffrey arrived. Black faces peered all about the tiny cabin. Anna Belle was still calling out for Jeffrey when he got to her bedside. He looked down on her. "Oh my God." This was not the face he had left last evening. One eye was swollen shut, and there was a small gash over her right one. Several cuts were scattered over her face from what appeared to be that of the print of a ring. Her lips were swollen as well. She laid there as her one eye searched until it fell upon Jeffrey. He could see she was trying to speak so he knelt closer to her.

"Yoooou's doesn't git to Masser Wellington soon enough. Masser Travor he busted in here shortly after you's be gone. He says he see'd you's when you's leave. Now look at my face. Misses over yonder says it doesn't look good I might lose my eye."

Jeffrey tried touching her on the shoulder as she pulled away.

"I'm truly sorry for what happened to you, Anna Belle. Travor will pay for this."

Anna Belle raised herself upon her elbows.

"Please, Masser Jeffrey. Leave it be. Masser Travor he be mean. He'll kills you's, Masser Jeffrey. I's see'd him does it before. Please don't fight with him." Jeffrey gave her one of his familiar warm smiles, as well as trying to comfort her.

"Don't worry, Anna Belle. I have no intentions of fighting with Travor. But I'm going to have it fixed to where he won't ever hurt you again." He looked at the women who had gathered.

"Take good care of her as well as the child."

"Yes, Masser. We's will." Mr. Wellington was on the porch when Jeffrey returned to the house.

"Well what the hell was all that yelling for? It's nothing serious, I hope."

"It's Anna Belle, sir. Travor saw me leave her cabin last evening and beat her up pretty good. It's a possibility she may lose her left eye."

"Has the world gone mad? Someone fetch Travor up here at once!" He looked back at Jeffrey. "You say it doesn't look good."

"Listen, son, I'm sure you think of me as being a tyrant, and I do believe in disciplining my niggers if they deserve it. But something of this nature disgust even myself. Wheel me into my study, boy. When I have this meeting with Travor, I want us to be alone." The wait was a long one. Finally, the door opened and a black face eased its head through the crack.

"Yes, Elsmeralda. What is it?" Elsmeralda curtsied to the master before speaking.

"Masser Travor be wait'n in the den to see'd you's." Mr. Wellington responded nicely to the message with a smile on his solemn face.

"Show Mr. Travor in." Elsmeralda suddenly disappeared, but her voice could still be heard.

"Masser Wellington says it be OK to come in now." Travor entered the study, rolling down his right sleeve then his left. Then he walked over to Mr. Wellington's desk. He stood in front of him, straightening his already perfect tie, trying to discard the uneasiness he was experiencing.

"I understand you wanted to see me, sir."

"I'll get right to the point." He lifted the lid of the box that sat at the corner of his desk and took a cigar, offering one to Travor. He took a match from the golden match box next to the cigars as he lit it to his satisfaction. Afterward he took the gold faced watch from the tiny upper pocket on his black silk vest.

"You're late. When I give an order here. I expect it to be carried out immediately regardless of whether it's one of my niggers or my employees." Mr. Wellington wheeled his way over to the wall where some pictures hung.

"You see these pictures? They may not mean a damn thing to you, but there's my life history." He pointed to the first photo.

"This here, he was my father, his father, and his father who got this place started." He sat there looking at the photos and talking as if he were speaking to them directly.

"When my grandpa started, it was only him and grandma. They worked hard for many years. Shedding plenty of blood sweat, tears, as well as falling on hard times. Their first home was a one room shanty. They planted soybeans, cotton, plus other crops. They did it all. Just the two of them. One day when they had enough money, they brought a couple of slaves. At the time they hadn't realized it, but the nigger bitch was with two niggers twins my grandpa said that was even better. The more niggers that were breed, the better the production. Meant more money." He collected his thoughts that had been entangled in the pictures clearing his throat, he turned again to Travor, wiping away the few tears.

"Anyway, to make a long story short, it took a long time." He repeated himself again so that Travor understood what he was saying. "A long time, mind you, to get this place where it is today. I'll be damn if I'll let the likes of a nobody like yourself try to destroy it because you can't control yourself." He moved over to the north window, pointing out toward the roll of cabins.

"Are you actually aware of what you did?" He banged his fist against the wall. "Don't you know how frightened these niggers have been since you came here? They're petrified. Several of them have come to me to ask if they may be sold off to someone else."

"You know a year ago when you came here, you weren't any better than they were. You barely had the clothes on your back. I felt sorry for you, and took you in under my wing. I even gave you highest authority over some of the overseers whose families had started out since the beginning of this place. I thought I was a man of good judgement, and character. But I guess everyone's entitled to a mistake now and again." He kept looking out the window as he yet spoke to Travor.

"When you got drunk and seduced the Hobsons' five-year-old nigger girl. I over looked the fact the alcohol might have played an important role, and that it made you act irresponsible. Then when they found that young nigger boy hanging from one of the apple trees. Your excuse was you caught him trying to escape, as you so put it. A good threshing would have taught him a very good lesson. It's worked on my niggers in the past. I even overlooked that knowing I should have done something then. It has been brought to my attention you've had several run-ins with Jeffrey, which you've instigated on both incidents. This, Travor, I'll never forgive, or tolerate any more of this behavior. Who gave you the right to beat that girl the way you did, and to keep her away from the others on this plantation?" He looked at Travor.

"There's only one Master here, and you're looking at him. I warned you what would happen if out paths should ever cross in the manner unpleasing to me. I want you packed and off my property in half an hour."

Travor started toward Mr. Wellington.

"Do you think I'm going to let an old shell of a man like you to tell me what to do? Hell, you can't even get out of that chair of yours without the assistance of that pretty little nurse maid of yours. What reason do I have to fear you?" The look of savagery was in his eyes as he started toward Mr. Wellington again. He removed his hand from beneath the blanket that he always had surrounding him to give him extra warmth. In his bony hand, he revealed a pistol. Travor stepped back as he heard it being cocked.

"I would say this is a good reason to be fearful. If you value your life, as I'm sure you do. I'd ease my way toward that door. I may be old as you so put it, but it won't take much for me to hit an easy target such as yourself. Understand this. Should you not be off my property at the given time, it shall be your body they will be digging a fresh grave for. Do I make myself clear?" Travor swallowed hard as he continued backing away.

"I've got it. But I've got some money due me." Mr. Wellington's eyes stared deep into Travor's with the most piercing, intimidating glare be could muster up.

"You'll be lucky to leave here with your life. Which is ticking away with every fleeting second you delay. I think you've been paid more than what you're worth. For this you won't be taking the woman nor her bastard with you." Once again, Travor made a gesture as though he was going to approach Mr. Wellington, only to be greeted with the pistol again. Travor clutched the knob of the door and flung it open with force.

"You haven't see the last of me, Wellington. I'm sure our paths will cross again. Then I'll have the upper hand." Mr. Wellington thumped the white ashes that had formed on most of his cigar.

"You're a bit confused, aren't you? Travor? For someone who's life is ticking away by the second, I'd be making as much haste as possible. As for your threat, that's all it is." He held up his gold pocket watch as it dangled and turned the face toward Travor.

"According to this, you only have twenty-three minutes and counting. If I were you, I'd start moving as fast as I could." Travor stepped on the other side of the door when Mr. Wellington called after him.

"Close the door behind you."

CHAPTER TWELVE

The middle of September had come. The rain was finally beginning to make way for the sun. Mr. Wellington's condition worsened. Doc McFallon said it was only a matter of months, even weeks, before Mr. Wellington might lose his sight and insisted he should secretly wire Matthew to come home.

Matthew is Mr. Wellington's son. Doc McFallon knew if he had mentioned to Mr. Wellington about his intentions he would strongly object. Their relationship was not that of what a father and son should have been. He had made that perfectly clear to everyone over the years. As he sat by the fireplace bundled up snuggly in his blanket among the stillness of the room, there came a knock at the door. Unable to turn his head, he gazed into the fire as though he was being hypnotized by the red and blue flames.

"Yes who's there?"

"It's me, Mr. Wellington, sir. I truly hate coming to you knowing your condition. I was going over the books and felt it imperative that we should talk."

"Reuben, Reuben, my boy. Come in." He managed to move his bony hand from beneath the covers that engulfed him so tightly. He signaled the young man to come join him by the fire, asking him if he might like some refreshments.

"A cup of hot tea would take care of this chill I seem to have gotten from the ride out here. That weather out there makes a person wonder if there's going to be any more signs of summer this year." Mr. Wellington tried to force his neck to turn the slightest bit, so he could see Reuben while he spoke.

"I know what you mean, sonny. But I've lived through worse than this, and we survived. We shall survive this as well."

"If you'll hand me that bell over there, I'll ring for some service. You know, back about three or four months ago, I might have challenged you to a bit of arm wrestling. Now it's hard for me to try and feed myself." Reuben put the bell in Mr. Wellington's old shaky hand as it rang out. Elsmeralda entered the study.

"Yes, Masser. What it be?"

"Mr. Jones here seems to have a chill. Bring him a cup of tea. also, go to the fruit cellar, get a bottle of that blackberry brandy and put a shot with it so it might warm his bones a bit faster."

"Yes sir, Masser," Elsmeralda said as she turned toward the door. But she was stopped by Mr. Wellington's voice again.

"Have you forgotten your manners, woman? Take the gentleman's coat and hang it on the hall tree, so it will dry out for when he leaves.

"Yes, Masser." She grabbed Master Reuben's coat and threw it over her forearm as she left the room but soon returned with the tea. Then she quickly disappeared again. Reuben took a sip of the hot tea but quickly rejected it away from his lips.

"Ah, I must say that really hits the spot and then some." He cleared his throat knowing what he was about to tell Mr. Wellington would upset him tremendously.

"Well, sir, I hate to be the bearer of bad news especially seeing you in this condition. But there's a big problem." Mr. Wellington tried to show some sign of life in his eyes.

"Go on, Reuben. What do you mean problems? What kind of problems are you speaking of?" He paused, awaiting a reply. "Well go on, boy, spit it out. You've never been one who's been lost for words in the past, so don't try to switch upon me now." He stopped himself. "Enough of that. I can see this problem is very serious. I've been accustomed to bad news before."

"Well, sir, as I was about to say, your financial status is very poor. You're lucky if there's a thousand dollars left in your account.

The bill collectors want their money. I've been stalling them as long as I possibly could. The reason for the delayed trip was because I saw Doc McFallon one day in town, and he said you were in no shape to be bothered by anything such as this. He said you needed your rest and feared the news might cause you to have a setback. Financial turmoil and personal problems wasn't one of the things you needed in your life right now."

"I'm tired of hearing about Doc McFallon's theory concerning my health. Everyone seems to think I've never taken severely ill before. I feel fine. We've been friends for many years. But if he doesn't stop meddling in my affairs." He paused for a second, and added, "I'm not going to let some old sickness called pneumonia whip me. At least not yet. You know I'm too evil to give up being captain of this ship. Did you bring the books?"

"Yes, sir. I happen to have them here in my satchel. Would you care to go over them with me?"

"That I would, my boy, that I would." He beckoned for Reuben to join him at his desk then he pointed toward one of the drawers. "There, boy, hand me my spectacles out of that middle drawer."

Reuben did as he was told. Mr. Wellington set the glasses upon his nose and held them there a moment until he was sure they were securely in place. Taking the books in his shaky hands, he sat them in his lap. Flipping through the pages with all the speed his bony fingers would allow him to. After a bit of frustration, he managed to get to the latest financial report. Using his fingers as a maker, he skimmed over the figures. There was a few moans and groans, even a few eyebrows rising now and then. He looked up at Reuben.

"You have done an extraordinary job on keeping these books. So well in fact your accuracy frightens me. I almost wish I wasn't seeing such outstanding mathematics. No matter how good in detail these books are. It doesn't kindle the fact I truly am in financial trouble. I was about to suggest you take out a second note on the plantation. But I see here written in black and white that it has already been done. You have to forgive my ignorance, but sometimes my mind has a tendency to forget."

"I'm telling you this damn rain's ruined everything. My cotton, crops, not a damn thing could be saved. Everything washed away. When the sun did come out what wasn't washed away was burned up. The only way out of this that I can see is to sell some of my niggers. I've surely got plenty of them."

"Listen, son, I understand another auction is due here the end of the month. I know that doesn't give us much time to work with. But I want you to go back to town and get started on it right away. Find out who's heading this auction and tell them I'll be bringing at least twenty of my best niggers there."

Reuben tried to force a smile of assurance on his face. But it didn't fool Mr. Wellington.

"Don't try hiding what you truly feel behind that faulty smile. I've been in this world a great number of years and I can just about tell what a person is thinking without him even saying a word. You don't believe we can pull this off. Do you, boy?" Reuben shook his head.

"No, sir, I truly don't." Mr. Wellington gave Reuben a fish-eyed look.

"First off, son, I'm a Wellington and around here that name carries a lot of weight. Do you actually think this is the first time the Wellington plantation has almost gone under?" He lifted his finger at Reuben and shook it sternly. "Well it ain't."

"I can recall a time back in eighteen hundred fourteen or was it fifteen? I don't recall, but it was some years back. I was a little one then. Under the rule of my papa, Theodore Wellington." He lifted his left hand and pointed to the pictures on the wall.

"The one on the end, he was the one mind you. We had the best of everything that year. Crops, every type of meat possible from slaughter. Everything was going so smoothly. Then all of a sudden out of nowhere the sky became very dark so it seemed there didn't appear to be a cloud in the sky. I felt something hit me on the top of my head like a little thump. It didn't bother me at first. Then came another and another. I went to focus my eyes upward when it hit me squarely in the face. Still not knowing what was happening.

Plus, the fact whatever had hit me in the face had brought tears to my eyes causing a burning sensation.

"Fighting with myself, trying to escape whatever was attacking me, I happened to look down. It was stunning. I couldn't believe what I was seeing. I bent down to see if I could touch this fictional thing that had built in my mind. I took both hands and scooped up a handful and brought them close to my vision realizing it was real. They were mangy little critters crawling all over my hands, even up my sleeves. I guess I was to shocked to be terrified. They were locusts. Thousands upon thousands of them. They were so thick, they completely blocked the sun's view.

"I threw the ones that were in my hands back to the ground shaking my arms, trying to free myself from the ones that had gotten under my shirt and went running toward the house. I guess some of the niggers had gotten to Papa before I did. "Cause when I got to the porch papa had already gone to start preparation on trying to salvage whatever could be saved. Bubba Smith. He's dead now God rest his soul. That ole nigger had been waiting for me on the front porch to tell me what Papa said." Mr. Wellington chuckled.

"I'll never forget the look on that nigger's face. For you see when I approached the porch he was sitting in the family swing. He knew niggers weren't allowed to sat anywhere on the front porch. Anyhown, when he saw me he jumped up. His eyes got as big as silver dollars. He also had the biggest lips I'd ever seen. His bottom lip was so huge you could have sworn it touched his chin. Of course, there's a bit of exaggeration there. But it did hang mighty low. He stood there trembling, lips and all. When he saw that streak of anger in my eyes. He became so nervous he couldn't remember what Papa had said. You see that nigger was so black till he shined. That wasn't why I was laughing. One day he was caught trying to run away and was beaten, and in the process he lost his front teeth. So you can only imagine how funny he looked especially from a young lad's perspective. When I saw that wide-empty space, I couldn't help but smirk a little. That nigger stood there trembling, trying to concentrate on what Papa had told him to tell me. Well go ahead, nigger. What was it you were about to say?" He bowed as he continued.

"Well, Masser. You's papa says fer me to stay here till you's come. He doesn't knows where you's run off to. He wants me to tell you's to take some niggers git out to the cotton fields and see'd what can be dun there."

"All right, Bubba, thank you. Now you can go back to your chores. I turned and stepped off the bottom step but turned quickly back to him. I could see he was yet trembling. I'm gonna let you be this time. But if I catch you in the family swing again. I'm going to have your hide tanned. An ole man such as yourself, I don't suppose will be able to with stand such treatment. You understand what I'm saying?" Bubba shook his head.

"Yeeees, sir I's understand perfectly."

"Good then. You can carry on."

Everything went silent. The only thing you could hear was the pitter patter of rain on the rooftop. Mr. Wellington gazed into the flames again as though that's where he'd been all along. A twig snapped, and he batted his eyes.

"Let's see now. Where was I?" He rubbed his chin.

"Oh yeah. I couldn't resist telling that ole Bubba story.

"We fought those locusts for three days and nights. We even tried drowning them, but the more we fought, the more we appeared to be defeated. On the fourth day after they had feasted and done their damage, they flew off leaving us with nothing but sorrow. Not one ear of corn, nothing. We sold most of our cattle and livestock. The rest we butchered as time went by. My papa got us through it, and I'll be damned if I'm going to let a little bad weather cause me to lose everything the Wellington's worked so hard for."

"I'm sure that's now your idea of a good story. It wasn't meant to be. I wanted you to know we Wellingtons aren't quitters. We weren't then and we aren't now." Waving his hand to Reuben, Mr. Wellington said. "Off with you now, son. There's a lot of work to be done if we're going to get them niggers of mine to the auction."

"You're absolutely right, Mr. Wellington sir. Shall I hand you your bell so you can ring for my coat?"

"That won't be necessary, my boy. You can ring for yourself." Reuben picked up the bell and let it ring out. The study door opened promptly as the black face appeared.

"Yes, Masser, did you ring?" Reuben held the bell out so that Elsmeralda was sure to see it in his hand.

"It was I, Elsmeralda. I've finished my talk with Master Wellington. Would you bring me my wrap?"

"Right away, Masser Reuben sir."

"I must say you handle that bell with very fine dignity."

"Why thank you, sir. But it really doesn't take talent to ring a bell. I bet as a matter of fact one of these niggers could even do it."

"Tish, tosh, enough hogwash, boy. There's more to ringing that bell than meets the eye. It shows authority. Who's in charge and that's a very important role." The door opened again.

"Here's be you's coat, Masser Reuben. It's almost dry, a bit damp about the cuff. I doesn't think about it till this minute. I could put the iron to them wet places and dry 'em out real quick ifin you's like." Reuben flashed a quick glance at Elsmeralda as he grabbed for his coat she had thrown over her left arm.

"That's very considerate of you. But there's no need, considering the condition of the weather." Reuben was about to put on his cost when something square and white fell out onto the floor. Elsmeralda noticed it the instant it hit the floor and stooped to pick it up.

"Masser Reuben, you's dropped this here out of you's pocket." Reuben took the envelope from her.

"Oh yes, Mr. Wellington sir, this is for you. It slipped my mind." Mr. Wellington took it but questioned Reuben while doing so.

"What is it, boy"

"I'm not sure. But I do believe it's a letter from your son. I noticed it was postmarked from England." Mr. Wellington flung the envelope on the desk.

"You could have gone without giving me that piece of trash or whatever the hell it is. Besides he knows better than to be writing me. As far as I'm concerned my son is dead don't you think you'd best be on your way and get things together for that auction?"

"Yes, sir. It will be a big task especially with such short notice." He looked at Elsmeralda.

"No need bothering to see me out. I can find my way quite comfortably, thank you."

"Yes, Masser Reuben." She walked a few steps ahead of him so she could open the door as he tipped his hat once again to Mr. Wellington. "I bid you a pleasant evening." Elsmeralda stayed on.

"Well, what the hell's your problem, woman? Standing there staring at me like you've got something on your mind."

"Noth'n, Masser. I's hop'n you's would open that letter so's I can heard what my Matt be up to all these years. Even though I never bore him. I took care of him from the time he comes into this world." She, like the others, took herself back to that particular day.

"Ifin that wasn't the most glorious day round here then. You's and the Misses be so happy." She chuckled. "You's be so proud you's give us niggers the day off." Bringing herself back to the present, she continued.

"Maybe what he dun be wrong but it be over and dun with, and you's can't change it. Ifin you's weren't such a stubborn old fool. You's realize you's still love that boy regardless of what kind of mistakes he made. You's sure as hell ain't perfect yourself you's knows." She closed the door behind her.

CHAPTER THIRTEEN

*M*r. Wellington sat in his study, looking at the envelope lying on his desk, wondering if he should see what was on the inside or pitch it into the fire.

"I guess it wouldn't do any harm to read what he has to say. After all, Elsmeralda can be right sometimes. He is a Wellington, my son." Taking the piece of paper out of the envelope, he held it in his hands for a moment. He looked at it then he crumpled it up, just to uncrumple it again as he started to read.

> Father,
>
> I know it's been a few years. That is why I'm sending you this telegraph to let you know Mary Lou died. I have decided there is no reason for me to stay in London. Will be home soon. By the way. You have a grandson named young Matthew Wellington.

Mr. Wellington crumpled the piece of paper with hatred, throwing it into the fire.

"What the hell does he mean he's coming home? It was made perfectly clear he no longer had a home or family. If that ain't enough, He's coming back with a bastard child he claims to be my grandson. Well, it ain't going to work." He wheeled himself over to the desk, picked up the bell, and let it rang out frantically. Elsmeralda rushed in.

THE LONG ROAD TO FREEDOM

"Yes, Masser."

"I want you to send Thomas to look for Master Robertson. Get word. I need to see him right away."

"Yes, sir, Masser. Everything be all right. You's look a bit upset."

"Hush, you fool of a woman. Just do as you were told." Elsmeralda threw up her hands as she went off mumbling to herself.

The rain finally ceased, only to be followed by a piercing cold-ness of the autumn winds. In the few weeks, Reuben had last seen Mr. Wellington his condition worsened, and each day he seemed more determined than ever to fight the fact he was dying. Jeffrey along with Doc McFallon tried to convince him that he needn't take the trip to the auction. They could take care of everything on their own. But he was very persistent, and defiant in letting them know should they not allow him to go with them. He would certainly get one of the other overseers to take him. Even though neither liked it. They knew the state of mind he had been in these few months. It was better to do just as he says then take it with a grain of salt.

Master Robertson had done an excellent job on the choosing of the best twenty slaves. As the last one was being placed into the back of the wagon. Mr. Wellington cautioned Robertson that every-thing needed to be perfect.

"It's important that they stay as comfortable as possible." "What he didn't need was a bunch of sick niggers. Especially when they were going to be sold." Mr. Wellington motioned. Robertson to go.

The fog was very thick, they had to use the light from the lantern to guide them. The city was filled with lots of slaves and buyers. Jeffrey couldn't believe his eyes. He had never been to such an auction of this magnitude until now. Back in Philadelphia, his folks had a few Negroes but they worked under their own accord. He wheeled Mr. Wellington into the building as he instructed Robertson to find their stable and start unloading his slaves in it. There came an announcement.

"Would everyone please be seated? The auctioning will be starting in a few minutes." Jeffrey wheeled Mr. Wellington toward the crowd of people when a familiar voice came up from behind them.

"Well, well, well, look who's here. If it ain't the old cripple himself in the flesh." The figure moved in front of Mr. Wellington making sure he would be quite visible.

"Fancy seeing you here, Wellington. I recall the last time we had a few words you seemed to have the upper hand on everything. Now things seemed to have changed a bit. Word is there's trouble on the old home front. It's also been said that you brought some of those precious niggers of yours here in hopes they'll make you some quick bucks. I was looking forward to having my day with you, wanting to be the first one to kick dirt on that old mangy body of yours." Mr. Wellington tried to stand up but was restrained by Jeffrey and Robertson.

"You low down, rotten heathen. You think just because I'm confined to this wheelchair I'm intimidated by you."

Jeffrey intervened.

"Sir, remember what doc McFallon said about your getting upset. You know the stress isn't good for your health." Mr. Wellington directed his attention to Jeffrey.

"Everyone seems to know better about my well-being than myself. Do me a favor, sonny, Keep yours and Dave's opinion about my health to yourself. It's beginning to upset me."

"Now what does the old man have on his mind? Does he plan on running over me with his wheelchair?" He went off laughing to himself.

"Ladies and gentlemen, if everyone would please be so kind as to be seated. We must get started."

"It was nearly two hours before they got to Mr. Wellington's niggers. Jeffrey could tell he was uneased.

"Mr. Wellington sir. If you'd like, I can stay and wrap things up for you. It appears you're a bit restless."

"You're damn right, boy. That's because I'm stuck in this old chair. I'm used to getting up and stretching my legs now and then. But all I can do is sit here and wait. It won't be long now. They're bringing my niggers upon the platform this very moment as we speak." They lined all twenty young black bodies across the platform single file as the auctioneer started the bidding.

"What is the opening bid I have on this nigger?" He nudged the first one away from the rest so the attention would be solely focused on him. "I understand these Wellington niggers are of the best prime in these parts. Just look at these muscular arms and this dynamic chest cavity. Not only do you find this nigger built like an ox, surely it's safe to say he has the strength of one too. He's very young, which means there's plenty of hard working years left in him. Not to forget the extra money he could bring in for studding purposes." He opened his mouth while he yet spoke. "His teeth are as white as pearls, and he still has all thirty-two of them. He's in perfect health and has never been sick a day in his life. So what's the opening bid for this magnificent black beauty?" There was a moment of silence. Then a voice shouted through the crowd.

"I bid twenty-dollars." The room filled with laughter.

"Come now," the auctioneer began. "There's no need for mockery. We all can see with our own eyes these are some of the most prized niggers. I ever saw. Do I hear an opening bid of fifteen hundred dollars?" Silence filled the room a second time as the auctioneer spoke again. "One thousand dollars. Do I hear an opening bid of one thousand dollars?"

"I'm here to announce that my father no longer wishes to auction off his slaves. So if you would so kindly escort them off the platform." A voice echoed from the back of the room. The whole room filled with chatter as heads turned. The auctioneer was so stunned he was almost speechless.

"You heard the man. Do as you are told. Start taking those niggers back to their stall." Mr. Wellington insisted on being taken home at once.

The fog was thicker than ever. The traveling by night didn't make the trip any easier. Mr. Wellington was seated by the fireplace when he heard the door open.

"Hello, Father. I've been in my room wondering whether I should come down or not. I knew we'd have to face off sooner or later. I'm sorry about Mother's death. You know I would have come home had I been notified. Why, Father, is your hatred for me so strong you couldn't share mother's death with me? Your own flesh and blood."

Mr. Wellington began to speak. "You did something that was forbidden to society, and our family heritage. You shamed our name, and you expect me to forgive and forget?" He spun his wheelchair around toward Matthew.

"Why did you come back here? I told you I never wanted to see your face in this house again as long as I lived."

"Father, that was many years ago. Things have changed. Time has passed."

"There will never be enough time as far as you're concerned." Mr. Wellington called out for Elsmeralda.

"That won't do any good, Father. Besides she can't hear you." Mr. Wellington whirled his wheelchair about again.

"What the hell do you mean she can't hear me! She's never disobeyed me before." He wheeled himself toward the door, trying to force his way past Matthew who was blocking it.

"Get out of my way!" He bellowed out again for Elsmeralda.

"It's no use, Father. I figured you'd try and pull something like this, so I ordered Elsmeralda and the other servants to their rooms with strict orders they weren't to leave them no matter what." Mr. Wellington was outraged.

"What did you say, boy? You're joshing me, ain't you?"

"No, Father. You don't see anyone coming to your rescue, do you?"

"How dare you come back in this house as though you've only been gone a couple of weeks on some kind of business venture when we both know it goes a lot deeper than that! You come back giving orders! You don't have any rights here as far as I'm concerned." Mr. Wellington started coughing and grabbed his chest Matthew reached out to console him. But he wheeled away.

"Stay away from me. I don't ever want you to touch this old body again!"

"Father, please, why are you doing this to us? I'm still your son."

"Correction, you were my son. I disowned you years ago. Or have you so conveniently forgotten that." Matthew threw up his hands.

"All right. OK, Father. I can see we're getting no place yelling at one another. I can also understand the hatred you've carried inside all these years. It happened, it's done. Neither of us can do anything to change it. I'm not asking you to accept me. You could show some compassion for me. My God, Father, Mary Lou is dead. What harm can she do you now? As though she were a threat to you before. Feel whatever you must toward me. But your grandson. Don't shut him out of your life. Regardless as to whether you accept it or not. Half that boy got Wellington blood in him. You're all he's talked about when he found out we were coming back to the States. Father, he wants to see you."

"That's very quaint. Do you think you can waltz in here after all these years and bring the likes of that so-called half breed in this house and take charge? Well, you're wrong. I'm the master of this plantation. Always has been and always will be. I want the both of you out of here." Matthew closed the study door.

"What I'm about to say, Father I didn't want anyone else to hear. I was also hoping I'd never have to say or go against you. It's obvious your respect for me left the same time your love did. I can see you never forgave me for marrying a Negro. You carry on as though I married a black woman to hurt you or to disrespect you. What you failed to understand is I loved Mary Lou very much. I don't know how or why it happened. I will admit when I found out she was with child I could have neglected them the way so many have done. But my feelings were to strong and sincere."

"Ever since this plantation got started. the Negro women have been used like savages to bore the white man's children so that when they're old enough they'll become slaves as well."

"You think it was wrong of me to marry a Negro but it's not wrong to abuse them. How do you suppose those Negro men feel when their wives, sisters, and sometimes daughters are being dragged from underneath them to satisfy the white man's sexual desires? Treating them like they're animals."

"Well they're human like we are. I fell in love, married, and she bore me a son out of that love. I loved her dearly." Tears came into his eyes. "If you're that full of hatred, you have to shut me and your grandson out for loving. Then its best he does keep his distance from you."

"At least when I slept with Mary Lou, it wasn't out of lust. I looked beyond her color. To me she was all your rich and sophisticated white girls are supposed to be. She was a woman, not a piece of property." He looked into his father's eyes.

"She was more innocent than your so-called lily-white girls, always trying to hide their promiscuous with shy tacts when in fact at times they were the aggressors. Believe me there were more of then who were willing to turn up their skirts to me than you could imagine. Because they're white makes everything all right. Quite frankly, she made me feel better than any of them possibly could."

"You don't know what it was like going through life not being able to take your wife to parties. To sat there watching her being groped like a piece of meat by your drunken upstanding friends. Watching that tormenting look in her eyes. I wanted so much to stand up and shout. Leave her alone, she's my wife. She wouldn't hear of it because she loved me too. To want her so badly, your whole body aches. Having to wait till the guest have gone to sneak off to her quarters to be intimate with her instead of making love to her the way I should in our bed. In our bedroom. Not some two-bit attic space you called her living quarters. Hell, your house servants had better living quarters than she did. Was that your way of punishing me, Father? If you thought it worked, it only made me love her even more." He stood there.

"I got word you were terribly ill, and that this place was about to go under. Whether you like it or not, I'm going to save this plantation financially and any other ways I have to. Not you or anyone else is going to run Matthew nor myself away. I made a vow to Mary Lou that Matthew would always be well taken care of, should anything happen to her, she wanted him to be raised where he was conceived out of love, and I'm going to honor that vow to her name. You may not forgive me, but you can't take away the fact

I'm a true Wellington. This is our home too." To his surprise, Mr. Wellington found himself applauding.

"How theatrical. Was that one of your traits you picked up while you were away? If you ask me, you got short changed. Do you think I give a damn about that so-called performance? It still doesn't change the way I feel about you. Hell, I can perform a bit myself. As a matter of fact, picture this being played out."

"Imagine one night when your son had to leave town because duty called. While he's away the father becomes restless because his wife is away as well. He starts drinking, he gets lonely. He needs the comfort only a woman can provide. All the other nigger women of the house have been broken in repeatedly. You have a desire. You want something different. Something new, fresh innocent. Then it comes to you. It's as plain as the nose on your face. She was right there all along. You hadn't noticed it before 'cause she never made herself visible. Then it hits you. Who would be better to accompany a lonely man in his bed, than his son's wench. One who has only had a boy to do a man's job." The corner of Mr. Wellington's mouth twitched as he continued his story.

"Imagine that son thinking the wench he put so much praise and trust in was keeping his father's bed warm whenever Margaret or yourself was away. How foolish you were to think you were the only one she bedded down with. I can agree with you on one thing, though. She was the best I ever encountered too."

"I can easily see where you might mistake lust for love. That nigger had all the right moves in bed." He chuckled Matthew's face became flushed as he lifted his father up out of his wheelchair by his lapels.

"You son of a bitch! You insane, sick son of a bitch! You despise me so much. You would even fabricate a lie such as this. I can see it all too clearly now. All your life you've been the controller. It wasn't just about Mary Lou. It was about your controlling my life. Which you were no longer able to do. So you thought if you disowned me this might possibly bring me crawling back to you. It didn't work, though. Did it, father?" He shoved his father back into his chair as he started pacing back and forth in front of the study door as he continued speaking.

"I've done very well for myself without your help. Lucky for you that you're my father, or you would be dead making a slanderous accusation such as this. You will never be able to let this thing between us stay in the past. Apparently, you are still living your life there. No matter what you say, I will always cherish the time and memories that Mary Lou and I shared the time she was here. I thank God for Matthew." With this he left the room, leaving Mr. Wellington a bit shaken by the ordeal he had just encountered.

CHAPTER FOURTEEN

November came, bringing with it one of the coldest month in history. Mr. Wellington's health had deteriorated to nothing. He was completely bedridden, stubborn as ever, still determined he didn't want to have anything to do with Matthew or his grandson. Matthew was seated in the study when both doors flung open as Pauline rushed in. She had a disturb look on her face.

"Matthew sir, come quickly. It's your father. He's not moving. I think he's dead." Matthew rushed to his father's room but stopped.

"I'm sorry Pauline. I would like nothing more than to go to him right now. I can't bear to see him suffer like this alone. Especially since it's not necessary. You know how my father feels about me as badly as I want to be with him. I have to respect his wishes, I will ride into town and get Doc. McFallon. Just keep a very close eye on him until I return with the doctor." It appeared no time had passed when Matthew came back with the doctor, and they both rushed to Mr. Wellington's room.

"I'm sorry Dave." He patted the doctor on the back.

"This is as far as I go until father and I can settle our differences. Maybe you can talk some sense into him." Doc. McFallon grabbed Matthew by the shoulders and smiled.

"I'll try, Matt, you know him as well as I. Once his mind's made up, there's no changing it. It wouldn't hurt for you to stay close in case though." He stepped behind the door and walked quietly over to Mr. Wellington's bedside where Pauline was seated, gently touching her shoulder. she jumped, startled, looking up to see who it was.

"Oh, Doc. McFallon. You frightened me. He's gotten worse his pulse is very weak."

"I came as soon as Matthew told me. Now if you will excuse me, I need to examine him. Go and join Matthew." Dr. McFallon waited until Pauline had left the room then he took her seat. He pulled back the eyelids of the old man to find that the pupils weren't dilating. Then he went to check his chest and pulse. There was no change.

"McFallon, is that you? I'm glad you made it in time."

"Yes, I'm here. But I don't want you to talk." Mr. Wellington opened his eyes.

"Oh hush, McFallon. What kind of nonsense are you talking? Don't be coy with me. I'm no doctor but I do have feelings. This old body has told me it's time to lay down and take a permanent rest. You know it as well as I. What I want you to tell me is how much longer before it happens."

Doc. McFallon sniffled as he took the handkerchief from his pocket to wipe the water from his eyes.

"You're right, Benjamin. We've been friends so long. I forgot just how hard it was to try and fool an old geezer like yourself."

"Ha," Mr. Wellington said. "I thought I'd never hear the day my own words would come back to haunt me." Doc. McFallon had a look of dismay.

"What did you mean by that?"

"Nothing really. Just tell me how long."

"I honestly can't say Benjamin." He paused. "I do know this. Matthew is standing outside that door. Ben, he's terribly concerned about you. He wants to see you. I reckon you're still bitter at him for marrying that negra."

"Quite frankly, it did devastate me and a few of our closest friends. In time we all went on with our lives. I didn't approve of his actions any more than yourself. But who am I to judge or condemn him? He made the right decision when he moved away."

"I know this is none of my business. But I think you're a damn fool if you don't settle this thing between the two of you. Your time is very short. What harm would it do for you to see him one last time? Things that have happened in the past can't be undone. It's the future we have to be concerned with. Let the boy in to see you. I can see in his face that he's suffering over this thing between the two of you. I have nothing else to say on the matter. You know I had to voice my opinion."

"You're damn right, Dave. It is none of your business. My son dishonored my name, I don't give a damn if it's a thing of the past." He looked at the doctor.

"Funny thing about the past. No matter how much you try to forget or escape it, the memories always have a way of resurfacing or coming back to haunt you. I shall never forgive him for it, and I will take this hatred and disappointment I have for him to the grave. Do you hear what I'm saying?" His voice weakened. "To my grave." His eyes closed on his last words. Doc. McFallon sat there a moment watching him, then he pulled the covers over his face.

"You ole fool, Benjamin. You could have at least told him good-bye." He wiped away the tears and walked over to the door, taking a deep breath to prepare himself for the bad news he was about to give to Matthew. Matthew rose slowly from the chair. He could tell from the reddish look of Doc McFallon eyes that the news wouldn't be good. Before Doc. McFallon could speak, Matthew was crying out.

"Father, Father, he can't be dead. I won't believe he's dead." Doc McFallon held on to Matthew with all the strength he had trying to keep him from entering the room.

"I'm sorry, Matthew, it's over." Matthew looked at him.

"Did he say anything about me? I mean, did he tell you to say anything to me?"

"I tried to get him to see you. But he said he'd rather take the hatred he had for you to his grave than to see you." Matthew sank back into the chair.

"It's a pity how hatred can consume a person up like it did Father." Doc McFallon tried to give Matthew some comforting thought.

"We both knew your father was a lot of things, and being stubborn was one of his stronger traits. But he loved you very much. It was his pride that wouldn't allow him to show you just how much he cared." Matthew gave Doc McFallon a firm handshake.

"Thank you, Dave, for standing beside him all these years. I know it wasn't easy to be his friend as well as his doctor. I know you did the best you could believe me. I appreciate everything. It wasn't easy for you to see a close friend like father suffer the way he did these past few months."

"No, son, it wasn't. It makes an ole man like myself begin to wonder if I might be next. I best be going. There are other patients I need to see. If you need anything, feel free to call on me any time."

The funeral was quite sizeable and tiring. Matthew had just gone up to lie down when a knock came at the bedroom door, then a head appeared.

"If you're wanting to be alone. I'll come back later." Matthew sat up in bed.

"No, that's perfectly fine. I was just lying here looking at the walls and finding it hard to believe he's truly gone. It's amazing how one knows that dying is part of a reality one must face sooner or later. It really doesn't take effect till it happens to someone you love. Or who was close to you at one time. Anyway, come in." Pauline eased her way into the room.

"I just wanted you to know I laid young Matthew down for the evening."

"Thank you, Pauline. You've done more than what has been expected of you already. You don't have to bother with him, there's someone who's in charge of him." She stood there in the doorway as their eyes connected with one another.

"Ah, I best be going. I wanted you to know about young Matthew." She turned to leave.

"Please don't go. I mean, do you have time to join me in a glass of sherry?" Pauline smiled before she turned back to Matthew, not wanting him to see it.

"I don't know. There's a lot of work yet to be done."

"I'll tell you what." Matthew began. "Just have one tiny glass with me. Then after that you can leave. Deal?" She nodded her head.

"All right, it's a deal."

Pauline sat down in the chair on the opposite side of the night table. There she sat under the window, watching intimately as he poured the sherry. He handed one to her then poured one for himself. As they sipped their sherry, their eyes met again. Pauline took the glass and placed it on the table as she ran her fingers up then down the glass, hoping Matthew hadn't noticed how nervous she felt. She picked up the glass again to have another sip. Matthew gulped down his sherry and poured himself another while Pauline sipped away at her first. Again looking into her eyes he spoke.

"You've got beautiful hair. I don't recall ever seeing you let it hang. Do you ever wear it down?"

"Occasionally, I've really had no cause to." By now she had finished her sherry and held her glass out to Matthew.

"Might I have a bit more to that sherry please, it's rather tasty?"

"Only if you'll do something for me." Pauline's eyes grew large as Matthew laughed.

"Don't panic. All I want is for you to let down your hair." You could see a sigh of relief come over her as her shoulders fell limp. She removed the pins from her hair that was pulled back into a ball, and let it fall freely beyond her shoulders. A gust of cool breeze rushed in and blew it gently. Matthew sat there staring into her innocent gray eyes.

"You know, I never knew how beautiful you were till now. Sitting here watching you, seeing how sensational you look under moonlight. So pure, so innocent. Like a beautiful, unspoken, seductive portrait." Red flushed into Pauline's cheeks while finishing up her second glass of sherry.

"What a lovely sentiment, Matthew. But I must be going."
She stood up. Matthew stood up as well and gulped down his second sherry.

"Please, Pauline. Must you go? I know I promised that you
could leave whenever you choose. But must it be now?" Matthew
moved over to where she was standing, grabbing her and pulled her
close to him, gently stroking her long beautiful brown hair.

"Pauline, I'm begging you, don't go." His lips pressed against
hers' with a burning passion as he continued to pull her body even
closer to him. For him the kiss was long and fulfilling. His hands
searched the back of her dress until he found the buttons and
started to unfasten the top ones. Pauline tried pulling away as she
felt his hot lips nibbling at her earlobe. He started to whisper to her.

"Please, Pauline, I need you. I'm so lonely. It's been a long
time. I want to make love to you." Pauline tried again to break
away, but Matthew held on tighter.

"Stop, Matthew. You're hurting me." She managed to get one
arm free, scratching him across the face in the process. Matthew fell
back onto the bed, grabbing the area as to where the warm blood
ran down his cheeks. Tears filled his face as he sat there bawling like
a child. Pauline wanted to run away. But she felt sorry for him. She
crept over to the bed and sat down next to him. He looked away
from her as he spoke.

"I'm sorry for what just happened. I never meant for it to go
this far. I've been so lonely since my wife died, and now losing my
father. There have been other women in my life. But none that have
interested me enough to want to take them to bed. You're different.
I don't know why I feel this way. I know that I want you. It's wrong
especially with your being a married woman and all. Can you ever
forgive me?" Pauline reached around and pulled Matthew's face
to hers'.

"Those scratches look like they could use some attention. Do
you have any clean cloth here?"

"Yes, over there in the top drawer of my chest." Pauline
walked over to the chest and took a handkerchief out of the drawer.
She came back and poured water from the pitcher into the bowl

and dipped the handkerchief until it was wet then she added a bit of alcohol to it, as she began to clean his scratches. Matthew pulled away.

"Whoa, that burns." She settled down next to him tending to his scratches while she continued to speak.

"Matthew, I've got a confession to make myself. From the first day you entered back into this house, I've had this desire for you. I knew this would be the best opportunity I would have to get close to you. That was my main reason for coming here in the first place.

"At first when you touched me, I was frightened. Then I felt something inside me I've never felt before. The way your hands felt touching my body. The burning desire. I truly didn't want you to stop. But I was afraid to let you know I wanted you also. I too am lonely."

"Jeffrey. What about Jeffrey?" Matthew questioned as his gaze became more intense. Pauline covered Matthew's lips with her hand.

"Shhh…I don't understand why I'm feeling this way. All I know is I don't want it to end. Jeffrey is the farthest thing from my thoughts at the moment. Please make love to me." Matthew still had that gaze in his eyes.

"My feelings haven't changed. I do still want you. Are you sure this is what you want?"

"Matthew, until a few moments ago. I had doubts about my still being a woman. Jeffrey and I haven't communicated for so long. I was beginning to wonder if it might be me. Tonight it all came alive, and I feel so wonderful. Something inside of me feels like it needs to escape. I'm with you here and now. That's all that matters, isn't it?"

Matthew slid the dress slightly off her left shoulder, gently laying her back on the bed. Afterward he stretched his body next to hers'. The warmth of his breath burning her shoulder with passionate lust. He could feel her body starting to tremble as she locked her arms around his neck, pulling him into her. Matthew pulled her dress down farther as his tongue slowly maneuvered down between her breast, his lips gently cupping her nipples. She closed her eyes, letting her mind venture into her fantasy world of passion, her body swaying with his, while a cry of ecstasy escaped her lips. By this time Matthew's whole body was upon hers. He could feel her body tightening again. He questioned her one last time.

"Are you absolutely sure about this?"

"Yes," she whispered softly in his ear.

CHAPTER FIFTEEN

*P*auline lay there with her eyes closed, indulging in the lovemaking. Suddenly the bedroom door opened.

"Excuse me, sir." Matthew rose up in astonishment. Who could this be entering his bedroom without knocking first? He turned to see who it was.

"What business do you have here? Don't you know its common courtesy to knock before entering someone's bedroom."

Jeffrey was very apologetic. "I'm sorry sir. Elsmeralda asked if I might check in on you. She said you seemed upset. She told me to come up and see if you might be ready for a bit to eat. She hadn't seen you for a spell. She wasn't sure if you were resting or not. She has some food if you're hungry." Jeffrey was flabbergasted as he and Pauline met face-to-face. she tried pulling the covering up around her.

"My intentions were genuine. I had no idea you would be preoccupied. And with my wife no doubt." Matthew turned away to put on his attire as Jeffrey turned on his heels. Pauline gathered the blanket about her and went after him.

"Jeffrey, honey, it's not what you think." Jeffrey shook her off and left. She fell to her knees, crying. Matthew put on his boots and stooped to help her up.

"Get dressed. Go to him. I must go downstairs and attend to my business. If you'd like, I'll try and explain it to him. But what does one say to another man when he's just been caught in the act of fornication with his confidant's wife? I can assure you everything about our relationship shall change after this." When Matthew got downstairs Jeffrey was standing at his study door. They stood there looking at one another. Matthew broke the brink of silence.

"I don't know what to say. Except that I was lonely and she was there. If you took your best shot right now, I wouldn't blame you one bit." Jeffrey stared at him coldly.

"Would it salvage the fact you made love to my wife? Maybe for you fighting is the answer. But it takes a far better man to walk away quietly and do nothing. After all, I've been hurt, which in time. I'll heal. If you're any kind of a man with a conscience, it should haunt you the rest of your days. My trusted friend." He silently walked away. Matthew stood there a moment trying to figure him out. Then he opened the door to the study and went inside. Pauline was waiting in their room when Jeffrey came up. Jeffrey picked up his coat and hat.

"I'm going to the cave. I don't know when I'll be back."

"Won't you even look at me? Is that all you have to say is. I'm going to that stinking cave! Shout at me! Slap me! Do something! But don't give me this silent bit!" Jeffrey turned to her.

"OK, Pauline. What do you want me to say? I approve of what you did. Well, I can't even though I'm not surprised by it. Ever since we've moved in this house, everything about you has changed. The way you dress, your attitude. Hell, I can't even get a kiss from you anymore. Don't think I hadn't noticed how you've been watching Matthew? I knew it was only a matter of time before he got you in his bed. You've gotten so greedy you'll hurt anyone to get to the top. Even the ones who care the most about you. Ester and some of the other Negro women here were good to you when we first got here. And you repay them by turning up your nose at them. One of these days you just might find yourself right back where you started. When that happens, I won't be there to comfort you."

"Go on, get out of my life. I don't need you, and I am going to make it big. All the way to the top. Matthew, he wants me. He said so. So you see I don't need you anymore. Why do I need a man who can only perform boyish acts anyhow? You never satisfied me in bed anyway. I only pretended because it was my wifely duty. Even that had its limit. But with Matthew. Tonight he showed me what a real man is all about." Jeffrey slammed his fist against the wall, causing Pauline to flinch.

"Go ahead, lay your guilt trip on me. You think just because a man is good in bed that that's all there is to it? Don't be fooled by a few words because they come cheap. Did it not occur to you that you were just someone to satisfy his needs at the particular time? Needing and wanting are two different things. Which apparently you haven't learned the difference yet. Besides, how can a husband give his wife what she needs if she doesn't give him what he wants?" She turned her back to him.

"Just go be with your nigger friend. He's the one you care about anyway."

"I feel sorry for you, Pauline. You're just another body to him. When the right woman comes along, and she will. He'll drop you like a hot potato. I'll be moving out of this room come first sight of day."

"That's right, run. You know why you didn't do anything when you caught me with Matthew. Because you're a coward! Afraid to stand up and be a man! You'll never be the man he is. Never!" She stood there shouting as he left the room. He wasn't sure why he mentioned to Pauline about going to the cave. Bobby Gene was in his usual place. He could tell from Jeffrey's mood that trouble was in the air.

"Bobby Gene, I don't have time to explain, but I'm afraid if you don't leave this cave tonight you may never get the chance."

"Man, what are you saying? You know I can't leave here. What if I get caught?"

Listen, Bobby Gene, this is not a joke. If you don't get out of here I can't be responsible for what might happen. It's Pauline. Bobby Gene, she's changed. She's not the same woman I married. I'm afraid that she's going to tell Matthew that I've been hiding you out here. Her mind has gone corrupt like these Missouri white folks."

"Just this very night I caught her in bed with Matthew. She has become so conniving. I wouldn't put it past her to go to

Matthew with this information. After catching the two of them together, she had the gall to try and talk her way out of it. She must really think I'm a fool."

Bobby Gene was startled.

"Damn, man. I know words aren't of much consolation during times like these. But I truly do regret something like this happening to you. You didn't deserve this. All my life as being a black man, something of this nature doesn't surprise me, since the white man didn't have to hide the fact when they wanted to be with one of our women was no problem. The question with them, was, which one this time? If what you're saying is true, then you could be in serious trouble too. What are you going to do?"

"Don't worry about me, I'll figure something out later. If we get this place looking like nobody's been here, then I can possibly play it off. That means we have to move quickly. Now hurry, grab your belongings and follow me. Hell, for all I know she's probably talking to Matthew this very moment she was a bit distraught when I left her. That's why we must make our move quickly. The only thing we have going in our favor would be the fact that Matthew doesn't know which cave to come to first. I never told Pauline which cave it was."

"If my calculations are correct, it's going to take him a while before he gets some of the overseers together. After all the drinking they were doing this evening. I've got to find a way to sneak you into Anna Belle's cabin. Contrary to belief it's the safest place for you to go right now."

So far everything outside was quiet. Jeffrey signaled to Bobby Gene that it was safe for him to come out.

"Hurry. We must take a different route just in case they are on their way here. Lucky for us the night is very dark. Follow me closely, so we won't get lost from one another."

Upon reaching the plantation Jeffrey beckoned Bobby Gene to stay put while he got closer to see what was going on. Jeffrey couldn't see very well from the distance he was at. But he could clearly hear Matthew's voice.

"All right, you men. I want you to break up into two groups of four. There are two neighboring caves close to here. I want them both checked thoroughly. I know the hour is late as well as cold. If there is a Negro hidden out in one of those caves, I want him brought back to me unharmed. Do I make myself clear?" All the overseers responded positively.

"Good, then be on your way." Jeffrey made his way back to Bobby Gene as they moved swiftly through the grounds.

"Quick, inside the henhouse. You'll be all right in here for the time being. I'll go check with Anna Belle and tell her what is going on, and see if she will agree to let you stay there for a few days."

Even though it was cold outside, sweat had engulfed Bobby Gene's body. He lay there on the floor listening and watching. Jeffrey seemed to have been gone a lifetime. Suddenly the door opened as Jeffrey softly called out to him.

"Everything's OK, Bobby Gene. But we must move quickly before the overseers get back. Are you ready?" Bobby Gene took a deep breath.

"Let's do this." They made a mad dash for the cabin. Jeffrey had asked Anna Belle to be on the lookout for them. As she saw them approach, she flung the door open so they could rush inside.

"Come sit down at the table, and I'll try to explain my intentions as best I can." He began.

"You see, there are other places where a man is not judged by the color of his skin or how he dresses. This is the place that I've been telling Bobby Gene about. It's also a place where you hear other blacks speak of where they can get their freedom." Bobby Gene looked at Anna Belle in astonishment while speaking to Jeffrey.

"It truly does exist?"

"Yes, we must find a way to get you on a stagecoach to Philadelphia. Once you're there you're home free. I have family there."

"Once Bobby Gene has gotten safely into their grasp, then he can explain the situation as shall I in the extensive letter Bobby

Gene shall be carrying on his person. My people are good people. They will help him to get his freedom papers and will teach him how to fight with the proper tools he will need when he comes back to face the enemy. Those freedom papers will tell any white man in the South, or slave state, that Bobby Gene is no longer a slave but as equal as they are." Bobby Gene cut him off.

"That sounds like a dream come true, Jeffrey. But how do you suppose I board the stagecoach. I have no money. And even if I did, I couldn't very well go and say I want to buy a ticket to this so called magic place of yours."

"I know that. But if you were a piece of baggage or if someone were to assume you to be." He rephrased his last statement. "The bottom line is this."

"Suppose we were to ship you away from here in something as to where it wouldn't be so obvious to the public, or naked eyes. No one would ever suspect anything now, would they?" There came a rap at the door. Bobby Gene and Anna Belle's eyes widened substantially.

"Open this door. We know you're in there, so open it right now!" Anna Belle looked at Jeffrey.

"What are we going to do? Someone must have seen you bring him here."

"First of all, we are not going to panic. That would give us away for sure. Quick, Bobby Gene, under the bed. Anna Belle, get the door and act yourself. Our lives are depending on the performance you give this evening. Remember what I said earlier. Be calm." This time there was pounding.

"If this door isn't opened in a few seconds, we'll kick it in!" Anna Belle sighed, giving everything a final look to make sure it was appropriate then she opened the door. The two men rushed in.

"Out of our way, nigger." They moved around Anna Belle. "Mr. Wellington said we might find you here. He wants you at the big house this instant." They spoke as their eyes wandered about the dimly lit cabin.

"Did he say what it was about?"

"Look. When the boss tells us to do something, we don't ask no questions less it's something we don't understand. We just came here to deliver his message, and that's that."

"I got the message so you can leave." They lingered a bit longer, scanning over the room finally leaving in the same abrupt way they had come Jeffrey stood up.

"Phew, that was close. I must go now. I have a feeling I know what this is all about. Tell Bobby Gene I'll get back with him as soon as I can about my plan." He left too.

Matthew seemed a bit impatient when Jeffrey got to the house. Pauline stood there massaging Matthew's shoulders, looking at Jeffrey with a deceitful grin on her face as he entered the study.

"I can see you didn't waste much time before running back into his arms. Have you no shame? I would have thought you'd at least use some scruples." Matthew cleared his throat, suggesting to Jeffrey that their behavior wasn't the issue at hand.

"Jeffrey, that isn't important right now. It has been brought to my attention this past evening that you have been harboring a runaway slave. Do you have anything to say on your behalf?" Jeffrey was misty eyed. Knowing he was put in a difficult situation, and realizing even if it meant his life, he was going to take the stand for Bobby Gene.

"I see Pauline is up to her old tricks again. When she can't have her way she tries to make trouble. I guess when I told her I no longer wanted her, she decided to retaliate by spreading some vicious lie. She's good at that, but you wouldn't know that part about her now, would you? I can assure you I know nothing of this matter except of your mentioning it this very moment." Pauline stepped away from Matthew.

"He's lying, I'm telling you. There's a nigger out there in a cave. He's even taken him clothing and food. He even told me his name was Bobby Gene."

Jeffrey looked at Pauline.

"You poor soul. Everyone knows Bobby Gene was killed several months ago." He looked a Matthew.

131

"If you should inquire about his death, I'm sure Mr. Dalton will verify this to be true. The reason for the lying is because she's hoping it will keep her in your good graces. You want to bed with him. Then you can have him. I want a wife. Not a slut or whore." Pauline turned to Matthew with a pleading voice.

"I'm telling the truth. If you doubt my word, then send some of your men out to search for the cave. I'm sure it hasn't disappeared into thin air. Maybe then you'll believe me." He stroked Pauline's face gently with his hand.

"I'm one step ahead of you, my dear. At this very moment as we speak, I do have men out with tracking dogs. They've already visited the neighboring caves but found nothing. If he is out there, they will find him." He looked back at Jeffrey.

"I do like you, Jeffrey and father had the highest respect for you. Should they come back with that Negro. You will answer to me, regardless as to whether you knew about him or not."

"I think that's only fair," Jeffrey replied. "Since we're on the subject of being candid, how can a man of your character display such a cheap standard of morals? Has all that wealth and power stripped you of your pride. Didn't you even care?" He looked at Pauline.

"I can see money doesn't always have to buy things. Sometimes, apparently if you're fortunate enough, you can have it for free." Pauline rushed Jeffrey, striking his face in the process.

"How dare you talk about me like that? What kind of husband have you been to me lately? Believe it or not, I do have desires which need to be met at times. You might have noticed had you not been preoccupied with that nigger." He grabbed her by her wrists and shoved her backward. Matthew banged his fist on the desk.

"Let's get one thing straight. I don't appreciate being talked down to by anyone. Especially the likes of you. Hell, you ain't even good enough to shine my worst pair of boots. I made a mistake and I'm sorry. She was a willing participant. We can stand here and fight it out. But that won't undo what has happened. She's free to come back to you any time. I'm not holding her to me."

Jeffrey looked at her once more before leaving.

"No thank you. Once a whore. Always a whore. I'll be moving my things to that empty cabin tomorrow if that's all right with you. Then I shall go into town and seek employment." He closed the door behind him and went upstairs.

Jeffrey laid there in the darkness until everything about the mansion was quiet. He went over to the window to see if everything about the grounds was the same. When he was sure, he put on his coat and pulled the collar up closely about his neck. He could feel the bitter coldness of the weather. He had chosen this room in particular. Outside the room was a vine that had grown alongside the wall of the house. This would make it easier for him to get to the ground without being noticed or to disturb anyone. He made his way down the vine. The frigid weather surrounded him from every direction. He knew that on this particular evening, as cold as it was, chances of him getting caught were slim to none. Everyone but him would be cuddled as close to the fire or one another as possible. He walked over to the window and whispered Bobby Gene's name. The door opened a bit. Bobby Gene stood there fully dressed as if he were prepared for any unexpected surprise. Jeffrey looked hazy to him. Then his vision became clear as he jerked Jeffrey inside.

"Man, get in here." He shifted his shoulders, trying to shake off the chill. "Are you crazy? This has to be one of the coldest nights of the year. And you're out here in it." Anna Belle came walking blindly through the dark calling out for Bobby Gene.

"Is everything be all right? I's thought I's heard voices out here." She stood there awaiting his reply. Bobby Gene walked over to her.

"Don't worry, Anna Belle. It's only Jeffrey."

"Masser Jeffrey," she said dryly. "What he be doing back here on a night like this? I's bet he be chilled. I's fix us some coffee."

"That sounds very good," Jeffrey responded.

"When I got to the house, they were both in his study. There she was marveling all over him." A grimace look appeared on his face as his right fist connected with his left hand.

"How could she be so stupid as to give herself to him so casually, when I know he doesn't want her?" He chuckled at his own disbelief as he continued. "And the sad thing bout it is what she said about my not being a man was true." Bobby Gene interrupted.

"Come on, stop belittling yourself. It took a man to walk away. One shouldn't have to always fight when there are somethings not worth fighting over. It's her loss, not yours. I'd say it's her who needs to grow up. Of course she's riding high now so she thinks. What's going to happen when that bubble she's riding bursts and she realizes she's back where she started? She'll be back pleading for you to give her another chance. You can rest assured of that."

"What you've done for me, I can never repay. How many so-called men do you think would be willing to put their life on the line for a complete stranger? I consider myself a man. But I'm not sure I would have done the same for you. Jeffrey, you've taught me many things, and I will forever be indebted to you." Jeffrey smiled as he patted Bobby Gene on the back.

"You know you're getting more intelligent every day, but you yet have a long way to go. That's why I'm here. I've been thinking and came up with a solution as to how we're going to get you away from here."

"Oh yeah, and how do you propose to do that, genius?"

"It's like this. Tomorrow, Elsmeralda the housemaid and myself have to go into town for supplies."

"OK, go on I'm listening. Not to mention my curiosity about it. Where do I fit in?" Jeffrey leaned forward in his chair showing his excitement.

"Well, here's the thing. When Pauline and myself left Pennsylvania, we brought with us this old trunk which carried our personal belongings. We found ourselves being robbed. After searching it and finding nothing of value, they left it with us. I'm going to ship you to Philadelphia to my folks, along with the letter I mentioned to you earlier explaining the circumstances surrounding you. While Elsmeralda is shopping, I'll make a trip to the motel where the stage coach will be. Once you're in Philadelphia, you will be introduced to a very good friend of mine." Jeffrey could see Bobby Gene was troubled. Before he had a chance to speak, Jeffrey assured him that the person receiving the trunk was a Negro he knew for many years. After they had discussed everything in full, Bobby Gene turned to Anna Belle.

"Do you think it will work?" She flashed him a smile.

"Anything be's worth a try. It couldn't be any worse than ifin they's found you's here." He looked back at Jeffrey.

"Then its settled. I'll do it." Jeffrey stood up.

"Great! Then understand what we've planned, and there shouldn't be any problems at all."

The few hours were endless. Jeffrey lay there watching the gold pendulum move from side to side as the hands on the clock slowly turned under the moonlight. Jeffrey found himself dozing off at the most unlikely time. When the hour had drawn near, he was fortunate that no one heard him drag the trunk to the back porch, namely Pauline, since he had to go into their room to get it. Luckily enough for him, she had spent the night with Matthew. It wasn't surprising since they weren't hiding the knowledge of their affair. The time had finally come. Jeffrey had only hoped that Bobby Gene was as accurate on his end of the plan as he himself had been.

Bobby Gene was impatiently pacing and watching through the window. The sun would be rising in a short while, then the whole plantation would be alive. At that moment. he could see the bunk board pull up in front of the back door with the two horses. Jeffrey could tell from the cold breath coming from their nostrils that the weather hadn't changed from the few hours he had been in it. If anything, it appeared to have gotten colder. He opened the door and rushed out to Bobby Gene who had just stepped down from the bunk board.

"Where have you been?" He wanted to know trembling from the cold. "I was beginning to wonder if you had backed out or something. It doesn't matter, you're here. Now quickly come help me lift this trunk in the back before we're found out." After the trunk was in the wagon, he looked at Bobby Gene.

"Now it's your turn. I can't guarantee this will be the most comfortable ride you've ever had, but if all goes as planned, you won't have to worry about anything anymore." After Bobby Gene was inside, Jeffrey reassured him he didn't have to worry about getting air.

"This old trunk is so ragged you'll have plenty of air to breath with the holes and all. I'm going to pull this canvas over you so that no one will notice we have a trunk back there. Are you all right?"

"I'm fine, except it reminds me of the times I've been bound and shackled."

"Lands sake. I's thought I's felt a draft com'n through this house." Elsmeralda got to the doorway just as Jeffrey finished pulling the canvas over the remaining of the trunk.

"Masser Jeffrey, what you's doing with that bunk board so early? I's still has to git the Masser breakfast before we start to town for them supplies." His face tightened as he stood there, silently trying to find the right words to say, hoping that she wasn't aware of what was going on.

"I…er, I couldn't sleep so I decided to go and hitch up now so I wouldn't have to do it later. I forgot something in the house and went back in to get it. It slipped my mind to shut the door behind me." From the look on Elsmeralda's face, he could tell she wasn't thoroughly convinced by his story.

"Well, whatever you's says, and speak'n of breakfast you's best be gitt'n yourself in here as well." She turned and closed the door behind her. Jeffrey made sure she had left, then he knelt down close enough for Bobby Gene to hear. The sound of fear still lingered within him.

"Well, buddy, it looks as though you're going to be in there a bit longer than expected. Will you be all right?"

"Yes, but I'm not going to pretend that I won't be happy to get out of this thing."

"I wish I could say I understand how you must be feeling. But I can't since I've never been in your predicament. We can't think about that now. There's a more urgent problem we have facing us." Even though Bobby Gene couldn't see Jeffrey's face, he knew from the tone of his voice he was frightened, and with a legitimate reason. Bobby Gene's voice rose through the trunk.

"What's happening, Jeffrey?" Jeffrey tapped on the trunk.

"Shhh, lower your voice before someone overhears you." Bobby Gene brought it down to a whisper.

"I'm sorry, man, but when I can't see what's going on around me, I get a bit nervous, I'm sure you would be as well."

"I won't dispute that, Bobby Gene. It's just that I've jumped the gun here a bit. It's because I'm overexcited about getting you on that stage coach than you are. I should have realized Elsmeralda had to fix breakfast before leaving."

Bobby Gene spoke again. "Excuse my ignorance, but could you fill me in on what you're babbling about?"

"I'm not sure. But there's a possibility Elsmeralda might have caught me talking to you. I suppose like all the other times; we just have to wait it out. That's the only way at this point. I'm going to take the rig around front and leave it there until we get ready to leave. You're warm enough, aren't you?"

"Are you kidding me? It's so tight in here, I'm smothering." Jeffrey had been notified Matthew wanted to see him in his study. He didn't bother knocking and went directly inside. Matthew was seated behind his desk and having a cup of coffee. He looked up at him with a bleak look.

"It appears you haven't learned anything about knocking before entering," he said sharply. You would think after that one incident you'd learn." He gloated at his very words as he sipped on his coffee. Jeffrey stood there grimacing.

"Anyway, we found no sign of anyone living there in either cave." The boasting look in his eyes ceased.

"Actually, I'm relieved that they didn't find anything. I know you don't like me very well, and that's understandable. I would have hated to think what your betrayal to me may have led me to do." He got up and walked over to the huge bookshelf.

Jeffrey spoke. "You don't fool me nor does your influence or money impress me one bit. Your arrogant behavior and the way you're using Pauline is what I despise. You don't love her. I can't figure you out." Matthew turned to Jeffrey, slamming the book closed he held in his hands.

"Even a farm boy like yourself should have figured it out by now. What I stand for, I have it all. Wealth, prestige and oh yes Pauline, such a presumptuous thing. Serves my needs quite well at the moment. But in time you shall have her back. Once I tire of her. You know what I mean. Or do I need to spell it out for you? She's a bit inexperience between the sheets, but that's what I prefer. Someone young and still unscathed. I promise you that when I'm finished with her, she'll possibly be able to teach you a thing or two."

"You egotistical son of a bitch! I could knock the hell out of you right now! But I won't give you the satisfaction. You're a very sick individual!"

Matthew smiled at Jeffrey.

"Not sick, just arrogant as you so politely put it. Now it appears you have some errands to run." He turned back to the books, leaving Jeffrey standing there. Jeffrey left the room, angrily slamming the door behind him. Elsmeralda was awaiting Jeffrey at the study door when he came out. She could tell from the redness in his cheeks that he was upset about something. She flashed him a warm smile.

"I's hope you's wrapped up fer this cold weather. We's got a long ride ahead of us. I's brought some extra quilts and a bucket of hots coals." Jeffrey could feel the heat penetrate his face as she lifted them upward to check and see if they were still red. "I brung along some extras in case these burn out.

Jeffrey spoke. "That was very thoughtful, Elsmeralda. Now if we're planning on getting this cold weather behind us, we best be on our way." For a long while, the ride was silent. Then Elsmeralda began to speak.

"That old trunk you's has back there must be of great value to you's ain't it? I's could swear you's be talk'n to it back yonder."

"You knew all along didn't you? I mean about me having someone in the trunk."

"Mmm. I's maybe dumb, but when I's see'd you's talk'n to that trunk, I's says to myself, Masser Jeffrey don't look crazed or act crazed. So's I's knows it had to be someone. He be that nigger Masser Wellington sent some of the overseers to find last night. Ain't he?

"Yes, but tell me. Why didn't you mention this to Mr. Wellington?"

"I's like you's, Masser Jeffrey. I's be watch'n you's around the plantation fer months. The way you's treat us niggers. I's knows you's care 'bout us I's doesn't knows why that nigger's back yonder in that trunk. But I's trust you's in what you's doing."

The little town was crowded and filled with bunk boards. Jeffrey gathered that everyone was there for the same reasons they were. He pulled up to the general store and let Elsmeralda off.

"I'll be back as soon as I get this trunk on the stage coach." The motel wasn't far. Jeffrey asked if he might get some help to lift the trunk onto the stage coach.

"That surely is a heavy thing. If one didn't know better, you'd think there was a body or some gold in there." Jeffrey gave him a stern look. He didn't like the candor with which the man had just spoken. If only he knew how right on he was.

"I didn't find that amusing." The old man wiped away his grin.

"I was only funning. It don't matter to me one bit what you got in that old trunk. All's that concerns me is whether you can pay for its fare. Which will be twelve bits." He took the money and went off mumbling to himself and shaking his head at the same time.

"You can't joke with folks anymore nowadays. What is the world coming to?"

"Oh, one more thing. Make sure the stage coach men handle that trunk with care. There's some very valuable merchandise in there. I'd hate to have damaged."

The old man waved him off.

"Sure, sure, sonny, everybody's cargo seems to be precious these days. I'll make note of it." Elsmeralda was still gathering supplies when Jeffrey got to the store. The crowds were still coming. Once they were back on the bunk board, Elsmeralda looked at Jeffrey.

"I's take it everyth'n be all right."

Jeffrey smiled and took her hands in his.

"Elsmeralda, everything is more than all right. It's perfect."

ive years had passed. Pauline and Jeffrey had gotten a divorced. Jeffrey had quit the plantation, and was now living in town and working at the saw mill. Anna Belle was living in the big house. She replaced Elsmeralda, who had passed on. Anna Belle heard from Bobby Gene time to time. She knew it had to be that way for everyone's safety. Oh but how she truly missed him. A war had broken out between the Confederate and United States at Fort Sumter, South Carolina on April twelfth eighteen hundred sixty-one. It was very brutal and had many causalities, till slaves were forced to enlisted to join in the fighting. Although they had to fight, they would still be slaves. For many, even though this might be a surety they would lose their lives. They jumped at the opportunity to at least be able to have space to breath. To be in wide open territory, no confinement. There were some who defected to the confederate side, who later helped them to obtain their freedom. But for others the masters and overseers still had the power to conduct their ways, and punishment when-ever they saw it necessary. While the confederates could only look on and do nothing. The majority of them ended back in Missouri, and other states who yet condoned it. Many with wounded bodies, and in some cases maimed.

Gabriel, Anna Belle's son, who was now five years of age found a friend in young Matthew Wellington who was a few years older than himself.

"I swear, Gabriel. If I hear you say that again, I'm going to clobber you one."

"Well, it's true, I heard Miss Molly and Ethel Mae. They said your mama was a nigger." Matthew shoved Gabriel to the ground and fell down on him, both striking out at each other. "I warned you, Gabriel." A cry for help filled the air. Anna Belle rushed outside, pulling the two boys apart and standing them both to their feet. She shook the both of them.

"What is the meaning of this?" Her eyes focused on Matthew since he was the oldest. He pointed to Gabriel as he spoke.

"It's all his fault, Miss Anna Belle. He's been saying that my mama was a nigger."

Anna Belle was stunned and quickly turned her attention to Gabriel.

"Is this true, Gabriel? Did you say that about Matthew's mother?" Gabriel held his head downward, kicking at the loose dirt beneath his feet. "Well, Gabriel, I'm waiting."

"Yes but I didn't mean any harm, Ma. Honest, I didn't." He looked up at her through his tiny tear-stained face.

"I only told him what Miss Molly and Ethel Mae had said. I didn't know it would make Matthew so mean toward me." He looked over at Matthew, who stuck out his tongue at him.

"All right, Matthew, we'll have no more of that." He then hung his head. "As for you, Gabriel, I believe you didn't mean anything by this. But if I should hear of your speaking in this manner again or find the two of you fighting, I'm going to warm the seats of both your britches. Do I make myself clear?" They both were in agreement.

"Yes 'em."

"Now get inside, the both of you, so you can get cleaned up. You look like you've been waddling in a pigsty." Matthew was standing in the door when she turned about. She was shaken by his presence.

"Oh, Master Wellington. You startled me. I had no ideal you were standing there."

He looked at her with a mystified stare.

"I'd like to see you in my study." He turned and left. She directed the children upstairs, informing them she would be there to attend to them shortly. She called after them once they had reached the top of the stairs.

"Remember what I said about your being good." They said they understood and disappeared behind the door to their rooms. Anna Belle tapped lightly on the study door.

"Come in," replied the voice on the other side. Anna Belle could feel her knees buckle as she crept through the crack of the door. Matthew signaled for her to come inside and close the door. He could see the door was as far as she had intended on coming.

"Well, suit yourself. I'm not going to bite you. Besides, Matthew Wellington don't beg nobody." He went on to say. "The reason I wanted to see you is because I wanted to commend you on the work you're doing around here. I was especially pleased with the way you handled the situation with the boys. It was remarkable." His voice suddenly froze as his eyes gazed into Anna Belle's.

"Er, Master Wellington is everything OK? You look as though you've taken ill or something."

Matthew shook his head. "Huh? What was it you were saying?"

"I was asking if you had taken ill. You appear to have gotten pale all of a sudden."

"Oh no, I'm fine. It's just that for a moment you reminded me of someone I used to know standing there like that." That bizarre look appeared once again. This time he arose and walked over to where she was yet standing, looking into her subtle face, touching it gently.

"My God, I never realized it until now, but you look like Mary Lou." He ran his tongue over his dry lips as his hands moved toward her blouse. She was frightened, and her insides were crying out for help. What kind of animal had this man become all of a sudden?

After several years of being his maid servant, he never reacted in this manner before. She wanted to strike out at him to protect her virtue. But she didn't know what his reaction would be. His face came closer to hers as his hot breath burned against her lips, pulling her body in close to him. Her inner feelings were completely uncontrollable. She had to get this man off her no matter what consequences she had to face. The door pushed against them as Matthew broke his concentration.

"Matt, are you in there?" There came another push. "Matthew, there's something against the door." Matthew cleared his throat as he helped a frightened Anna Belle pull herself together.

"Just a moment." His eyes were still mystical as he looked at her.

"We'll continue with this later." He pulled Anna Belle away from the door, knowing the state of mind she was in she couldn't have done it herself. Pauline was in question about Anna Belle's strange behavior as she quickly excused herself.

"I can see you've picked up some of your ex-husband's bad traits."

"Don't be coy with me, Matt. My not knocking has never been an issue before now. Maybe that's because there has never been a reason to knock until now. What were you doing? Trying to seduce that nigger into your bed? I saw the way she looked when she left. Frightened, scared out of her wits. Isn't she a little old for you to try and break in? It appears to me that you're about some years too late for that." Matthew grabbed her arm and squeezed it firmly. A fierce look came into his eyes as he struck her face.

"Let's get one thing straight! Whatever I choose to do with my life is none of your damn concern! You're only my mistress. Don't mistake that for being my wife, which is a big difference. Don't you forget it! If I want that woman or any woman for that fact, it will be my choice to make. Not yours. Besides you're old merchandise to me, so why don't you go and see if you can find loverboy Jeffrey? I told him when I had my fill of you I'd send you back to him. I only wanted you to fulfill my momentary needs until I found that right woman."

His mind started to wander.

"After all this time, I do believe she does exist."

"That housemaid of yours. You've got to be joking. What can she give you that I can't? The only purpose I can see is her accompanying you in your bed, which is already occupied. Or have you forgotten?"

Pauline ran her fingers through Matthew's hair, trying to entice him with charms and kisses.

"It won't work, Pauline. Your seduction I mean. You can be replaced at the snap of my finger if I choose. So if I were you, I'd watch myself on being so loosed lipped about certain things. It's over. The woman I truly want is Anna Belle. I'm a man who usually gets what he wants." He looked at Pauline. "You've been a good example of that. I intend on having her as my permanent mistress. Maybe even my wife." Pauline was furious. she lifted her hand, which caught Matthew alongside his face.

"You bastard, all this time you lead me to believe that you loved me! That one day we'd be married. Only to turn me out for a worthless nigger? You even told me you loved me. It was all a lie, a game. I was someone to keep your bed warm, to be your whore, till you found that right woman, when all this time I thought it was me!"

"Correction. I told you I loved the way you made me feel. There is a difference and as far as my marrying you, that was out of your own presumption. The thought never entered my mind. Not once." She threw her hand up again, hoping to make another connection to Matthew's face. He grabbed it and clinched it tightly.

"I've never made it a practice for a person to strike me once, let alone twice." He sent her sailing into the study door. "Remember that, won't you? Gather your belongings and be out of this house immediately. You're no longer welcome here." He brushed past her as he left the study. She followed after him, ranting and raving.

"You won't get away with this, Mr. High and Mighty! I'll get even with you for this!" He walked on ignoring her totally. Stopping at the gun display and lifting out one of its pistols, she took aim at him.

"I'll kill you for this, you bastard! You think I'm going to roll over for some black bitch? Then you're sadly mistaken." Matthew could hear the click of the pistol as he quickly turned to find it pointed toward him. He rushed up to her, knocking her to the floor.

"Did you honestly think I'd leave a loaded gun in the open like that? You're more naive than I thought. If you're so hell bent on shooting me." He took the gun from her hands and retrieved some bullets from the locked drawer beneath the gun display, filling the pistol with them. Putting it back into her hands, he said. "Here, it's loaded. Take your best shot. Now is your chance." Pauline sat on the floor, sobbing. Hugging the pistol tightly with both hands, she raised it slowly toward Matthew again, shaking while focusing on him through a flood of tears. She cocked the trigger and held it there a long moment then laid it down beside her. "Just as I thought. You have the gall to say Jeffrey was less than a man. What nerves do you have? Where's that boldness you displayed a short while ago. You two deserve each other. Get the hell out of my house, bitch, never to return! I want a real woman. A strong woman. Of which you are neither. I need someone with back bone to carry me when I'm down. All you're after is material things. that don't set well with me. You've got to have strength, respect, but most of all dignity. Look at you. You can't even defend yourself. So be gone, my decision has been made!" She could see Matthew turn on his heels and walk away for the last time.

CHAPTER SEVENTEEN

The saloon was filled with wails of laughter. The thickness of smoke left a gray film in the air as the stranger entered and strolled calmly up to the bar. His hair was midnight black, accented with a touch of gray on his right side, neatly combed backward with each strand in its proper place. The dark skin coincided with the silky black mustache and its neatly shaved side burns joined with his full beard. His body was well mature and perfect in build. The gray three-piece suit he wore was that of the best tailor-made and stayed in contrast with the black silk lapel that was dressed up with a gray corsage. His boots were so shiny that they glimmered from the lantern light. He stood bold and proud at the bar.

"Barkeeper, give me a shot of whiskey." The man behind the bar stopped his conversation long enough to see who was speaking to him.

"Don't you know the rules here, boy? Niggers ain't even allowed in here. What gives you the right to feel you can come in here to have a drink? I suggest you get on out of here and get you some water out of the horses' trough. That should quench your thirst." The loud laughter was now quiet. This time the man's voice was demanding.

"I said I want a shot of whiskey! Now! This piece of paper says I have as much right to sit here and drink it as well as anyone else." He took the white piece of paper that was neatly folded from the inner pocket of his suit and laid it upon the bar. The barkeeper walked over and picked up the paper, giving the man an unfriendly glance.

"Didn't you hear the barkeeper, boy? Niggers aren't served in here. Now are you going to walk out of here on your own? Or are you going to have to be thrown out?" He grabbed the man by his lapel when the barkeeper intervened.

"Hold on, Travor. I don't want no trouble in here. This here paper does state that a Bobby Gene Watson under the state of Pennsylvania declares him a free man. He's no longer to be treated under the boundaries of slavery in any city of the United States of America." Travor was mystified as he snatched the paper from the barkeeper giving Bobby Gene a through looking over.

"Well I'll be damned. Speaking of coming back from the grave. Nigger, you surely pulled a good one over on me." He examined the piece of paper held in front of him. "I don't believe it." He read the words on the paper silently to himself, crumpling it up as he threw it to the floor and stomped on it.

"This is irate. Are you telling me that you're going to let a small piece of paper stand in the way? Well, I'm not." He again grabbed Bobby Gene by the lapel when he heard the cocking of a gun.

"The man has the right to be served, and I'm not going to turn him out as long as he's willing to pay. I can't say I approve of this. But as long as he's on my property, there won't be any trouble. Once he's outside my place, well, that's another story." Travor loosened the hold he had on Bobby Gene and staggered off into the smoke-filled room. Bobby Gene straightened his clothing stooped down and picked up his paper, and drank down the shot quickly, dropping the glass sternly to the counter.

"Barkeeper, I'll have another." The barkeeper strolled back to Bobby Gene and poured another shot. Then he looked him squarely in the face.

"Listen here. Just because you got some paper doesn't mean I have to like you, nigger. I want you to finish your drink and be on your way." As he sat there sipping his drink, he could feel the burning hatred of the eyes that were focused on him. He took the last swallow of his drink.

"I'll be taking a bottle with me." He took some money and threw it on the bar.

"Keep the change." He turned to walk away from the bar when the thought came to mind.

"By the way. Could you possibly tell me where I might find one Jeffrey Turner?" The barkeeper hollered out to him.

"You'll find him at the motel across the street. The man behind the desk will be able to tell you what room." He tipped his hat with gratitude.

"Thank you kindly." He was at the door when a pale, fragile figure approached him. She stood in his way, gawking at him with fiery red eyes. The stale smell of alcohol was on her breath.

"Did I over hear the name Bobby Gene?" She wanted to know, swaying forward then backward, waiting for her reply. He smiled, speaking in his gentleman-like manner.

"Yes ma'am, that's me. Bobby Gene Watson is the name." She stood there a moment, searching him upward then down. Then she spat in his face. He closed his eyes, gritted his teeth, and took the handkerchief from his pocket, wiping the saliva from his face. He stepped around her and walked through the double doors. the silence was faded out by laughter once again.

The weather outside was hot and stuffy, except for the pleasure brought on from a gale of cool wind racing by now and then. He stood there in the middle of town, admiring its beauty. Even the old abandoned buildings were a beautiful sight to him. Looking at the motel across the street, it didn't appear as ravishing as it did when he first arrived. It could have been because he was too tired to notice the real world around him. To think. The one who made everything possible for him was staying at the same motel as he. He inhaled a large gulp of the fresh air as it passed by him, standing there a moment taking in the view of the people. Negroes who had stopped to marvel at this strange person. Oh how wonderful it felt to be free to be able to roam wherever he chose. His reentering the lobby of the motel startled the man behind the desk. The man jumped straight way in the air though he was still half asleep.

"Yes, can I help you?" He stood there rubbing his eyes when Bobby Gene's face became visible to him. "Oh Mr. Watson, sir, it's you. I must have dozed off. Are you in for the day?"

"Yes I am, thank you. That long stage coach ride has finally caught up with me. I think I'll just retire to my room for a nap." A look of relief came on the man's face.

"Good then. I'll just bid you a good day and go rest these weary bones of mine for a few hours then." He walked over to the door and shut it.

"I'm sorry to disturb you again. I have one last request before you retire. I understand Jeffrey Turner has residency here. Would you be so kind as to tell me where his room might be?" The man stood there, rubbing his chin.

"May I ask why you would inquire of him?"

"Let's just say," Bobby Gene said as he slipped the man a five-dollar piece. "We have some unfinished business we need to wrap up." The old man pointed up the stairs.

"The second door on your left. I warn you, sir, if you should cause any trouble. I will have to be obliged to shoot you." He reassured him that wouldn't be necessary.

Bobby Gene stood at the top of the stairway, watching the brown faded door in front of him. He knew seeing Jeffrey was only a knock away. What would his reaction be after not hearing from him but only a few times? Had he changed much in the five years they've been separated?

The only way to find out was to knock. He lifted his hand to the door but pulled it back. The suspense was killing him. He could feel the blood running warm inside his heart, racing rapidly. His hand went up again. This time it connected with the door. He waited to see if he might here some response on the other side, but heard nothing. His hand rapped again.

"All right, all right, don't knock down my door. I'm coming. who is it?" Jeffrey asked from the other side. From the laziness in his voice one could detect he had been sleeping. Bobby Gene stood there in silence, knowing if he spoke his surprise would be discovered. Besides, he wanted to see the look on Jeffrey's face when he opened the door to him.

"I said who's there?" Bobby Gene refused to respond. The door unlatched from the other side his one eye bucked as the door swung open.

"Bobby Gene! Is it really you?" He snatched him by his arm as they caressed one another, overwhelmed to see each other again. They got so involved with themselves, they hadn't noticed anyone else was present.

"My, my, now ain't that a sight for sore eyes." They both pulled away as their eyes focused on the voice. The joyful look that was on Jeffrey's face became vexed.

"What do you want, Pauline? I thought I told you to stay away from me." She staggered up the stairs, speaking as she did so.

"Pauline? This is your wife?" Bobby Gene wanted to know. "I should have suspected as much when she confronted me over at the saloon."

"My ex-wife," Jeffrey corrected. "We're divorced. So you ran into her at the saloon?"

"One would call it a chance meeting. Good seeing you again, Miss."

"So this is what you gave me up for, a no-count nigger."

"I suggest you leave now, Pauline. It's quite obvious you've had a bit much to drink. Besides, shouldn't you be at work this time of day?" She stood there swaying as she held on to the rail for leverage, looking up at him, her eyes rolling to the back of her head.

"Ha," she tried to laugh it off. "Indeed, I should be, but you see Katie seems to think I've been boozing it up too much, and just a few minutes ago told me I was dismissed. Can you believe that? She fired me, but I don't need her or her stinking job. I was the best saloon gal she had. If it weren't for me, she wouldn't be getting the business she has acquired over the past few years. This is how she repays me. By firing me." She held on to the rail while speaking.

"Not to worry, though, she'll be begging for me to come back. Especially when she sees her establishment start to die off. Anyhow,

I don't need her. I don't need anyone!" She looked up at Jeffrey, the webs of her eyes were with moisture. "That's not true. I need you, Jeffrey. Won't you please take me back? I'm begging you."

"What's the matter Pauline? I recall a while back you were gloating because you were the mistress of the town's most affluent man. You even put me down and made fun of me. I needed you to be my wife as well as a friend; But you turned your back on all of us. Everyone who was ever good to you. You turned your back on them. Now you're down and out, you come to me expecting me to be forgiving? You've wasted your time. Look at you. You're a drunk. You can't even hold a decent job, if you call what you did decent, and God only knows how many men you've whored with to get a drink." His eyes became vile and cold and the tone of his voice was ruthless.

"Even whores have some dignity about themselves. They know when they have had their limit with the booze. But look at you." He pointed to the rail that was supporting her.

"You can't even stand on your own accord. When you thought everything was going all right for you. You never gave me a second thought. Remember my trips to the saloon, trying to get you out of that way of living? You wanted no part of what I was trying to say to you. At the time I pleaded with you. Were you there for me? Of course not. You sicken me, Pauline." She managed to top the stairs and over to where they stood, as her hand caught the side of his face. The muscles in his face flexed with anger as he moved toward her. Bobby Gene braced him.

"Come on, man, just ignore her. You can see she's drunk." Jeffrey looked her solely in the eyes.

"You're right. Besides, she's not worth dirtying my hands over anyway. How quickly she forgets we're divorced." They went inside the room, slamming the door behind them.

CHAPTER EIGHTEEN

*J*effrey was awakened by a loud thump and the shouting of voices. He rushed to the door and cracked it in hopes he might be able to detect what was happening.

"What the hell is going on in this town? At first it was the barkeeper, now you? Have yaw lost yaw mind? I mean when did it become a law for us to protect these niggers?" The old man spoke while Travor yet had him in his grasp.

"It's not only about the law. It's about a human being such as yourself and me. Until today It was as hard for me to accept the fact because of my upbringing, these niggers are human too. I'm not agreeing nor disagreeing with you. But I see where I've been wrong. I don't believe they should have the same rights as us. But I do think they should be treated like people, not animals."

"Mr. Watson has done nothing but showed me respect. Which is hard to get even from my own kind. Do what you feel you must do. I'll have no part of it." Travor slapped the man across the face as blood start to flow from his mouth.

"Don't you ever put that nigger in the same category as me. You think because he's got some damn piece of paper or wears the white man's clothes he deserves special privileges? Then you're a blinded old fool. Strip away the clothing, and you've got nothing but a common branded nigger. Scares to prove his true identity. He's a slave and always will be." He drew back his hand again.

"This is your last chance, ole man. Are you going to show me that registration book? Or do I have to come on the other side and get it myself?"

"I'm sorry, Travor, but that's against the regulations. I could lose my job over this." The rugged voice came again.

"I don't give a damn about your job. I'll find that nigger if I have to kick in every door you've got in this place."

There was another thump, Jeffrey gathered that the old man was probably being thrown around a bit more. It was quite obvious that Travor was in search of Bobby Gene. Jeffrey shut the door as he sat there in the darkness trembling, wondering if Bobby Gene, like himself, had been awakened by all the commotion. And if so, how would he handle himself? Travor was very dangerous as well as threatening. Not only to Bobby Gene, but to him also. How would Bobby Gene escape? Even though there were two ways out of the motel, the only way right now was the front. That wasn't too advisable at the present time.

He sat there as the roaring of wood fell around him. He wanted to rush outside, but something wouldn't allow him to move. The stillness led him to believe he had finally reached Bobby Gene's room and was dragging him out. When he heard a different voice. Apparently the old man had managed to get away and fetch the sheriff.

"All right, Travor. Hold it right there." Jeffrey's body relaxed. He knew all was well now that the sheriff was there. Jeffrey slipped into his trousers and made his way outside. Just as he had suspected, Travor had found Bobby Gene and was making his way down the stairs with him. Travor was reluctant to let Bobby Gene go, even to the sheriff's warning.

"Go ahead, Sheriff, shoot." A wide grin filled his face. "This nigger will be the one to die not I. So why don't you go back to the jail and let a man do a job that you should be doing?"

"I can't do that, Travor, especially when a man's life is at stake. You know I can't let you walk out of here with him regardless of whether he's a nigger or not I'm the law."

"Man, huh? This ain't no man. This here is a nigger that need be taught a lesson. He's been wanted for five years. He led everyone to believe he was dead so they'd forget. Hell, I haven't forgotten. This nigger cost me everything that was of value to me, and I ain't never going to forget it. He made a fool out of me, and that don't set to kindly with me,"

"You're wrong, Travor, I don't see where this man has done any harm, and if he has that's for the law to decide. Not you."

Travor was hostile.

"He's trying to live in a white man's world! Ain't that reason enough? This society ain't for niggers, and he need to be taught a lesson." The sheriff stood there in the doorway as Travor eased closer toward him with Bobby Gene leading the way.

"You won't make it past me, Travor. You know that, don't you?"

"Well shoot then, Sheriff."

"I can't Travor. I can't shoot an innocent man." The grin of confidence returned to his face.

"Then step aside. Cause this nigger and I will be heading out that door." A voice from behind took him by surprise.

"The sheriff might miss, Travor. But I can assure you I won't. Now let him go!" Jeffrey's voice was demanding. Travor dropped the hold he had on Bobby Gene as the sheriff rushed him.

"You'll have a while to sleep this one off Travor. You're going to be in jail for several days." As he was leading Travor off, he thanked Jeffrey for his help. Then he turned to Bobby Gene.

"I don't know where you came from, but if you're smart you'll go back." Bobby Gene thanked the sheriff for his voice of suggestion, then he turned to Jeffrey, trying to convince him as well as himself that he wasn't the least bit scared.

"Thanks, man. that's two I owe you." Then he went silently back to his room. Bobby Gene sat straight up in his bed, blindly looking toward the door. He wiped away the sleep from his eyes and picked up the pocket watch and read it as the rapping continued.

"Come on, Bobby Gene, open up. It's Jeffrey." Bobby Gene put on his trousers as he went to the door and opened it. Jeffrey pushed his way in.

"Well, come right in why don't you. I'm usually up at five in the morning. Especially after only getting to bed a couple of hours ago."

"Don't be sarcastic, Bobby Gene." Bobby Gene turned to Jeffrey.

"Sarcastic? That's quite the understatement. My life was almost taken away from me last night, and you have the gall to tell me not to be sarcastic. What should I do? Up and run?"

"That's why I'm here. Bobby Gene, because of last evening. Do you think you're the only one who was affected by that ordeal? I was just as frightened as you. Travor has had it in for me for a long time as well, friend. His eyes met Bobby Gene.

"Listen, Bobby Gene. Maybe you should just pack up and leave on this morning's stage coach" Bobby Gene slammed his fist down on the nightstand next to the bed.

"Man, do you know what you're saying? You told me I should run away from life instead of facing it. I can't believe I'm hearing something like this coming from you. You're the one who helped me all those months. Gave me courage and support. You helped me continue on when I was ready to give up."

"You even convinced me that I could help my people. Now all of a sudden you're telling me to give it up like that. Well I'm sorry, friend. I've come too far and worked too hard to get where I am today. I'm a free man, and I'm going to stay that way. I came back to keep my promise, and that's what I intend to do. I knew I would be taking a chance on my coming back here, but it was my choice to make. If I must die, then it's going to be for something worthwhile. Something you taught me to believe in. I will continue on with or without you. I know you've got my best interest at heart. When I was younger, I always heard my mama say. God knows what's best. I'm not leaving, Jeffrey. I've got a job to do, and I'm going to do it. Look around you at my people. They need me, and

I'm going to help them." When he had finished, he turned away from Jeffrey, looking out the window on to the street below.

"Do you know how good it feels for me to be able to look outside this window at the people below without having to worry about being whipped or shot at, or even have things thrown at me because I'm black? Not to say it will never happen." He paused a moment.

"That smell of breakfast is very inviting. I don't suppose I could talk a friend into joining me. Maybe we can talk about what you've been up to for the past five years." Bobby Gene whirled about.

"You're on. I'll even buy."

The dining room was crowded. The busy chattering ceased with Bobby Gene's and Jeffrey's entering the room. Bobby Gene could feel their eyes all over his person as they were being seated. The old man who was at the front desk approached them.

"I tell you, good help is hard to find these days. This is the third time this week I've had to cover for one of our waitresses. Coffee?"

"Yes," they both said. He left to get their coffee. Coming back quickly.

"Oh, Mr. Watson, I wanted to apologize for last evening. I had no idea there would be any trouble such as that. Have you decided as to what you're having for breakfast?" He looked over at the waving hands.

"Excuse me. Take a bit more time if you will. They're signaling for me in the kitchen. I do hope nothing's gone wrong again." They looked at each other and grinned. Low whispering surrounded them as they sat there ignoring it.

"Good morning, Mr. Watson." Bobby Gene took his face out of his cup of coffee. The sheriff was standing over him. "I hope the rest of your evening was peaceful. I also hope you gave thought to what I suggested." Bobby Gene stood up.

"Good morning to you as well. I do appreciate your coming to my rescue last evening, and I did give some thought to your sugges-tion." He paused as though he wanted to keep the sheriff in sus-

pense. "I decided to stay. This is my home. I grew up in this town."
A look of disapproval seemed to come over the sheriff's face.

"Suit yourself. I can't always be there to protect you from the
likes of Travor."

"Not to worry yourself sheriff, I can handle myself if need be."
He bid them both a good day and excused himself. Bobby Gene sat
back down.

"Nice fellow that sheriff."

Looking over Jeffrey's shoulder, he said. "Don't look now, but
here comes our friend again. I hope he will take our order this time.
I'm starving." The old man stood in front of them, looking down
on them with his rotten teeth.

"I'm back. It appears breakfast is a bit short this morning."
They looked at him with questionable eyes, afraid to ask the question, but doing so anyway.

"Just how short?"

The old man's grin disappeared. He could see the impatient
look in their faces as he blurred it out.

"Eggs. We only have eggs."

"Eggs," Bobby Gene repeated.

"Coffee. there's plenty of coffee," he said nervously. They
could tell the old man had a lot on his mind.

"Eggs will be fine." They smiled.

"Yes, sir, right away." When he left, they couldn't help but look
at one another and chuckle. Bobby Gene sat there stirring the refill
of his coffee, looking over at Jeffrey with sincerity.

"I'm sorry I didn't bring this up last evening. But I was so
excited about seeing you after so many years. I'm truly sorry about
your breaking up with Pauline. I had no idea. I can't recall your
writing me about it." A sulking expression came over Jeffrey.

"I didn't mention it because it was too painful." His mind
began to venture back.

"The sad thing about it all is I really loved her. I even thought
we had the perfect marriage, but that just goes to show you don't
know a person the way you think you do." He brought himself back.

"Enough feeling sorry for myself. Tell me, what have you been up to these past five years? Were you treated with respect by everyone I had you to get in contact with?" Did you find Pennsylvania as magical as I had mentioned?" He leaned into the table as he continued his conversation. You had mentioned something about becoming a lawyer. You also mentioned you were a minister as well. There should be an interesting story behind that one." Jeffrey could tell Bobby Gene was anxious, but it had nothing to do with his endeavors, but about something else altogether.

"I'll tell you everything later. I want to know about Anna Belle. Not once have you mentioned her since we've sat down to talk. Hell, now that I think about it, you've hardly ever mentioned her in any of your letters. Everything's all right with her and the kid, isn't it? After breakfast, I'm going out to Wellington's plantation. You know, these past five years have brought me a long way and taught me a many things as you had said. I think it's about time I shared them with someone."

"Jeffrey, I'm going to ask Anna Belle to marry me." The news startled Jeffrey as he choked on the coffee he had in his mouth.

"Marriage. Don't you think that's kind of sudden?" I mean, don't you think the two of you should get reacquainted first? You just got back after being away for five years. A lot could have happened in those five years. Look at yourself, that should be evident enough."

"Believe you me, Jeffrey, that's all I've been doing is thinking about this. I know when I wrote her there was no indication of any proposal in the future. But for me its personal, and I think it deserves an in person proposal. Plus, the fact I had no idea I would ever see this town again let alone Anna Belle." He stood up.

"Yep, my mind's made up. The sooner I get myself together the quicker I will be able to see her. Are you coming?"

"Mmm...er...no. You go ahead and do what you must. I have to be leaving for work at the saw mill anyhow. But listen, before you go out to Wellington's place..." He stopped himself.

"Never mind, I'll see you back here after work." Bobby Gene was puzzled. What was Jeffrey not telling him and why did he stop so sharply.

"What were you about to say Jeffrey? And why did you stop so abruptly. Does it concern Anna Belle?" A worried look filled his eyes. "Everything's all right with her, isn't it? I mean, the child and what not."

"Listen, man, I've said too much already. Go see Anna Belle, talk with her. If there's something for you to know, then she should be the one to tell you. Not I."

CHAPTER NINETEEN

The trip to the plantation seemed like a never-ending journey. Anna Belle was in the sitting room when word was brought she had a visitor.

"Who is it, Sadie?"

"I's don't knows, ma'am. He's don't gives his name."

"That's all right, then show him in."

"Yes ma'am." She disappeared. Anna Belle stood when she saw the figure being escorted to the room. She was speechless. Could this really be? Her mouth fell open, but her words wouldn't come. She ran to the figure with open arms, tears streaming down her cheeks, as she held on to him tightly.

"Dear God, thank you for answering my prayers." She stood back where she could get a good look. She wiped away the tears with her hands. Bobby Gene offered her his handkerchief. She stood there, admiring his sleekness.

"You're looking mighty distinguished. Like one of those city gents you see in the catalog. I must admit getting away from here was the best thing that could have happened for you. From your appearance, I'd say you've done all right for yourself?" He hunched his shoulders.

"I can't complain. I'm a lawyer now. Even got myself a document here." He removed the paper from his pocket and handed it to her. "I'm a free man to go wherever I choose." As Anna Belle was reading, she could feel his eyes upon her.

"It would appear that I'm not the only one who has changed I noticed you observing that paper. I just handed you as though you knew what you were looking at. Are you pretending to read it? Or have you been taught to read as I have?"

"I also couldn't help notice your attire is none of which a housemaid or servant usually wear. You're pretty fancied up yourself. Things around here must be going good for you as well. His eyes wandered about the beauty of the room as he spoke. Anna Belle neatly folded the paper and handed it back to him.

"That's wonderful, Bobby Gene. I'm happy for you. Truly I am."

"If that's true, then why are you looking at me like that? Aren't you glad to see me?" Her soft brown eyes met his.

"Of course I am. If only you knew how I'm feeling inside this very moment. Your being here has nothing to do with it. Not directly." He moved closer to her as their eyes started talking, then closer he came. Pulling her to him, pushing back her hair and softly compressing his lips to hers, only to get rejected as she turned away.

"I'm sorry, Bobby Gene." He was now troubled as he laid his hands upon her shoulders.

"Anna Belle, there is something wrong. I can hear it in your voice. Whatever it is, you're being very evasive about it. Jeffrey mentioned something of it earlier, but when I insisted he tell me, he only said if there were something to tell you should be the one to hear it from. I'm waiting, Anna Belle. Is there something to tell me?" Anna Belle dropped her head.

"There is something. Before I begin, you must realize that sometimes in life people do things they have no control over. There isn't really any way to escape it. So I'll get right to the point."

"Mommy, mommy," a voice was shouting as a little body ran blindly into Bobby Gene. He looked down upon the little boy.

"Hey, watch out there, little one, you almost ran me down." He could see blood trickling down the front of the boy's shirt as he bent down to see where it was coming from. He removed the boy's hand from his mouth.

"You've been fighting again, haven't you Gabriel?" His mother wanted to know. He shook his head yes as Bobby Gene looked on.

"It's nothing serious. Just a minor cut on the bottom lip. Whoever hit you must have a mean right." Gabriel by now had forgotten about the cut.

"Heck, that wasn't nothing. You should have seen the way I clobbered him."

"Enough of that young man. How many times have I told you not to fight?" He looked up at her.

"But I had to, Mommy. They said ugly things about us. They said the reason why my skin is light is because my papa is a white man. They even said that you and Master Wellington go to sleep in the same bed, that's why we live here in the big house and have nice things." Anna Belle was astonished as she scolded Gabriel.

"Hush talking like that." She held his face closer so she could get a look at it also. "It looks as though the bleeding has stopped. I best attend to it before it gets bigger." She gave him a tap on the bottom and scooted him toward the door. He turned in the doorway, looking up at Bobby Gene with the same identical eyes as his mother's.

"Hey, Mister, thanks. It don't hurt much anymore. I hope to see you again." He then looked at her again.

"Please Mommy. Can we?"

"We'll see honey." He waved as he disappeared behind the door. It was only a short while before Anna Belle came back. Bobby Gene could see the uneasiness about her.

"That's a handsome boy you have there. I can see he's being well taken care of too." Her voice was subdued.

"Bobby Gene, please. Can't we get back to what we were discussing earlier?" She contorted the handkerchief she had in her hands.

"What Gabriel said is true. I mean about my sleeping with Matthew and all. I was hoping he would never find out but something of this essence is hard to keep quiet." She lifted her face her brown eyes met Bobby Gene's. Traces of water began to fall to her cheeks.

"You see, Bobby Gene. I'm Matthew mistress." Bobby Gene turned his back to her so she wouldn't see his bewildered look.

"Well, say something." She broke the circle of silence. "I'm sure you've got plenty of thought in that head of yours."

"What do you want me to say? I'm happy for you. Or that I give you my blessings. Well, I can't. I've patiently awaited this day when I would be able to see you again. I always kept you in my thoughts and my heart. I came here today a free man, hoping to buy your freedom so we could finally be together. I came here to propose to you, and you have the audacity to tell me you've been sleeping with Wellington of your own free will." He turned to her with fire in his eyes.

"Boy, I've really been the fool. I should have listened to Jeffrey when he said to take it slow on this marriage bit. No, I had to be such a dumb wit. All this time I thought that you were saving yourself for me, when all along someone else was keeping that lonely fire burning." The anger in his voice rose.

"Well, tell me. Is this big house your just reward for sharing his bed? You're no better than a prostitute. A woman who would sell her body or do anything for prosperity or power." With this remark, she tore into his like a tigress with all her strength, striking at his tall, lean body.

"You son of a bitch! How dare you speak that way to me after you've being gone for five years? You think it was easy for me? You think I didn't hurt or yearn for your touch? For your making love to me? You think because you wrote me a few letters from time to time that gives you special privileges to come back and expect things to fall right back into place? I don't recall you ever asking for my hand in marriage the few time you did write. Or was I to assume this day would happen? I will admit there were times when I dreamt of nothing else. But there also comes a time when you realize that's all they were. Just dreams. I lived on those hopes and dreams for three years. Nothing happened."

"So what if I turned to Matthew for comfort and strength? I like yourself, saw an opportunity to better myself and took it. Instead of criticizing me, you should be happy for me."

"I know what's truly gnawing at you. It's the fact that he's a white man. How quickly we forget, especially when it was a white man who helped you. I did whatever it took for me to survive. Why should I have to live like my people? Afraid, ignorant, nothing good to look forward to in the future except more hard times. I may not have my freedom yet, but in a sense I'm free. Anyway. Who are you to judge me?" He snatched her into him and kissed her furiously. She struggled with him till she was free.

"My goodness, you're even feisty like a white woman. Did Wellington teach you that as well?"

"What I teach my mistress is none of your concern." Bobby Gene loosened the grip he had on her. He stood there face-to-face with Matthew. He looked very gallant there in the doorway. The expression on his face lead Anna Belle to realize she should leave the two of them alone.

"I'm sorry, Matthew. It's not what it appears to be." He cut her off.

"Silence! I shall tend to you later in the substance as too which I choose. Close the door behind you." Anna Belle doing as she was told, modestly left the room. Matthew walked farther into the room eyeing Bobby Gene from head to toe as though he were on display.

"Bobby Gene Watson, I presume. I must admit, until now I thought you were dead. You've been the talk of the town." The arching of eyebrows showed his approval of this man.

"You seem to have gathered yourself some very distinguished attributes and abilities, as well as being very dauntless. I approve of those qualities in a man. Shows me acuteness, I like that in my competitors. But you don't want to mess with a man of my status. I'm sure you're understanding what I'm saying to you." The tone in his voice was menacing.

"I don't take kindly to strangers coming into my home and helping themselves to whatever is appealing to them. Especially when that something is of interest to me as well. You see, Anna Belle is my woman now, and she doesn't have room in her life for anyone else if you know what I mean. She's given me something I thought impossible for me to recapture, and I'm not going to let her leave me."

"What do you intend on doing? Keep her here with your intimidations. She'll soon tire of that. Since we're on the subject of being candid, if there's one thing I've learned in the white man's world, is not to be intimidated or afraid of whatever stands in your way of success, or to go after whatever you want—even if it means fighting to the finish. I've learned that very well. I'm not intimidated or frightened by your small innuendoes. I don't know what your game is as far as she's concerned. But I love that woman, and I haven't waited all this time for nothing. I intend on having her as well. She's a bit distraught at the moment but shall soon come to her senses. Especially after seeing me. She loves me and always will. Let's hope when she makes her decision you will be man enough to accept it. For it shall be me who will prevail. As you shall see." Matthew grasped Bobby Gene in his collar.

"I want you off my property this instant, and if you ever in any way attempt to see or try to persuade her to leave me, I'll kill the both of you. You comprehend?" Bobby Gene broke away from Matthew's grip.

"As I said earlier, I'm not one who scares easily." He tipped his hat to Matthew before leaving.

"May the best man win." The door closed behind him.

Anna Belle was standing at the top of the stairs when Bobby Gene abruptly left the setting room. She silently stood there watching as he walked through the front door, wanting so badly to call out after him, just hoping he might have glanced her way before he left. But why would he? He wasn't aware of her presence being there. Or at this point he probably didn't even care. The door to the sitting room opened again. Matthew looked up at her from the bottom of the stairs.

"I thought I told you to make yourself scarce. What were you trying to do, get his attention?" Anna Belle was afraid to answer but knew if she didn't it would make matters worse for her especially when he was in this state of mind.

"I only wanted to tell him good-bye Master Wellington."

"Master Wellington is it now? My, haven't we gotten formal all of a sudden? After months of sharing my bed and calling me plain old Matthew. You suddenly decide to call me Master Wellington. It couldn't by chance have to do with seeing that nigger, now could it?" Anna Belle was astonished by Matthew's vocabulary.

"Yes, I said nigger. Does that surprise you?" Anna Belle became humble.

"No, I guess I'm shocked after not having seen him for several years."

"Good. I hope that's all it is for the both of your sakes." He entered his study.

After pacing the floor Matthew picked up a glass and poured some whiskey from the canister that always occupied his desk. He drank down the shot and helped himself to another one, also gulping it down quickly as well. The words that Bobby Gene had spoken to him earlier yet rang out in his ears. Pouring himself yet another drink, he found himself speaking out loud.

"I'm Matthew Wellington. Nobody dare go against me, be he black or white, especially the likes of one Bobby Gene Watson." He became frustrated as he swallowed down his third shot, yet pouring another one.

"Anna Belle is my woman, and that's the way it's going to be." He swallowed the fourth and final drink before he sent the glass sailing across the room as it hit the hearth of the fireplace and shattered into small pieces. He stood up, staggered to the door, opened it as he looked toward the stairs.

"She loves me and I'll prove it." He staggered up the stairs and into their bedroom. Matthew stood there in the doorway, watching Anna Belle as she quickly turned from her reading. His tall frame leaning against the door, using it for leverage to keep himself afoot, looking on at a very frightened Anna Belle. She laid the book down on the table. Stammer was in her voice.

"I'm sorry about earlier, Matthew. I meant no harm nor disrespect." He stood there, still looking on, eyes blazing as he closed the door.

"Oh, it's Matthew again I see. How quaint of you. If my memory hadn't escaped me, not so long ago when that nigger was here you couldn't hurry quick enough to call me Master Wellington. What the hell kind of mind games are you playing?" He took a step away from the door but fell back against it. Anna Belle became meek.

"I have no idea what you're talking about. I thought I explained to you earlier why that came about. Were you not listening?" With this statement, Matthew made a gesture as though he were going to approach her. Instead he found himself falling backward for the second time against the door to stay on his feet.

"Bobby Gene Watson. I must say he's a very impressionable man. Seems to have been a bit misinformed about something, though. He seems to think you're going to leave me for him." He chuckled in dismay.

"Ironic, isn't it? He stood there, awaiting his reply.

"You're drunk, Matthew, I don't think now is the time to discuss this." Matthew banged his fist against the door, prompting Anna Belle to become afraid.

"I think now is the perfect time to discuss it! I ain't going to let no bitch dictate to me when's the proper time to have a conversation!" The room became silent as he stood there staring at her.

"I'm waiting for your reply. Are you planning on leaving me for that nigger? Why do you find it difficult to answer? It's a fairly simple question. Don't you think?"

"Please, Matthew, can't we discuss this another time?" Anna Belle knew she couldn't reason with him no matter what she said or did. She stood up and started toward the door. But he caught her as she brushed past him.

"Oh no you don't! Not this time!" He tried kissing her, but she pulled away from him as he held on tighter. She became frantic, pleading for him to loosen the hold he had on her.

"Please, Matthew, let me go. You're hurting me." He continued to try and kiss her, pulling her even closer to him. She pleaded again. "Matthew, please I beg of you. Let me go." He again ignored her plea. She bit at his chest, hoping this would break her free. She had never seen him this violent before. She fought against him as best she could, but it still wasn't enough. He lifted his fist to her face as it connected with her jaw. She fell onto the bed as he fell upon her, ripping at her clothing, his body completely covering hers'.

"You're my woman! You got that? You're mine! I love you, and I know you love me too! Tonight you shall prove that love for me, or I shall be obliged to kill you!" His tears fell upon her face as they intermingled with hers', his vicious green eyes glaring savagely into hers.

"Don't challenge my threat. Even though I love you, I can just as easily kill you. If I can't have you, then no one shall. I should not want to live if I ever lost you again!" His glare oblivious.

"I need you Mary Lou." With these words, Anna Belle could feel him as he entered inside her.

Jeffrey greeted a grim Bobby Gene at the motel. He could tell Bobby Gene had heard the news from Anna Belle.

"From the looks of you, I'd say you had that little chat with Anna Belle. Did she tell you about her being—"

Bobby Gene interrupted him gruffly. "What were you going to say? Did she tell me about her being the mistress of one Matthew Wellington? Yes, she told me and you don't have to make a mockery of it."

"I don't think that was fair, Bobby Gene. Do you see me enjoying this? Remember, I'm the one who tried to talk you out of going there to talk to her about this marriage thing in the first place. But you were insistent on doing so."

"You're right, I'm sorry. I just didn't expect to come back to this type of situation." His face tightened. "But it doesn't matter. I love that woman and I will have her regardless of Wellington's idle threats."

"Threats? What kind of threats?" Jeffrey wanted to know as his eyebrows rose. Bobby Gene reassured him it was nothing to concern himself with he could handle everything just fine. He literally changed the subject.

"Listen, I just had a great idea. On my way back to the motel. I noticed this bulletin in the window at the bank that some property was for sale at a reasonable price." A gleam filled his eyes.

"Do you understand what this means? This could be the beginning for us. I'm going over right now to see if I might be able to purchase it. Then we can start fulfilling my promise to Joseph Dale. You coming?"

"I reckon; work has been slow at the saw mill. It's boring trying to keep yourself company."

Bobby Gene had gotten used the whispering that followed him wherever he went. Being gentleman-like he tipped his hat to all the ladies he passed on his way to the bank. Many of them turned up their noses, while others crossed the street so they wouldn't have to walk past him. While the men made their comments.

"Move along nigger before we take the whip to you." He took a seat in one of the wooden chairs that rested against the wall, awaiting his turn. Jeffrey decided he would sit outside and do some people watching.

"Next please," Bobby Gene stood up and strolled over to the desk and sat in the chair on the other side of it. The man was busy scribbling on a piece of paper.

"I'll be with you in a moment. If I don't get this down while it's yet fresh on my mind, I'll forget it." When he finished, he neatly placed the pen back on its ink plate.

"Now what can I…" His voice froze as he looked over his reading glasses into the face of Bobby Gene. Clearing his throat, he started again.

"Pardon me, won't you. I just---"

"I know, Bobby Gene interceded. My color threw you. It happens quite often. I can assure you." The man cleared his throat once again then balanced the glasses back onto his nose.

"Indeed, is there something I can help you with?"

"There is. I'm interested in that property bulletin you have posted in the window."

"The Taylor place. But why would you be interested in that? And what makes you think I would sale it to you a nigger.? He wanted to know.

"That's none of your concern. What I want to know, is it for sale?" The man removed his glasses and laid them gently on the desk.

"Again my question to you is. Why should I sale anything to you? Nigger."

"Because my freedom paper states that I'm a free man. I have the same equality as you white folk. If I have to take this matter all the way to the supreme court. I'm willing to do so."

"Ah, you're one of those smart niggers ain't you. I've been hearing about you around town. Seem like people don't think they can touch you because you're free. But I can assure you, that most of the people round here ain't like that. They could care less about some damn freedom paper. If I were you, I'd be watching my back very closely. You never know when the cobra will strike." He replaced the reading glasses back on his face as he fumbled through the pile of papers in front of him until he found the ones he was searching for. Bobby Gene could sense he was none too pleased with the situation before him.

"Here they are, and at a reasonable price. Only two thousand dollars."

"Two thousand dollars?" Bobby Gene chocked on his words. "But I just overheard you telling someone else it was only fifteen hundred." The man gave Bobby Gene an evil look.

"If you want this property, you'll pay two thousand dollars and that's that. Besides, we bankers have to make a living too." Bobby Gene stretched his body over the desk.

"Listen, Mister. I'm certainly not stupid. I detect a sense of greed going on here. I wonder what would happen if I were to take a fine upstanding banker such as yourself to court on charges of embezzlement. Do you think business will be good after that?"

"Do you honestly think anyone will believe you. I mean a nigger's words against a white man's."

"Maybe not, but you know about rumors. All it would take is for me to start planting the seeds of doubt and suspicion in people minds. Funny thing about rumors, once they get started, they're hard to stop. I don't have anything to lose myself now, do I? Plus, I'll make sure you'll be investigated. With my credentials of being a lawyer. I'm sure some of my friends up north would like nothing more than to come to the aid of one of their brothering." There was a moment of quietness.

"The choice is up to you. Either you sell me that property for what is was agreed upon, or I will walk right now, go to the post office, and send that telegraph to my friends up north. What is it going to be?" Bobby Gene stood up waiting for a rejoinder then turned on his heels.

"All right. You may have won't this round. but I'll get even with you if it's the last thing I do. I'm not going to let no nigger come in my bank and make a fool out of me. Come back in an hour. All the necessary documents should be ready by then." Bobby Gene turned back to the man.

"Good then, so there won't be any misunderstanding I'll make a down payment." He took five hundred dollars out of his wallet and laid it on the desk as the man quickly snatched it up.

"I'll be needing a voucher on that." The man looked at Bobby Gene and rolled his eyes.

"You truly are an intelligent nigger aren't you? He pulled out the drawer and took out his voucher booklet. "And who shall I make this out to?"

"Bobby Gene Watson will be sufficient enough." He took the voucher and left. Jeffrey was still waiting outside. Bobby Gene could tell by the expression on his face he was excited about what was to come. Yet on the other hand a bit nervous too.

"Well, don't keep me in suspense. How did it go? Did you get the property? You surely were in there a long time." Bobby Gene, seeing he wasn't going to get a word in edge wise, held the voucher up for Jeffrey's reading. He could see the excitement even more in Jeffrey's eyes as he grabbed for it.

"Does this mean what I think it does? You got it! You son of a gun! You got it!"

"Correction, we got it. I owe my life to the good Lord and to you. You've helped me to accomplish something I never dreamed possible. You were there for me from the beginning. Did you honestly think I would forget all that? Remember, friends forever. Besides, I'm going to need you to help me with something else."

"I hope you're still willing. I'm no fool, I know any day now these people can turn on me and I'll be right back where I started, a slave. It's a miracle it hasn't happened yet. If that happens, I'm going to stand straight and tall and take it like the man I've become, not a frightened nigger. I've had a taste of the good life. I can at least say I'm thankful to have experienced it. Even if it should only have been a short time. To me it will always be a lifetime of memories." He smiled at Jeffrey.

"What do you say to our going back to the motel and gather our belongings? The papers won't be ready for an hour yet. I can't wait to get to our new home."

Hours turned into days and days into weeks. Bobby Gene and Jeffrey stood back to admire the hard labor they had done to the house. Jeffrey beckoned for Bobby Gene to come join him on the porch.

"Look, Bobby Gene. I never thought I would ever be bringing up this subject after so many years." Bobby Gene noticed a change in his demeanor while speaking as though he had traveled back in time.

"Remember the first night we came face-to-face? The truth of the matter is, I was terrified of you. Then when I saw you were just as frightened, I was no longer afraid. Being around and seeing your hard work and the determination to work hard at learning how to read and write and all the other things. I started seeing things in a different light. Then when you chose to come back here, knowing what the outcome might be you, made me strong. I realized you can't keep running because a man speaks acuteness or threatens you. You're not the only one who's grateful." Jeffrey walked to the end of the porch as he looked out over the land.

"When we first came to this part of the country, we weren't much better than you Negroes. Today I've got a wonderful friend and a beautiful house to live in. No, Bobby Gene, it's time I became a man as well. You've taught me the true definition of being a man. I've always been one who has ran from problems instead of facing them."

"Pauline was right on the money when she said I was a coward for not facing her father to ask for her hand in marriage. Instead, I talked her into marrying me, then after that we left, and they haven't heard from us since." Bobby Gene joined Jeffrey at the end of the porch.

"Being a man comes in many different forms. Just because you weren't able to face Pauline's father doesn't mean you weren't a man. To be honest with you, had Anna Belle's father been alive, I don't know if I would have been that bold with him."

"You must realize when you and Pauline left Pennsylvania you were still quite young. I think it showed strength as well as courage to strike out across country like that, and to make it this far is amazing to me. Especially when you've never been on your own." He put his hand on Jeffrey's shoulder.

"Most importantly, you showed your manhood all those months you kept me hid. You can look at it as being nothing, but at any given time you could have been discovered and suffered dire consequences. Did you leave me? No, you stayed there and saw me through it. How many so called men do you think would have done that? I can't think of any. I would even have to question my own loyalty on that one." Bobby Gene looked back at the house.

"You know this place is quite large for only the two of us. What do you say to our getting some company around here?" Jeffrey looked at Bobby Gene with excitement.

"My thoughts exactly. This is where I come in."

"For the past few weeks I've had my eyes and ears open to see if anyone was selling any of their Negroes. Or if there might be any slave auctions to come to this area. I didn't have any luck in either department. So I came up with this idea. I could. go to some of the neighboring plantations and see if I might purchase a few of their

Negroes. I've got good credential from working at the saw mill. Not to mention how hard times have been lately." Bobby Gene smiled. "You know, that's exactly what I had in mind. first of all, I want you to go over to the Dalton's plantation and buy Mrs. Thompson. That shall be one of my gifts to Anna Belle when she comes here to be with me." Jeffrey had a demure look on his face.

"I'll do as you ask. But I must warn you that you shouldn't get your hopes up about Anna Belle. Matthew Wellington is a very powerful man around these parts. I don't know what's going on between the two of you. A word of advice from what a wise man once told me a long time ago. No woman is worth fighting over. There are too many to replace her. Keep that in mind, my friend. I just ask that you be careful."

CHAPTER TWENTY

*J*effrey was only able to acquire a handful of Negroes for their plantation, including Mrs. Thompson. Mr. Dalton was more than willing to get rid of her. The day when she tried to stop Travor from harming Anna Belle, when she was thrown against the stove and hit her head as a result became blind. The doctor informed her it was due to the blow she had sustained to her head. When Jeffrey offered to buy her, he told him he could have her. Without her sight, she was useless not only to him but to anyone." Mrs. Thompson sat there under the window in her room when there came a knock at the door.

"Come in."

"Good morning, Mrs. Thompson. Master Watson asked me to come and see'd ifin you's like to go fer a walk or some'n." Mrs. Thompson positioned her head as to where the voice was coming, with a smile.

"Tell Bobby Gene that be kindly of him, but I's just want to be left alone. Besides, what be the use go'n fer a walk ifin you's can't see'd the beauty of it?

"Yes, 'em, but ifin you's should change you's."
Lorene interrupted.

"I's won't. Now please, I's like to sit here and feel the heat of the sun." Bobby Gene and Jeffrey were in the study when Gertrude approached.

"Excuse me, sir." The black figure stood in the doorway, waiting to be asked inside. The two stopped their conversation and turned toward her.

"Yes, Gertrude, what is it?" Bobby Gene wanted to know.

"I does what you's asked about my going to see'd ifin Mrs. Thompson wanted to go fer a walk." Bobby Gene nodded.

"Yes, well go on. What happened?"

"She doesn't wants to go. She says she wanted to be left alone."

"All right, Gertrude, thank you. That will be all." He slammed his fist on the table. "This can't go on any longer. That old woman is like a mother to me, and I can't stand to see her spending the last of her days cooped up in that room, shut off from the world. I'm going to do something about it right now."

"Come on, Bobby Gene. We both know if you had told her about Anna Belle when I suggested, maybe she wouldn't be in the state she's in right now."

"That's right, go ahead, blame me. But you know the situation. What do you suppose would happen if we were to get her hopes up, then Anna Belle refuses to leave her lover?"

"Do you honestly think she would deny her mother? Or are you saying that because she's hurt you."

"I'll ignore that last statement." He walked over to the door and called out. Gertrude came running.

"Yes, Master Watson. Does you's need some'n?"

"Yes tell Kuta to hitch up the horse and buggy. I shall be leaving shortly."

"Yes, sir, right away." She turned back to him.

"Will Masser Jeffrey be going too?"

"No, I don't believe so. This is something I have to do on my own." She turned away again when Bobby Gene called to her. "Remember, you are to call me Mr. Watson. Remember the conversation we've had about calling me master."

"Yes sir, I does Masser. I mean Mr. Watson. I's does my best in the future to remember."

She bowed then disappeared.

The Wellington plantation was only a short distance from Bobby Gene. This time he didn't wait for the house servant to announce him but showed himself to the sitting room, hoping he might find Anna Belle there. Instead he found the room empty. He paced the room impatiently. Then he heard voices come up behind him.

"I's sorry, Mistress, but he just shoved me out of the way."

"That's fine Constance, I'll handle this. You may go back to the kitchen now." She entered the room, shutting the door behind her.

"How dare you intrude like this? After our last encounter, I assumed you to be out of my life for good. You have gall!"

"Cut the white woman's act, Anna Belle, I've come to take you away from here." She stood there with a smirk.

"Is that so? And suppose I don't wish to go?" Bobby Gene became imprudent.

"Oh you'll go, all right. That's if your mama really means anything to you" Anna Belle was baffled.

"Mama? What about mama? Is she alive? How do you know about Mama? Have you seen her?"

"All your questions will be answered if you trust me by coming with me now." Anna Belle stood there, trying to shake the scrambled thoughts in her head.

"I don't know, Bobby Gene. This could be a trap of some kind to get me away from here. Matthew did tell me to be weary of you. Also there's a very important aspect here. Matthew mentioned he would kill me as well as yourself. Besides, it doesn't make sense that Mama should want to be in touch with you, especially when she believes you're dead."

Bobby Genes' eyes waxed cold. "Listen, woman, and listen good. I'm fed up with these games of yours. It's true I want you. And as far as Matthew goes, I have no fear of him. I don't play games. They're for children. Another thing, I wouldn't stoop as low as to pull a prank such as this to use your mother. Excuse me for wasting my time. I was looking for Anna Belle Thompson. Undoubtedly you don't know her." He turned away.

"Wait, Bobby Gene, please I'm sorry I've distrusted you. You've never given me any reason to before. I guess I really have changed. I couldn't see it until now. Just give me enough time to get a few things for Gabriel and myself, and we'll be right with you." Bobby Gene turned back toward her with a sedate look on his face.

"You realize when you walk out that door there's no turning back?" Her big brown eyes twinkled at him.

"I know, that's my intentions."

"Bobby Gene, I truly have been a fool. I don't know if this will be of any consolation to you, but I haven't been with Matthew since I saw you. He refuses to give me up, but if that marital invitation is still open. I'd be honored to be your wife. That's if you'll still have me."

"If I'll still have you? I was determined on this day you were coming with me even if I had to come over here and drag you away." He extended his arms to her as she ran into them but quickly pulled away from his embrace.

"We best be getting a move on it. Matthew had some personal business that needed tending to in town. I'm sure he should be on his way back. I just hope we don't run into him on the way."

Anna Belle was surprised to see Bobby Gene taking a trail that wasn't familiar to her. She sat upright on the buggy seat, speaking as she looked at all the exotic surroundings amongst them.

"Bobby Gene, where are we going? This isn't the way to town. I thought you told me you lived in town at the motel."

"Sit back, Anna Belle. Relax and enjoy. Don't worry, everything will be quite clear to you shortly." Anna Belle still couldn't comprehend what was happening. Every now and then Gabriel would ask a question or two. The team of horses seemed to know where they were going. Once they were in front of the big house they came to a complete halt. A tall frame of an older man came out of the house and grabbed the reins.

"Master Watson, you's back. Shall I's put up the team now, sir?"

"Yes, Kuta that will be fine." He stepped down from the buggy and went to the other side to help Anna Belle then Gabriel down.

Then he grabbed the luggage and clutched it under his arms. Anna Belle stood in front of the big house, mesmerized.

"It's absolutely beautiful, Bobby Gene. I'm truly amazed. Does it really belong to you?"

"Yep. Signed, sealed, and all paid for. I must confess that it's not as fancy as you're accustomed to. But it's ours. There's also someone else waiting to see you too."

By this time, Jeffrey appeared from behind the door making his way rapidly down the steps to greet the two of them. He grabbed Anna Belle and whisked her off her feet, whirling her around with excitement.

"Oh how wonderful it is to see you again after all this time." Then he focused his attention on Gabriel with an extended hand as he greeted him. "You must be young Gabriel." Gabriel bowed.

"That I am, sir. that I am."

"Strong grip I see, as well as being well-mannered."

"Well, thank you, sir. I owe it all to Mama and Sir Wellington. Oh and I can't forget the servants too." Anna Belle then clutched Bobby Gene's hand, pulling him toward the house.

"Well, come on. I can't wait to see it. And Mama, why isn't she here to greet us?" Bobby Gene stopped Anna Belle in her tracks.

"Hold on a moment there's something I think you need to know." Anna Belle, not listening to what he was saying, ignored him totally.

"It's just going to have to wait. If Mama's in there. I want to see her this instant." Anna Belle stepped inside the doorway, dragging Gabriel in one hand and Bobby Gene in the other. They were greeted by Gertrude.

"Masser Watson, sir, it's good to see'd you's back. I took care of them rooms the way you's asked."

"Thank you, Gertrude. Oh how thoughtless of me. Gertrude, this is my soon to-be bride, Anna Belle Thompson, and her son, Gabriel. This is Lorene's daughter." The young girl bowed to the introduction.

"Please to know you's, Madam, and young'n."

"Likewise, Gertrude." She turned to Bobby Gene again.

"There's been enough talking. Now where is Mama?" Bobby Gene couldn't get a word out before Gertrude was speaking.

"Mrs. Lorene, she be at the top of the stairs, the last door on the left." Realizing what she had done, she excused herself and went back to her chores. Anna Belle knelt down before Gabriel.

"Listen, honey, I haven't seen grandma since before you were born. Would you understand if I went to speak with her first?"

"Sure, Mommy, I understand." He looked up at Bobby Gene with his toothless smile.

"Besides, us menfolk have some talking to do." Once again, Bobby Gene tried to get her attention.

"Anna Belle, before you go upstairs to see your mother, we have to talk."

"It's going to have to wait. It's been too long since I've see Mama." She dashed up the stairs and into the room. The old woman was startled by this irregular outburst.

"Who's be there?" She wanted to know with a bit of fright in her voice.

"Does someone be there?" She felt for the stick next to her chair with her hands. This gesture took Anna Belle by surprised as she realized her mother was blind. Unable to speak, she ran over to her mother and fell upon her knees in front of her.

"Mama it's me." The woman sat there until her voice registered in her mind.

"Anna Belle. My baby, is that really you's?"

"Yes, Mama, it's really me." By this time tears were streaming down both of their faces. Lorene lifted Anna Belle's face with her hands.

"Oh dear God, thank you's. It truly does be my Anna Belle." She bent over and caressed her very tightly in her arms. Anna Belle raised up as she looked into her mother's worn face.

"Oh Mama, it's been a long time. I've tried so hard to get in touch with you, but it was next to impossible. I didn't know if you were alive or dead." Anna Belle paused.

"Mama, your blindness. When did you…I mean how?"

"On the day Masser Travor comes and take you's away with him. Member when my head hit the stove?" Anna Belle could detect a bit of anger in her voice for a moment or two, then felt the soft gentleness she was so use to.

"That be the past. I just thank God that you's alive. And Bobby Gene." A bit of excitement entered her voice.

"I was so surprised when I's found out he be not dead after all this time. He tells me he's gonna ask this young'n fer her hand."

"It's me, Mama. Bobby Gene, he asked me to marry him, and I said yes."

"I's had no idea it be you's." A smile came on her face. "He be a wonderful young man. I's almost fergit. The baby. What it be?"

"A boy, Mama, a handsome little boy. He's downstairs right now with Bobby Gene and Jeffrey. I told him I wanted to be alone with you first. I'll go and get him right now if you'd like."

"Don't be silly, child. Course I's like to see'd him."

Gabriel was still in the study with Bobby Gene and Jeffrey when Anna Belle came down. He could see the hurt in her eyes.

"Are you all right? I tried to prepare you, but you wouldn't hear me out."

"I must confess, seeing her like that did throw me, but I'm just grateful she's alive. She seems to have let herself go as though nothing mattered. She did ask to see Gabriel. Maybe that's a good sign." She moved past Bobby Gene and went over to the desk where Gabriel was scribbling on some paper. He looked up at her with the same identical glare as hers'.

"Did you see Grandma, Mommy?"

"Yes, baby and she wants to see you now." Gabriel jumped off the chair and rushed past her. She grabbed his arm.

"Hold on there, young man. There's something you should know first."

"What is it, Mommy?" Anna Belle knelt down to talk with him.

"Listen, Grandma is what you might call ill. You see she's blind."

"You mean she don't have no eyes?"

"No honey its's nothing like that. She has eyes the way you and I do. Everything is just dark to her. She can't see anything." Gabriel's eyes widened with curiosity.

"You mean even if it's day outside to grandma it's still dark?"

"That's right, honey. No matter what, Grandma will always see black."

"Then Grandma, she won't be able to see what I look like. Will she, Mommy?"

"Sure she can, honey. Not the way you and I can. But she can see you with her hands."

A curious frown covered his face.

"That's neat, Mommy, is it all right if I go see her now?"

"I suppose, but don't tire her out. There will be plenty of time to be with her." The little boy's eyes grew large again.

"Do you mean that we're going to stay here with Grandma, Master Watson, and Jeffrey too? Anna Belle glanced at Bobby Gene as she spoke.

That's right, honey, this is going to be our home." Gabriel jumped up and down.

"All right did you hear that, Master Watson? We're going to stay here. I'm going to see Grandma now." The rest of the evening was filled with cheers and laughter of a happy reunion.

CHAPTER TWENTY-ONE

"Bobby Gene Watson get out here!" The sound of breaking glass surrounded them prompting Bobby Gene and Jeffrey to enter the darkness of the hallway. Then Anna Belle appeared with the dim flickering of candlelight.

"Bobby Gene what is it? I thought I heard glass breaking." Bobby Gene quickly brushed her off.

"I don't have time to explain. Take everyone and go to the hideout until we come for you."

"But, why, Bobby Gene? Who is it?"

"Don't ask any more questions. Do what I say and now!" He then instructed Jeffrey to follow him. The voice came again.

"If you're not out here within the next minute. I shall be obliged to come in and get you myself." Anna Belle spoke again.

"That's Matthew's voice. Bobby Gene this doesn't sound too good." Bobby Gene instructed her again.

"Anna Belle, please do as I ask." They grabbed their guns as they stepped out onto the porch. The silhouette of a man on horseback approached the two of them. His face wasn't visible in the dark, but the voice was familiar.

"I'm not here for any trouble, Bobby Gene. All I want is my woman and boy. For a man of your status, it was very cowardly of you to wait until I was gone to take her. I told you what I would do if you tried to come between us. Apparently I underestimated your intelligence, which shall never happen again. I can appreciate a man who keep me on my toes, thinking one step ahead of himself. As I said before, I like competition. I have no qualms with you. Now, if you would kindly escort the young lady and the boy out here, we shall be on our way." Everything was silent except the singing of crickets in the distance.

"You're also very stubborn, so I see. I'll just have to get the lady myself." Bobby Gene and Jeffrey both cocked their guns.

"If you value your life, you will stay on that horse and leave here now. This is private property you're on, if you didn't notice." Bobby Gene continued to speak while they yet held the gun on the silhouette in front of them.

"You speak of belittling you. Everything I've learned, I learned from the white man. I know there has been a time or two you've done some underhanded things yourself?" The man sat there a moment then continued to speak.

"Do you truly believe I was stupid enough to come alone? It's you who should think about whether your lives mean anything to you." They heard the clicking of triggers surrounding the both of them as their guns fell to the porch with a thump.

"I thought you gentlemen would come around. Like you said, you're sure I've done a few underhanded things in my days. You're absolutely right." He beckoned for the two hidden men to check the house. While the others continued to hold them captive.

"You're a bad loser my friend. It's quite sad we became adversaries. Who knows if we had of become friends. It might have been profitable for the both of us." The two men came back outside. "Mr. Wellington, sir. The house is empty."

"What do you mean empty?" He said angrily. That can't be possible. She's got to be here. There's no place else she would go. Are you sure you checked the house thoroughly?"

"Yes, sir. Room by room." They tried to reassure him.

"But we can tell you these two aren't the only ones residing here. Several of the other rooms have been occupied. It would appear they left in a hurry, sir."

"Well now, how interesting. If everything is legal and all. Why do you find it imperative for you to keep your slaves out of sight? My concern isn't about the others you have here. There's no reason to fear that I will take them away from you. Granted, if that is what I should choose to do. There is nothing you can do about it. I only want the two of them. Give them back to me and we shall be on our way."

"I have no idea as to what you're referring to. It's true I have acquired several slaves. But Anna Belle isn't here. Could it be she got tired of your mistreatment of her. I told you she might leave you one day. Her and the boy's whereabouts is of no concern to me. She told me she didn't want to have anything to do with me. Ever."

"You're an obstinate man. I can see we're going to have to use some persuasion tactics on you and your friend here." There was a shrewd tone in his voice.

"Take them over to that tree under the moonlight and string them up by their wrists. I want them to see my face when I put the whip to them. Strip them to the waist." He stepped down off his horse and lifted the whip that was attached to his saddle. The cracking of it rang out as he approached the two of them.

"This shall be the moment of truth. We shall see just how brave you truly are." He let the whip glide through his hands as he propositioned them one last time.

"It's still not too late. You would be saving yourselves a lot of torment and torture. Tell me where the woman is."

Bobby Gene opened his mouth. "Oh to hell, Wellington." The whip rang out as it connected with Bobby Gene's body repeatedly. He closed his eyes and gritted this teeth, trying to bear the pain. After a while, his body fell limp as he hung there unconscious. Matthew moved a few steps over to Jeffrey.

"Who would have thought you'd side with a nigger? I'll give you the same opportunity I gave him. I hope you won't be as unwilling to cooperate as he was." He waited for Jeffrey's response.

"You heard the man, Wellington. That goes double for me."

"You ignorant fool. I should have known you'd side with him no matter what." The echoing of the whip rang out again. Jeffrey moaned as the whip tore into his naked flesh. Then he too hung there lifeless and limp.

The hot rays of the sun made it hard for Bobby Gene to focus on anything. He could hear their names being called by Anna Belle, but he was unable to answer her. He tried to swing his body to see how Jeffrey was doing. The voices got closer then stopped in front of them.

"My Lord, Bobby Gene. What happened to you? Gabriel, go get Kuta. tell him to come quickly, and get Gertrude. Tell her to bring water." Gabriel took off like a bullet as Anna Belle called after him.

"Oh and tell Gertrude to bring a knife and some liniment. Hurry, Gabriel!" Anna Belle stood there looking at the brutally beaten bodies. She could see Bobby Gene was trying to speak.

"Don't worry, Bobby Gene. Everything is going to be all right. If only I understood what you were trying to say." She stood there as Bobby Gene's eyes moved in the direction of Jeffrey.

"Jeffrey. Are you concerned about Jeffrey?" Bobby Gene blinked once at her. "I gathered that meant yes." He blinked again.

"I really don't know, Bobby Gene. He hasn't moved or anything."

At this time Kuta and Gertrude joined Anna Belle. The both of then stood looking up at the two as though this were the first time they had experienced something of this nature.

"What happened, Mistress?" They both inquired at the same time.

"I can't really say," Anna Belle responded. I can only speculate when we heard the breaking of glass last evening when Bobby Gene sent us to the hideout is when this took place."

"Why, Mistress? Who's would have dun such a horrible thing as this? Gertrude wanted to know.

"It was Matthew Wellington."

"Masser Wellington?" Kuta seemed astonished by this.

"Can you's be sure 'bout this, Mistress? I's mean he be a fair man with us niggers in the past. Why should he want to do some'n like this fer? I's can't see'd any reason fer it."

"People do change over the years. Some for the best, some for the worst." The heat from the sun was beginning to beam down up on them severely.

"Please, Kuta, Gertrude we've wasted enough time by standing here chatting. The sun has begun to reach its peak of the day. Give me that water so I can give them a drink." She motioned to Kuta.

"Quick, Kuta. Cut them down. Gertrude, get on the other side so we can catch him before he hits the ground. Be careful with him. We want to move him as little as possible. Let's lay him down gently on his stomach." Once Bobby Gene was placed on the ground. Anna Belle gave him a bit of water.

"We need a doctor out here quickly, and the sheriff too. Kuta, I know it's risky, but upon cutting down Jeffrey, do you suppose you might ride into town and get the doc and the sheriff? Please, tell them to come quickly!"

"Yes, Madame."

"Excuse me Madame, but Masser Jeffrey, he's be dead." Anna Belle stood up and walked over to him.

"Are you sure, Kuta?"

"Yes 'em, he's be not breathing, and his body be cold." Anna Belle tried to control her emotions and the anguish she was feeling. The tears blinded her momentarily.

"All right, Kuta. Please cut him down. We'll have to bury him after you get back. Besides, I would like for the doc to take a look at him as well."

"Yes 'em." Bobby Gene was trying very hard to move his body. Anna Belle could tell he had heard everything. There were small dark circles in the dirt as the tears ran off his face and onto the ground. Anna Belle looked up to Gertrude.

"We can't leave them lying out in the sun like this. We've got to move him to the house. Do you suppose the both of us might be able to carry him to the house ourselves?" I'll send someone else back for Jeffrey. Just remember, we have to be gentle with him."

"I's think we's can, Madame."

The doctor and sheriff arrived at the same time Gertrude took the doctor upstairs, as Anna Belle talked with the sheriff down stairs in the study.

"I'm truly impressed with the way he's fixed up the place, and to think." He chuckled. "Even got himself some niggers working for him, I see."

"Pardon me, Sheriff. You didn't come out here to marvel over the way this place has shaped up. You're here on official business. So I thought." The sheriff redirected his attention.

"Right. You mentioned something about a death and a beating."

"Yes, that's correct."

"Well, what do you want me to do about it?" Anna Belle couldn't believe what she was hearing.

"Am I hearing you correctly? You're the sheriff. I told you about a serious crime here, and all you have say is what do you want me to do about it?" The anger rose as did her voice.

"I'll tell you what I expect you to do! Your job!" He took a cigar from this pocket, bit the tip off, and sent it sailing to the corner of the room. Anna Belle watched it as it landed.

"This is my home, and I expect it to be respected."

The sheriff walked over to the place where the piece of cigar landed as though he was about to pick it up. Then he turned back to Anna Belle.

"Well it might help if I had something to go on. Like for instance, what happened and who did it."

"It's obvious they were beaten with a whip. You can blame Matthew Wellington for it." The sheriff gagged on his smoke.

"Matthew Wellington? What are you talking about? How does he tie in with this? It really doesn't make much sense."

"You're here to uphold the law, aren't you?" The sheriff squinted his eyes at Anna Belle.

"Are you absolutely sure that Matthew Wellington did something of this nature? It's not likely. What reason would he have to be on this property?"

Anna Belle shuffled her feet several times.

"Well, I actually didn't see him do this. But I know it was him because I heard his voice last night."

"Nigger, are you crazy? You expect me to arrest someone for something they possibly had nothing to do with at all. Well, you've just wasted my time by coming way out here." The study door opened and the doctor stepped inside. Anna Belle turned to him.

"Bobby Gene, Doc is he going to be OK?"

"He'll be fine after a bit. It's lucky for him that he's a strong man after that beating he encountered, it's a miracle he's still alive. I gave him something to make him sleep, and there's some medicine for the pain and some liniment for his back. He's still unable to speak right now. That's nothing to alarm yourself with. His voice should come back in a few days when his strength gets better. On the other hand, I'm truly sorry about Jeffrey. He was a fine young man. Apparently his heart couldn't sustain the abuse his body had taken and gave out on him." Anna Belle thanked the doctor, as he was about to leave, the sheriff stopped him.

"Dave, did I hear you say Bobby Gene wasn't able to speak at this time?"

"Yes. He's just to weak." The sheriff picked up his hat and put it on his head.

"Well, it looks like I've done all I can here. I'll just ride back with you then, if you don't mind."

"I don't mind one bit. As a matter of fact, I'd welcome the company. I get tired of talking to myself." He bid Anna Belle a good day.

"Excuse me, Sheriff, but aren't you going to make an arrest?"

"I'm afraid not. I have to get the facts from Bobby Gene before I can take any actions. If it was Matthew Wellington, then I need to hear it from Bobby Gene himself."

"But I told you, Sheriff, it was him." He pointed his finger at her.

"No. You said you heard a voice that sounded like him but you saw nothing. I can't put him under arrest without knowing the facts. He's a very influential man, and I could lose my job over this I've had this job for eighteen years. This is my life, and I'm not going to jeopardize it. I'll come back in a few days or so when Bobby Gene is able to talk. Now good day!"

With every passing day, Bobby Gene's strength gradually came back. They held a short service in remembrance of Jeffrey. Pauline realized after it was too late she had been a fool and decided she was going back home. She was also sure Jeffrey's family would want his body back there as well. Bobby Gene had given her money to ship his body back with her. Anna Belle and Bobby Gene were in the study when Gertrude knocked on the door then stepped inside.

"Sir, the sheriff be here to see'd you's."

"Good, send him in."

"Well. Hello again, Mr. Watson. It's good to see you up and about. I understand you had a close call with death. If I'm not mistaken, this is the second time your life has been threatened. Maybe you should have heeded my advice. Pack up and leave here before it's too late." Bobby Gene had a grimace look on his face.

"You know, Sheriff, the way you're good with offering advice, maybe you ought to change your profession of work besides, you can't be that naive to not know I'm from around here, given the fact there were reward posters posted all about the town. The sheriff cleared his throat.

"Mmmm…well, I came to get that statement if you're up to it." He pointed to the chair that was in front of the desk as he signaled he would like to have a sit down. Bobby Gene let him know it was all right for him to be seated. He continued on with the conversation where he had left off.

"Now I want you to tell me exactly what happened."

Bobby Gene began. "Well, it was late one evening. Everyone was asleep. I heard someone calling my name, then the breaking of glass. I told everyone to hide. Jeffrey and myself went outside to see what was going on. When we stepped out onto the front porch, there was a man sitting on a horse, I couldn't make him out at the time because of the darkness. But the voice was familiar as he spoke. He said he wanted no trouble. He just came after the woman and the boy. I had taken them earlier that day. When I refused, he had a few of his men search my home. After he had found nothing, he asked again where they were. I still wouldn't respond. He had Jeffrey and myself tied to a tree, and he beat us with his whip. I was beaten unconscious. But while we were being tied to the tree. I did see his face under the moonlight. As matter of fact, those were his specific orders. To tie us to the tree under the moonlight so we could see his face." The sheriff stood up as he started to pace the floor as though he had become nervous all of a sudden, finally, the words came.

"So you say Matthew played a part in this drama?"

"That's exactly what I'm saying. Now answer me one question. What are you going to do about it?"

"Well, I really don't see that I can do anything. First off, you brought this on yourself when you decided to go on his property and take something that belonged to him. Don't you know I can arrest you for that? But being the kindly sheriff that I am, it's your lucky day. I'm not going to take you in on kidnapping charges. I can lock Matthew up. He'd be out of jail within the hour. Even if you took him to court, he'd have it thrown out before it got to the judges' chambers." Bobby Gene stood up. "Just what are you saying, Sheriff? That you're going to sweep this under the rug?"

"That's precisely what I'm saying. Because you have no other choice."

"Yeah. Well that's where you're wrong, sheriff. Because I'm going to do something. Ain't no man going to come on my property, beat me like an animal, kill my best friend then walk. He's going to pay and I'll see to that."

"You know, I feel sorry for the towns people. If they were ever in a critical situation. Or is it because I'm black? Better yet, because I'm black, educated and free. You know what you can do with that badge you're wearing as well as finding your way out. So goodbye." The sheriff strolled boldly to the door, turning once again to Bobby Gene.

"I'm warning you. If I hear you've made any kind of trouble, even if it's only spitting on the street. I'll have you for company in my jail a long while and you can bank on that." Bobby Gene walked to the front of his desk as he leaned back against it crossing his legs, making himself comfortable.

"Hear me out, sheriff. And make no mistake about this, Matthew Wellington shall pay for his wrong doing. I didn't attend four years of law school for it to be ridiculed by the likes of an under the table sheriff. I also want to remind you the law required a man to face a judge and jury when the laws of the constitution have been broken." The sheriff had a bewildered expression on his face.

"What's wrong sheriff. Does my knowledge and wisdom surprise you? You must remember. I'm an educated nigger now. I've learned a lot in the white mans' world." He raised his eyebrows with pride as he yet spoke.

"You don't want to challenge my capabilities as far as the law is concerned." A confident smile came on his face. "Unless you want the towns folks to know how ignorant their sheriff truly is. Granted you might have your hooks in some of them, but most of them are God fearing, law-abiding citizen." The sheriff stood there just as assuredly as Bobby Gene.

"Boy, I think you've lost touch with reality. I can haul your ass off to jail this very minute, and you couldn't do a damn thing about it." He grimaced at Bobby Gene while he shifted the brim of his hat in his hands.

"I hope you take heed to the warning I gave you."

"As far as Matthew Wellington, I'm not at liberty to arrest him. There are higher authorities who are underfoot, as you so graciously put it. Someone shall we say who wears his black very loosely." He pointed his finger at Bobby Gene.

"If you repeat what I just said, I'll deny it. Plus, your life won't be worth a plug nickel. I've given you advice in the past. This time it's an order. I want you out of this town immediately. Or that threat about having you in my jail will become a reality."

"Please, Sheriff. You have to do better than that to make idle threats. I've been in shackles and bondage for most of my life. Do you think that frightens me? I think not. Matthew will pay for his wrong doing. If you think you can take me to jail, then here's your opportunity. Don't underestimate my potential. I will fight." The sheriff stood there a long moment, silently looking on.

"I don't see where at this time you have done anything wrong. Just remember, I'm going to be watching you. And make no mistake about that." They both watched him leave, Anna Belle walked over to Bobby Gene.

"Can't you see, Bobby Gene? We've lost. Don't you realize, no matter how intelligent we might be, we have no place in this society. We must surrender before it's too late. The white man has abused our people for years. Look around you. Do you see any of the old folks complaining about freedom? They seem to be content with the way things have turned out for them. Why start a war when the battle is already lost? Maybe the ole-timers are our example. They didn't get old by being foolish. We need to take heed. We see the young has tried to escape and it has mostly been the young who have paid the price." Bobby Gene looked at Anna Belle with a cumbersome glare.

"I can't believe you're falling back into the old way. I can understand why I get the stares and ridicule from them. They're ignorant to the fact. But you. You've experienced the other side even if it maybe for only a short time. Why do you think we've accomplished what we have, and where we are today? Plus, we decided that we were tired of living like our ancestors or the other slaves." He chuckled to himself.

"How strange to use that word slave when they're just like yourself, black, but with a completely different definition, even though we're Negroes, we're free Negroes. It's amazing how one can live in the same atmosphere but live different lives. We learned just as they can learn." He stood up and walked over to the window as he looked out across the fields.

"You're wrong Anna Belle, we have everything to fight for. Freedom for our bodies, mind, and souls. The white man has abused our people for too long, and I know it can happen for the rest of them if they truly believe. Look at you for instance."

"Can you honestly tell me that after tasting the good life like a white woman, you would want to go back to being one of the slaves? Jeffrey was willing to risk his life for me and you to the very end. He never gave up knowing what dangers lay ahead, and he was a white man. That's enough to let me know whenever a white man gives his life for a mere slave, I'm worthy of something. Jeffrey's believing has made me more determine to carry on. The worst that can happen is I might get killed. Ironically, tomorrow is not promised to us anyway."

"That's just it, Bobby Gene, you could get killed over nothing." He turned back to her.

"How can you call freedom nothing? Nothing to help your people to a better way of life. Then maybe it was a mistake, your coming back with me. The door is always open. You're free to leave any time you choose." She strolled over to the window to join him, gently stroking his cheek.

"I'm sorry, Bobby Gene. I know, that you're wanting to put this to a good cause, but it's just frightening me so. I don't want to leave you, and I'm not going to. It's just that Matthew isn't a stupid man. He knows you had something to do with my leaving his plantation. Just like he knows he could have killed you that night. This 'is his way of causing you to be uncomfortable. To try and break you down. To weaken you. He's a shrewd man, Bobby Gene, and he's going to make you pay for invading his territory. He's the type of man who thrives off the anguish he gives to others and right now you're his prime target. I won't go back to him because he shall surely kill me. He's a man of his word." Her brown eyes tightened with worry.

"Please Bobby Gene. Don't challenge him for you'll be fighting a losing battle."

"Woman of little faith. You think because Matthew is white that makes him invincible? He's only a man like myself. He frightens like myself. He hurts like myself. He bleeds like myself. He can die like myself. I hear what you're saying, Anna belle, but I'm a man and a free man at that. I can't express how much that means to me. I'm not about to let any man run me away from some place I have as much right to be as himself."

"I can see your mind is made up. Anna Belle replied. You should be able to understand when I say I can't marry you until this thing is resolved. I've lost too many loved ones in my life, and I don't think I could cope with losing another."

CHAPTER TWENTY-TWO

The fully blossomed trees that had once pressed against the clear blue skies were no longer. As the leaves began falling to the ground, filling it with their lively autumn colors. There hadn't been any more trouble with Matthew, Bobby Gene knew he was just waiting for the right moment to attack again. This time, Bobby Gene swore to be ready. Lorene was doing much better and had even decided to come out into the world again.

Bobby Gene, Anna Belle, and Lorene putting their heads together decided the best way for Bobby Gene to get to the other slaves was for him to us his preaching credentials. This way he'd have a better chance of getting to speak with the slaves on the other plantations. The black suit Bobby Gene had put away would finally get its proper use again.

"Ah, just perfect," he said as he held the piece of paper on his lap.

"Reverend Franklin Tindall at your service." Anna Belle took the piece of paper and read it.

"It might be perfect to us, but do you think the white man will fall for it?" Bobby Gene sighed.

"Why is it, Anna Belle, that you have to be so negative all the time? I don't know. All I can do is try. It won't be long before we'll know though." Anna Belle was a bit stunned by his statement.

"What do you mean, Bobby Gene? You aren't planning on leaving soon, are you?" He walked over to the window using the autumn's scenery as an excuse for not having to face her as he spoke.

"As matter of fact, I'm going to be leaving tomorrow. I have to go. It's been delayed long enough." Anna Belle stood and joined him at the window where he stood.

"Tomorrow, Bobby Gene? Does it really have to be that soon? Couldn't it wait till the next day? Maybe even the next one."

"I can't, Anna Belle. Don't you see if I put it off tomorrow then there will be other excuses? I must go tomorrow. I don't like the idea of leaving you and the others here alone, but I believe Kuta and the other young men can handle everything that need be tended to. I'm hoping not to be gone that long."

Anna Belle grasped Bobby Gene on the shoulders and turned his face toward her when she noticed the tears. She caught them with her tiny brown fingers and brushed them away.

"You're crying. I've never seen you cry before."

"That's because I've never felt so unhappy before. I love you, Anna Belle, but I have to do this." Water was starting to form in her eyes now.

"I love you too, Bobby Gene." They embraced as their lips touched each other. Anna Belle whispered through her tears.

"Make love to me tonight for we may never get the chance again."

Bobby Gene stood there a long moment, watching Anna Belle as she lay there sleeping so calmly. He walked over to her bedside and kissed her gently on the forehead. Then he went downstairs to give Kuta and the others his last minute instructions. He threw the satchel on his back and started his journey.

The winds were very cold. He knew eventually his body would adjust to it. But he also knew he would have to seek refuge before too long. The first stop on his journey would be the Wellington plantation. He knew if he were to pull off this masquerade, he would first have to hit the place that would be the most threatening to him.

The start of the evening moon was beginning to appear through the naked trees. Although Bobby Gene had been traveling only for a short time, the aching of his body told him it had been a lot longer. The distant to the Wellington Plantation was quite lengthy on foot. He could tell he was nearing the plantation for he heard the barking of the hound dogs and the smell of chimney smoke. The uneasy feeling he had gotten so many times before had caused sweat to start forming all over his body. The tingling of his spine almost overpowered him as he stepped onto the property. He was greeted by the howling dogs and a couple of the overseers.

"If you're smart, nigger, you won't take another step. Now why don't you tell us what you're doing here and why?" Bobby Gene looked at the dogs that had formed a circle around him, snarling and showing their white teeth.

"Well, sir. If you'll be so kind as to call off your dogs. I'd be mighty glad to explain myself."

"Never you mind 'bout them dogs, nigger. They ain't going to attack you unless we tell them to, and if you don't want that to happen, you best start talking right now."

"Yes, sir. You see, I'm known as a wandering preacher. My name is Franklin Tindall, and I got my freedom papers to show who I say I am." He slowly removed the papers from inside his suit coat and stretched them out to one of the men as he beckoned the younger overseer to dismount his horse. Keeping a close eye on Bobby Gene. The young man snatched the papers from his hand and gave them to the man who examined them very thoroughly. Looking back at Bobby Gene, he said. "These papers say you're from Pennsylvania. What are you doing so far away from home? Don't you know it's not safe for a nigger to be traveling in these parts? One might mistake you for one of them stray niggers and decide to make a slave out of you." Bobby Gene shook his head.

"Yes, sir. I do know this, but I heard there wasn't many Negro preachers out this way. So I decided to take out one day to become a wandering preacher. To preach the word where and whenever I can in exchange for a bit of food and a little comfort." The overseer

threw the papers back at Bobby Gene, who could sense the vicious-
ness in his eyes.

"What do you think, Bud? Shall we turn him over to
Wellington?" All was quiet except the dogs. The man's eyes yet fixed
on Bobby Gene.

"No, I don't see as to where this need to be brought to his
attention. This here nigger sure can't do any harm. He's all by himself. Might be of some help to them niggers though. Being they just
lost that ole nigger preacher of theirs. I don't understand it. but if
it's one thing these niggers love is the speaking from the Good Book
so they call it. Why don't you show this nigger where they are??

"All right. He spoke to Bobby Gene.

"You've got until tomorrow at daybreak. Then you'll have to
be on your way. Just a word of warning. Don't try anything stupid,
or the only place you'll be going is in shackles." He grinned.

"You comprehend what I mean?"

"Yes, sir. I understand clearly."

The church was a small one-room shack with a few worn
benches. The congregation had just finished singing when Bobby
Gene was noticed. The man standing in front of the altar smiled.

"I's see'd we's have a new face here with us this evening. He
stretched out his hand in welcome.

"Won't you please come forward, introduce yourself, and join
us?" Every eye was on Bobby Gene as he walked to the front. The
man took Bobby Gene by the hand.

"My name is Emmanuel Bell. I's be asked to lead this people."

"Mine is Franklin Tindall. Reverend Franklin Tindall." A voice
spoke within the congregation.

"Thank you's, Lord fer answer'n we's prayers by send'n us our
new young preacher." The ole man pointed Bobby Gene toward the
altar. Then he took a seat as Bobby Gene took the pulpit. Bobby
Gene studied the black faces as he began to speak.

"Brothers and sisters. I thank you for welcoming me a stranger
into your family. But I must say right off that I'm only here for a
short stay. Being informed by the kind gentlemen who is standing
back yonder. I must be on my way by morning. Which is fine.

For we know Jesus was here for only a season himself. If you don't mind, I'd like to read to you a little from the Good Book." He reached into his satchel and took out the small square black book. He opened it as he began to read from it.

"And the Lord spoke to Moses and Aaron in the land of Egypt, saying…" As he read on there was moans and groans amongst the congregation.

"This nigger talk he's speaking don't make no sense to me. What do you say we go get something to warm these cold bodies of ours, and I don't mean just whiskey. This dumb nigger surely can't do no harm." The young man smiled at Bud who had decided to join him after all.

"You know, that don't sound half bad. I've been watching that Sherman girl for sometimes now. I do believe she's ready to be broken in. I don't see why tonight wouldn't be as good as any." Bud ruffled the young man's hair.

"You know, kid that's not a bad idea. We know how them new bitches get to bucking and kicking when they're first saddled. That alone is enough to keep one's, body warm. Hell, there might even be enough for the both of us." Bobby Gene waited until he was sure they had left.

"Brothers and sisters this concludes our sermon for now. Again I thank each and every one of you for listening to me. God bless you. But now, brothers and sisters, before you leave, there's something I'd like to speak with you about." He stepped down from the pulpit and continued to speak while he yet stood before the small crowd of people, looking into their mysterious eyes.

"If you're wondering why I'm not speaking from the pulpit, it's because I don't feel it proper to deliver a personal message from where God wants his word to be delivered. Part of Jesus' message was about honesty. That's why I feel it's important I be totally honest with you. First off, I want to tell you that my name isn't Franklin Tindall but Bobby Gene Watson." The moaning and whispering started as they got up to leave while one of the old-timers turned back to Bobby Gene as he addressed him.

"It be's clear now. I's thought some'n be's familiar with you's. Until now I's couldn't put my finger on it. But I's remember now that night when Masser Travor thought you's be dead. I's doesn't understand it. But I's feel evil in you's. Ain't no nigger 'pose to be's like you's. You's the devil I's say, and I's not gonna to listen to what you's has to say."

"Please wait. Why are you leaving? I haven't finished what I have to say." Another of the old-timers responded to Bobby Gene's plea.

"Why should we's listen to you's after all you's dun lied to us." They continued toward the door. Bobby Gene looked over at Emmanuel with begging eyes.

"Brothers, sisters, please wait and see'd what this young man has to say. He may have lied, but hasn't all of us at one time or another. There be's one thing I's sure of. And that be. He be the man of God. Please sit and heard what he's has to says." Bobby Gene waited until everyone was properly seated then he thanked Emmanuel for his help.

"Before I say anything else, I want you to know I am a certified preacher, but that is not my only profession. You will not understand what I'm saying, but I'm a lawyer too. That means I help people, and that is why I'm here. To give you a chance to be free like myself and not have to worry about being misused or abused by the white man ever again. Tonight I'm asking you to put your trust in me and come away with me." There was an outburst in the crowd.

"Be's gone with you's. We's doesn't want you's kind with us. You's be an evil man like Jeremiah says. Why does you's come here to torment us? We's dun noth'n to you's. Go away, and leave us be." A wail of noise came again. Bobby Gene tried to speak above it.

"Listen to me. I'm not here to cause you any harm. I've come to help. To give you a chance to live your lives like people. Not like animals."

"Lies does you's see'd. It be's the devil himself. Listen to the way he talks doesn't none of us use any of them fancy words like that. We's doesn't know how to speak from no book. Then what be's worse. He tries to tell us that ifin we's trust him. He's take us to freedom. How it be's he can offer us some'n our people have died fer, fer years to try and run away to."

"Now I's ask you's. Does that be one of us? I's says we's goes and tell Master Wellington. I's sure he knows how to handle this evil man." Several of the others jumped up in agreement to what the woman had said.

"All right!" Bobby Gene shouted.

"If that's the way you feel about it, then I'll save you the trouble. I'll turn myself over to your master. But before I do, I have this to say. I thought when I decided to give up everything to fight for what I felt would help my people that it would be something to look forward to. I knew it wouldn't be easy, but I never thought the battle would be so easily lost."

"You think because I come here with some fancy words or can read from a book that I'm an evil man. Well, that's not true. It was a white man who helped me. I was a runaway for a long time. I hide out in a cave right on this very plantation. Some of you may have even known Master Jeffrey. From the first time Jeffrey saw me, he could have turned me over to the master or even killed me. But he helped me by bringing me food, taking care of me when I was sick, and even taught me how to read and write."

"There's nothing evil about that. You can all do it too if you choose. Most importantly. He helped me to escape to the north where slavery is but a word. After I got all the learning I needed. I decided to come back here and fight for the promise I made to a friend on his deathbed. I promised him I would help our people to freedom." Tears started forming in the web of his eyes.

"The sad thing about it is when I came back, Jeffrey stuck by my side even to his death. Granted he could have lived his life like other overseers, but he wasn't raised that way. So instead he taught me a lot of things. Tonight you make me feel like why I even bothered about coming back. Ashamed to be black. I've come back to some broken down gutless people who chooses to continually be controlled and torched by the enemy. When are you ever going to start acting like the men and women that you are?" He stepped into the aisle making his way toward the door.

"Go ahead, nigger turn yourself over to the master. You's can't make us feel guilty fer the death of you's white friend. Doesn't no body ask him to git involved with us niggers anyhown." Bobby Gene rushed at the young man but was quickly restrained.

"What about all the forefathers who have died before us? Was their dying none of our concern? If I wasn't being restrained by these gents. I'd make you eat those words."

"Enough of this the both of you's. This be's the house of the Lord, and there will be no fight'n in here, now or anytime. Is that be's understood?" Emmanuel's dark eyes frowned upon the both of them.

"Yes," they both replied.

"Fine. Now that everything be's back to normal. I's say we's sit down and heard what Bobby Gene has to offer us." Another one of the females in the congregation spoke up.

"Ifin you's think I's gonna take a thresh'n, or possibly even git sold away from my family 'cause some strange nigger come here and tells us he's can offer us a better life than what we's has now. That all's we's has to do is trust in him. Well, you's can count me out. Besides, how does you's knows this ain't a trap he be's try'n to git us into."

"Ifin you's be's smart you's git up right now and goes as I's does." She stood up as others followed, leaving the church almost empty. Bobby Gene cleared his throat.

"Those of you who have decided to stay won't regret your decision. That I promise. The only thing that worries me now are those who just left. If they should get to your master, it could be the death of me. There are things I still need to discuss with you, but most importantly right now is for me to get out of here before Wellington and some of his overseers get here. I don't want any of you harmed because of me. If you're questioned, you know nothing." They listened for a moment.

"It's too late, someone's coming!" Mr. Bell grabbed his arm.

"Quick, follow me." He led Bobby Gene up to the pulpit where he asked some of the others to help him move the stand.

"Come, git in this hole. No one knows it be's here till now. I's started digg'n it out long time ago. Hop'n I's could hide out here then later escape to my freedom. But I's never git the courage."

"Quick, inside!" He instructed them to put the stand back in its place. The door to the church swung open as several overseers and Matthew rushed in, frightening the few blacks that remained. Mr. Bell and the others slowly turned towards them.

"Does there be's some'n wrong, Masser?" Why such an outburst in the house of God?" Matthew approached closer while the others stood guard.

"That's what I'm hoping you'll tell me. My understanding is that there's a nigger here trying to turn some of your minds against me. Is that true, Emmanuel?"

Emmanuel stuttered. "Why no, sir Masser. You's knows we's never does noth'n like that know'n what would happen to us." Master Wellington walked about the room, showing that he wasn't thoroughly convinced, looking over the room as he slapped the handle of the whip against his left hand. He stood there staring Emmanuel sternly in his eyes.

"You know, Emmanuel, I've known you for a great number of years, and I can generally tell when you're trying to cover something up. It's quite obvious that y'all are nervous about something, so I'm giving you and the rest of y'all niggers one last chance to save yourselves from a good threshing."

"Honestly, Masser. There be's noth'n to tell, and you's can surely see'd that we's hid'n noth'n. we's nervous because of the way you's come burst'n through the door." Matthew started pacing again as he continued slapping the handle of the whip in his hands.'

"Contrary, Emmanuel, it's what I don't see that lets me know you're lying to me. That nigger preacher. How did it come about that he's not here? One of the overseers told me he told him he had tonight to bed down. It's awfully odd that one wouldn't stay on overnight, especially when one confesses he's been wandering over strange country he knows nothing about." He looked at the overseers.

"Since these niggers find it so imperative to lie, take all of them to the barn, shackle them. We shall tend to them come the first sign of day break. Who knows, maybe by then one of them will decide to talk. I want two of you to keep watch in case that nigger tries to come back. The rest of you come with me. If that nigger did leave, he can't have gotten far on foot."

CHAPTER TWENTY-THREE

"Masser Watson, can you's heard me, Masser?"
Bobby Gene knocked on the bottom of the
stand. "Hold on, Masser, we's have you's out of
there shortly." Bobby Gene could feel the cold air surrounding him
as the altar was being lifted away.

"Here, Masser, take my hand and I's help you's out." Bobby
Gene felt about the darkness till their hands connected. Once he
was out of the hole, he thanked the stranger.

"Man, am I glad you came along. I've been trying to push
that altar aside for what seemed for hours. By the way, how did
you know of this dugout? Your voice sounds a bit familiar to me."
Bobby Gene inquired.

"You's be's right, Masser. I's Emmanuel son. Many has said
we's talk alike. I's guess it be's true. The Masser Wellington give me
the OK to take my pa some grub, that be's when he tells me you's
be's here. Come, we's must leave here. I's made sure we's not be's followed. Also we's have others look'n out fer us. Ifin anyone decides
to come back this way, they's gonna give us a signal. Maybe we's can
make it to my cabin without be'n see'd." Bobby Gene pulled the
young man back.

"Are you sure you want to do this? After all, your father and
some of the others are in trouble because of me."

"Masser Watson, my pa didn't git old by be'n no fool. He
believe in you's and that be's enough fer me. Now come quickly,
time at the moment is not on our side."

The weather outside was still old, which made it much easier for the young man and his accomplices to get to his cabin without being noticed. The other young men decided it was best they went back to their cabins before someone becomes suspicious of them as the young man and Bobby Gene went inside.

"Come sit by the fire. I's sure the heat should feel good to you's right about now. Toby, git the Masser a cup of coffee. The boy did as he was told constantly observing Bobby Gene in the process.

"Boy, where be's you's manners. You's knows it be's not polite to stare at someone."

"I's sorry, pa, but you's calls him Masser like you's does the white man when he be's a nigger like us. He's be that nigger Masser Wellington be's look'n fer this night, ain't he? The man slapped the boy alongside his face.

"I's not tell you's again, boy, mind you's manners. Off to bed with you's anyhown." They waited until Toby had left the room before they continued their conversation.

"That boy of mine, he hates me because of his ma's death. Ifin he knows the truth. I doesn't knows what he does." Bobby Gene could see the young man was hurting inside.

"Don't think I'm trying to tell you how to raise your son, but you could be a little less critical of him. He's only a boy. I know how he feels as far as his mother's concern. It took me a bit to accept the loss of my ma. Even though she was sold away from me at a young age, it was as though she had died. To this day I have not been able to get in contact with her. For all I know she might be dead. He gave the young man a reassuring glare.

"I know some things are difficult to talk about. But if you'd like to lift that burden you've been carrying on your shoulders I'll be more than glad to listen." The young man looked back at Bobby Gene.

"Has you's ever be's deeply in love with someone?"

"Yes, for many years." Bobby Gene replied. "We're going to be married."

"Then you's understand what I's feel'n. We's be's happy, my woman and me, then one night when the overseers had their fill of whiskey, they's wanted to have some fun with her. Toby be's our first born. I's be's tied to this chair gagged and forced to watch as they used her. Shortly afterward, she be's with child and died at childbirth. A few days later the baby died too. Toby thinks that I's be's the cause of her dy'n 'cause she died giv'n birth. He's never knows that the baby be white, and I's never has the heart to tell him. I swore they's would pay." There was a long moment of silence.

"And they's will." Bobby Gene touched the young man on the shoulder.

"I'm sorry about your wife, and I empathize with you because I lost two of my very best friends. We can't dwell on the past. We can only concentrate on the future. Did your father brief you as to why I'm here?"

"Yes, but I's doesn't understand. What can one nigger do, Masser?"

"First of all I want you to stop calling me 'masser. The name is Bobby Gene, and I'm no more your master than Wellington or anyone else. It would also be better for the both of us if I were to know your name."

"How silly of me. The name is LeRoy." He extended his hand out to Bobby Gene as he accepted it.

"Well, now that's out of the way, let's get back to your question. Actually there's really nothing one man can do alone. But if he were to band together, then there's nothing we can't conquer. That's if he's determined and willing." LeRoy looked back into Bobby Gene's eyes.

"Then count me in."

"I was hoping you would say that. But before you accept the challenge you should know up front this decision could be detrimental for you and the others too. Do you understand what I'm saying?" LeRoy nodded his head.

"I's understand fully, and my decision still stand. Ifin I's should die, it's gonna be fer a cause. I's may not be free from the white man. But in my head and my heart I's can say I's be."

"We must move quickly while it is yet dark. This is what I want you to do. I'm sure you're familiar with a knife. But other than killing and skinning animals." Bobby Gene looked sincerely up on LeRoy's face.

"I mean if you had to use it on a person. Would you hesitate?"

"Maybe up until now I's would have been. But since you's come along and showed me life is worth living and fighting for. No I's wouldn't."

"Good, then here's the plan. You said your father and the others were being guarded."

"Yes. Two overseers be's standing outside the barn door to make sure no one can git to them."

"Namely me." Bobby Gene added. "Well, we'll have to see about that. Do you by chance have another hat and coat I can wear? I shall dress up like you and pretend I had gotten drunk and decided to pay my pa another visit to check on him. I'm sure they won't recognize me due to the fact it's night time. I will approach one of the overseers in an aggressive manner knowing they like nothing more than to give us a good beating whenever the circumstance was allowed. After I've lured him off, then it will be up to you to handle your father and the others till I'm able to rejoin y'all again to help. Now how about that coat and hat? You should also wake your son have him bundle up with as much clothing as possible because we've got some traveling to do in this bitter weather. I suggest you do the same thing. I'll go out, scout a bit to make sure things are still quiet." He opened the door as the wind made its way to the fire as though it were seeking refuge.

"Take only what is of importance to you and any kind of weapons you might have on hand. We'll be traveling light." He shut the door behind him.

CHAPTER TWENTY-FOUR

"Toby, Toby. Wake up son." LeRoy stood over the boy, shaking him out of his sleep.

"Whatsa matter, Papa? Does some'n be wrong?"

"No, son. Finally, everything be right. Here, put these clothes on and add over top on what you's has on, make sure you's bundled up real good. You's heard?" Toby inquired again.

"Why's I's gitt'n dressed in so much clothes fer, Papa?" LeRoy took Toby by the shoulders and shook him.

"I's haven't time to answer you's now but trust me. When I's come back I's want you's to be's ready."

"Trust you's, Papa? After what happened to Mama? I's wish it be's you's that died." LeRoy slapped Toby again.

"I's won't have no son of mine talk to me that way. These years you's blamed me fer you's ma's death when you's knows she's died giv'n birth. What you's doesn't knows is that the child be white, not you's papa. So ifin you's want to hate. Hate the one who be responsible not you's pa. I's going now, and when I's come back you's leav'n with me whether you's want to or not." Bobby Gene came back into the cabin with good news.

"All is clear for the time being. But we must get a move on it. You haven't changed your mind, have you?"

"No chance of that I's had a bit of a problem with Toby." A worried look came over Bobby Gene.

"He won't cause any trouble for us, will he?"

"No. I just told him the truth about his ma's died baring the white man's child. I's think that hatred he be's keep'n lifted away. Doesn't we's have some'n to tend to?" Bobby Gene slapped LeRoy on the back.

"That we do. Do you have your knife with you?" LeRoy checked to make sure. He held it up.

"Right here."

"Good. I'm going to need some liquor. Do you by chance have any around here?" To Bobby Gene's surprise he watched. LeRoy, as he strolled over to the bed, reached down as he came up with a jug and handed it to Bobby Gene. He stood there stunned while he watched him pour some of the liquor down in the front of his shirt, then he rubbed some down his coat. Finally taking a big gulp he swallowed it down quickly so his breath would reek with alcohol.

"Wow." He shook his head. "I almost forgot what kick that corn whiskey carries. Shall we go? When we reach the barn. I'll go on the one side and you the other. Don't forget after I've lured off one of them The other will be your responsibility. Bobby Gene staggered to the front of the barn.

"Well, well, Masser. I's see'd you's still here," Bobby Gene said as he staggered up to the overseers.

"What is it nigger?" One of the overseers asked as he pushed Bobby Gene.

"It's that nigger, Emmanuel's son again" The one replied. "Looks like he done got himself liquored up pretty good." Bobby Gene approached them again pretending as though he was about to break through the two of them.

"Come on, Masser, I's want to see'd my pa one more time to make sure he be's all right." For the second time he was pushed away.

"Go home, nigger, before you end up in there with the rest of them." Bobby Gene rushed at the two men, again striking one of them as he did so. The man stood there as he wiped the tinkle of blood from his chin. He became irate.

"This nigger done attacked me." He grabbed Bobby Gene around the neck.

"Boy, I don't give a damn if your pa is in there or not. You've crossed the line this time." He beckoned to the other overseer.

"Take over while this nigger and I go out back." He chuckled as he dragged Bobby Gene away. When he felt they were far enough away so that no one could hear anything, he threw Bobby Gene hard to the ground.

"OK, nigger. You want to play rough? I'll show you what rough can be." Bobby Gene lay there watching as the overseer took something out of his pocket. He could tell it was a knife from the way it reflected under the moonlight. As the overseer went to land on top of Bobby Gene, he quickly rolled over to the side, leaving the man to fall upon the bare ground instead. Bobby Gene jumped to his feet. He now looked down upon the overseer who quickly got back to his feet as well.

"Look a here, a nigger with spunk. Well, that's the best kind." He swung at Bobby Gene and there was the sound of fabric ripping Bobby Gene jumped back.

"Quick too, aren't you nigger? He came at Bobby Gene again as their bodies collided. Bobby Gene shoved the overseer sending him to the ground once again. This made the overseer more angered as he came back at Bobby Gene full force, only to catch the hidden blade of Bobby Gene's knife he had stationaried tightly in his right hand. Standing there he watched the overseer fall to the ground for the last time, after which he headed back toward the barn. Peeping around the corner but seeing nothing, he waited a few moments, hoping that either LeRoy or the overseer would present themselves, but still nothing happened.

Sweat started to form about his body as it had done many times in the past when he was not sure of the situation. He would allow himself a bit longer, then he would have to proceed on with or without LeRoy. As he allowed himself to wait for a few more moments, he was distracted by a noise behind him. He positioned his knife to attack as he turned about, only to find his assailant to be that of a mere raccoon. He would wait no longer. He eased his way to the barn door, slow to open it, whispering out LeRoy's name in the process so he wouldn't be mistaken for someone else.

"LeRoy, is everything all right?" He called out. He heard a sigh of relief as LeRoy emerged out of hiding, knife erected trembling, and ready to strike.

"Man you's scared me. I's doesn't knows ifin it be's you's or the overseer." Bobby Gene could tell he was a bit shaken. He slowly walked over to him and relieved him of his knife.

"LeRoy are you OK?" He asked. LeRoy batted his eyes several times.

"Pa and the others, we's must free them quickly? They called to Emmanuel out of the dark.

"Pa, it be's us. LeRoy. We's come to free you's." They could tell by Emmanuel's voice he was dumbfounded.

"LeRoy son, that be's you's? How you's make it past the overseers?" He made his way to his father and started to free him while Bobby Gene started freeing the others.

"Bobby Gene. He be's the how." LeRoy finished freeing his father. "I's must help with the others." When each person was freed, Bobby Gene informed them with the same instructions he gave to LeRoy. Gather whatever family they had who would be willing to come along. Put clothing on top of their other clothing. Bring only their personals, and any kind of weapons they could muster up. Travel lightly for they would be traveling through the night to make it to his place. He told them to meet him at the end of the crop fields as quickly as they possibly could. Emmanuel and one of the other old-timers volunteered to hang back for a few more minutes then would catch up with them soon.

"I see more of you have decided to join us. This is good. I know it's cold out here, and for a few of you, you're frightened. Frankly so am I. That's why I want to specify to you this decision you made is very important. It's not going to be easy, and no doubt some of us standing here will die. We're going to have to fight, but that's the choice you're making for your freedom. It's not too late for you to go back to your cabins and act as though nothing has happened. But we must leave now. Tomorrow will bring Wellington to my door for the murder of two of his overseers and the abduction of his slaves." He waited, but no one budged.

"I guess that means we're ready to go."

CHAPTER TWENTY-FIVE

*I*t was daybreak when Bobby Gene and the others reached his plantation. Anna belle had been watching from the window to see why the dogs were making such a ruckus when she spotted them. She grabbed the shawl she always kept on a nail by the kitchen door. Wrapping it around her, she ran out to greet him.

"Oh Bobby Gene I'm so glad to see you. I thought something bad had happened to you." He held her in his arms trying to keep her quivering body warm from the cold.

"Come let's all go into the house. These people need to get warm and some food into them so we can prepare for battle." Anna Belle was puzzled but decided to wait until they were inside before she pursued this any farther. Everyone greeted Bobby Gene as he entered the house.

"Masser Watson," Kuta greeting him with a huge smile.

"Boy is we's glad to see'd you's." Bobby Gene embraced him tightly.

"Likewise, Kuta, likewise. Now I want you to take my guest into the dining area, and feed them some food and coffee. We will decide later where they shall bed down. I shall be upstairs changing my clothes. Then I shall join all of you later. At that time, we will get acquainted with one another." Anna Belle smiled at the strangers faces as she followed Bobby Gene upstairs to the bedroom.

"Oh, Bobby Gene, I was so frightened. Not only for you, but for us as well. I thought for sure Matthew would come back, trying to cause more trouble. Maybe I was wrong about him. Maybe he decided to give up and leave us alone."

"Don' be too sure. As a matter of fact, I'm sure we'll be hearing from him before this day is over." Anna Belle again was puzzled.

"You act as though you know something." She nervously started pacing the floor.

"Does those people have something to do with Matthew?" She stood there a moment.

"Oh my God, they do." She said as everything started coming back to her. "Those people down there. They aren't really strangers anymore. I can remember seeing some of their faces at Matthew's." A bewildered look came over her as she looked at Bobby Gene.

"Dear God, Bobby Gene, what foolish thing have you done?"

"Look here, woman. I'm not in the mood for questions. Nor the time to explain. My main concern right now is for our lives and the lives of those people downstairs." Anna Belle fell upon her knees as the tears started to flow.

"We're going to die! Just as I said we would!" Bobby Gene pulled her to her feet.

"If all you think about is dying, then you can go back to Matthew. It seems to me you can't get adjusted to this lifestyle. You're afraid of doing something that is unavoidable." She screamed at him as she broke away.

"I realize that dying is part of living. But why should one want to bring it upon himself instead of letting is happen naturally? Why should we have to die for a few niggers anyhow?"

"Niggers. They're just niggers to you now. Have you forgotten you're one of us too? Or has that white woman exterior been embedded in you so deeply you feel superior to us?" He walked past her toward the door.

"I'll be downstairs with my people. You know where your bags are." He opened the door but spoke again before he left.

"What makes you feel so much better than us? Because you've slept between the sheets of a white man and been his mistress. What makes you so sure Matthew would even have you back. I'm through fighting with you, Anna Belle. I have to save my strength for where it will be needed most" He was gone.

Everyone seemed to have saddled in the dining room area. Bobby Gene interrupted the many different chatters that filled the room.

"Excuse me, folks. But there are plans we have to make. I'm sure you've gotten warm by now, which brings us to the seriousness at hand. As I explained to you last night. I'm sure by now Matthew has discovered the bodies of his two men and the fact the bunch of you are missing. "I'm just as sure it didn't take him long to figure out I'm behind this. He will be coming with overseers to try and force you to go back with him. But you don't have to go. You're free, and he can't take that away from you no matter what he does. Do you understand? Kuta, Emmanuel, and the rest of you ole-timers. I want you to go with the children. Kuta will show you the hideout where you will all be safe from danger."

Emmanuel interrupted. "Listen, sonny. This maybe your spread, but as long as I's can talk. I's shall speak my say. I's might be's an ole-timer as you's so puts it, I's yet have some fight in me. Therefore, I's stay'n ifin you's don't mind." The others agreed.

"I've lived long enough to know when the ole-timers has made up his mind. There's no changing it. So then, Kuta, take the children and Mrs. Thompson to the hideout."

"That won't be necessary," a voice sounded from the back of the room. "I'll be more than happy to show them myself. Afterward, I'll come back and help fight this battle with you. We've come too far to turn back now." Bobby Gene looked at Anna Belle and smiled.

"All right, children, you heard the lady. Follow her, and no matter what you hear, stay put till someone comes to get you." His eyes wandered about the room.

"I need one of you women folks to keep watch over them to make sure that nothing goes wrong." a voice came from within the crowd.

"I's choose to stay by my man. We's feel the same hatred and bitterness, ifin not more than you's. They's owe us, and I's not

gonna let my being a woman stop me from gitt'n what be due me."
There were other women who were in agreement with her.

"Alrighty, women." He walked over to Lorene.

"Do you think you can manage the children?"

"Course I's can, and ifin need be, I's sure there be's some of
the older ones who can help me out. It be's time I's start pull'n my
weight around here. Children, come quickly. Anna Belle can take
us to the hideout." Bobby Gene immediately directed his attention
back to the eager faces.

"Now that's out of the way, we have to get some of you to a
couple of cabins on each side closest to the house. The only way
you'll be able to keep warm is by the clothes you're wearing. A fire
would arouse their suspicion, and we don't want them to know
they're being surrounded. The rest of you I will distribute around
the house. You women folks can fill in wherever needed. Now that
everything has been discussed, we must get ready. As each one was
leaving he reminded them not to forget their weapons.

CHAPTER TWENTY-SIX

Sure enough, midday brought Matthew and a few over-seers with him.

"Hey, nigger, bring your black ass out here this instant!" They heard Matthew say, then the breaking of glass while his voice became more vicious and demanding.

"You hear me, nigger? I said get out here! It appears to me we've gone through this before. It's like having déjà vu all over again, huh? Everything was quiet. "You haven't forgotten about that. Now have you nigger?" Another voice rose over Matthew's.

"Forget the talking. Why don't we just rush them niggers? What are we waiting for anyhown?"

"Quiet, Travor, you fool. You'll get your chance soon enough. I want them to squirm. He has no place to go. No one to turn to, ain't that right, nigger?" There came the sounds of broken glass again and again.

"That's enough Matthew." Bobby Gene called out from one of the broken windows. "I want you off my property right now." Matthew started to laugh.

"Did you hear that? He wants us off his property. You've got to be kidding, after what you tried to get away with. I want my niggers back plus my woman. I warned you once before what would hap-pen but you refused to heed the warning. You think because you've gone unscathed these past few months, all was forgotten. You're only fooling yourself. I knew you would never be a threat to me. So I decided to go along with your little charade. After this stunt, it has to end now. You seemed like an intelligent man for a nigger. That's why I'm going to give you one last chance. If my niggers and that woman ain't our here in five minutes, we're going to come in and get them." The door to the house swung open as Anna Belle ran out into the court yard between Matthew and Bobby Gene.

"Please, Matthew. Leave them alone. What harm can they do to you? You want me? Here I am." He approached her on his horse, taking the heel of his boot, he kicked her to the ground.

"You stupid little bitch! Did you really think I would have you back after your being with that nigger? Apparently you didn't believe me when I told you I would kill you if you ever left me. You're nothing more to me than another nigger, a whore." He signaled to Travor.

"Kill the bitch!" A shot rang out, and the horses pranced nervously from the explosion. Travor fell dead as more shots rang out. Matthew rode to safety as he watched a few more of his men fall dead. Then he called off the others. When it was quiet, he called out to Bobby Gene.

"This war has just begun, nigger. You hear me? You won't get away with this. I'll be back." His voice faded in the distance. Bobby Gene dropped his gun to the floor as he ran outside to get Anna Belle. She had been hit by a stray bullet, but it wasn't too serious. As Bobby Gene carried her into the house, he was surrounded by cheers.

"Hooray fer the Masser. We's dun it, Masser." They patted him on his back as he walked past them to lay Anna Belle on the couch in the study. He closed the door behind him to drown out the sounds. Then he went over to the cabinet took out a bottle of whiskey, pouring some in a glass. He brought it over to Anna Belle and ran it under her nose. She choked on the aroma as her eyes open substantially. Her vision was blurred for a moment, but she knew it was Bobby Gene who stood before her.

"I did a dumb thing, didn't I?"

"You did a deadly thing." She turned her head.

"I'm sorry, Bobby Gene. I guess for a moment I forgot who I really was and where I came from. All I knew is a white man wanted me as a woman. Not a nigger. Today, I was proven wrong. I'm nothing. The nobody I've always been." Bobby Gene knelt down in front of her.

"How can you put yourself down like that? Undoubtedly there was something in you Matthew loved. Remember, he did choose you over Pauline. A white woman. Besides, you're very special to me, and that should mean more to you than anything any white man could ever say to you. I love you." He waited for her to respond, but she didn't.

"Well, if you'll all right, I'll go out and see what kind of damage was done on Matthew's part. I'll send one of the ladies in to take care of that flesh wound on your shoulder."

When Bobby Gene came out of the room, everyone inquired of Anna Belle's condition. He assured them she would be fine but was more concerned as to if anyone else was hurt or even dead. The report was good. Not one person except Anna Belle was injured. There wasn't anyone killed. As they gathered back into the dining room area, Bobby Gene spoke.

"We were blessed this round. They'll be back. This time with more men and more power. We still have to fight. Ladies, we're going to need all of your support this time. That's all I have to say. I suggest you go back to your posts and pray while you yet have the chance, for we may not be as victorious next time."

They sat waiting quietly when the roar of horses' hooves shook the ground about them. Echoes of shots roared through the air. Bobby Gene and his people returned fire. There were moans and cries of death all about them. But there was nothing they could do. The shooting went on for what seemed to have been hours, with the intermission of reloading their guns. Matthew had made his way into the house and to where Bobby Gene was.

"I found you at last nigger. I must commend you on this almost perfect battle, but this is where you lose." He slowly raised the gun at Bobby Gene and pulled back the chamber, easing his finger onto the trigger and ready to shoot. There came a shriek and a cry of pain as the gun fell to the floor followed by Matthew. Anna

Belle stood there face-to-face with Bobby Gene as she rushed into his arms.

"He's dead, Bobby Gene. I've killed him." They stood there looking upon him as the knife protruded out of his back. A voice awoke them from their trance.

"Hold your fire! Hold your fire!" The rider was yelling as he galloped into the yard. "Sheriff sent me out here with this telegraph."

"It says, as of this day January first, eighteen hundred and sixty-three, the Proclamation Emancipation has just been passed by President Abraham Lincoln. This means these here niggers are free."

Anna Belle and Bobby Gene stood there in the bedroom window looking down upon the black face that remained as they danced to their victory in the center of black and white bodies that lay all around them. Bobby Gene turned to Anna Belle and looked deeply into her eyes.

"The long road to freedom has finally come at last." Bobby Gene said. Anna Belle's eyes answered back inquisitively.

"Or has it?"

To be continued…

Carolyn Harris was born and raised in Marshall, MO. She currently resides in Paris, MO.

In 1971 she graduated from Marshall High. Upon graduation Harris moved to Denver, CO and lived there for several years. She is a divorcee.

Harris takes pride in being a Christian. She also thanks God for not only bringing her through her spiritual journey, but also through the 27-years journey. He brought her through in the writing of this book. That's why she dedicates this book to Him and Him alone.

In 1973 Harris became the proud mother of a beautiful baby girl, Giselle Harris Ballenger, who now resides in Columbia, MO with her husband Kelley Ballenger. Harris has four grandsons, Jarrell Harris, Drevon, Kendrik, and Jaidyn Ballenger, a step-grandson, Kelyn Johnson. A step-granddaughter, Charlene McLendon, a great granddaughter, Jantel Harris, and a step-great grandson, Jamarion McLendon.

Harris would also like to thank Janel Rhodes for the outstanding job she did on the photographs. As well as everyone who kept encouraging her to continue on, and Mr. Erik Rowlett who is very dear to her heart.

CPSIA information can be obtained
at www.ICGtesting.com
Printed in the USA
FFHW020156281018
48961357-53200FF